MAFIA HEIR'S SECRET BABY

AN ARRANGED MARRIAGE ENEMIES TO LOVERS ROMANCE

VIVY SKYS

D1714329

Vivy Skys
CONTEMPORARY ROMANCE

MEL

"Did the ring have to be red too, father?"

A blood red dress, red roses, and a ruby red ring worth millions. It sounds more like the beginning of a bad joke than a marriage, but at this point, I feel more like I'm being bought rather than married.

Father's face creases and he sighs for the second time in two minutes.

"Baby, I don't know. That's what he sent."

Yeah. Being bought sounds about right.

I sigh and look at the ring again.

On top of everything, red is not my color.

And, I hate rubies.

Xander knows this too, which makes all of this even worse.

I stare mindlessly into the mirror, admiring the drape of the dress around my body. The dress hadn't been my idea either. Nothing on my skin had been my idea.

I chuckle, the sound catching in my throat as I press my eyes closed and let my head tilt forward so he can drape the accompanying diamonds on my throat.

I'd known this day would come. There's no need to pretend otherwise or even feel sorry for myself.

Six years was more than enough respite.

"Where's Lucian?" I turn to Father and let him press an almost tender kiss on my forehead.

"Sleeping. He's not coming tonight, Mel. You know why."

He sounds sorry, and my breath catches in my throat.

"How bad is this going to be?" I ask in a whisper.

He takes my hand in his and squeezes softly. "Only as bad as you want it to be. I support you, baby, but you knew this day was coming. I've protected you as long as I can."

And he has, too.

I inhale a deep swell of air and smile as widely as I can, hoping it doesn't look as much of a grimace as I think it does.

"You smile at Xander that way, and he's sure to run screaming for the hills." My brother Daniel is at the door, his navy-blue Brooks Brothers suit unbuttoned.

He holds his arms out, and I walk over to him, hugging him tight. I pull away and tuck my arm into his when he offers. He smells of mint and Lucian's powder.

"Is he sleeping yet?" I lean into him and tone my voice low so Father can't hear me.

"No, but Hailey will make sure he does. And no, do not go in there, Mel. You'll never leave." He tightens his arms around me and leads me to the door away from the stairs.

I nod and follow Father's brisk strides to the door, shaking my hair away from my face and straightening my shoulders out.

Outside, a cool breeze blows through the palm trees planted on the property, the moon just sneaking out of the clouds. The air smells of cherry blossoms, light and airy, nothing at all like my mood.

Daniel opens the car door and holds it for me, lifting the train of my dress carefully and sliding it into the car after me.

I smirk at him. "If I didn't understand better, I'd think I wasn't your sister."

He glares playfully. "Shut up, Mel."

He pushes the door closed, walks over to the passenger door of the SUV, and slips in beside me.

I turn to him and whisper the words I've kept to myself this entire time, festering in my stomach like worms. "I still hate him."

Daniel turns to me, his hazel eyes deep and hard. "He probably hates you just as much. The past didn't wound you alone. You know he was just as hurt as you were."

"And then there's Lucian. How do I explain that?" Daniel is right. And I can't deny it. Xander had been just as hurt as I was. Maybe even more broken. The split had, after all, been my idea.

Daniel sits back against his seat and, resting his head against the headrest, closes his eyes. "There's going to be hell to pay. Even his family won't survive it."

"Why can't we cancel this? We don't need the money. Father certainly has enough."

Daniel opens his eyes and takes my hand. The car pulls out of the driveway, and we're on our way to the lion's lair.

. . .

"The Russians are getting stronger, Mel. He needs the combined power of our family and his. Father is worried handing our business to him without some leverage will spell doom for us, but he also understands we can't not do anything."

I feel a twinge of guilt as I ask a question I've asked one too many times. "Why don't you take over the business?"

Daniel's eyes darken. "I can't. I don't want it. My law firm cannot be associated in any way with the Mafia, Mel. You know this, someone has to keep the legit side of the business up."

He squeezes my hand a look of guilt in his eyes, "I'm sorry we're throwing you under the bus like this, but you know we have less than no choice. Father doesn't even want to do this."

Which makes my reluctance so much worse. Father is probably festering in a soup of guilt right now. I bite my lip and nod.

I inhale harshly and close my eyes. "You're right. I just hate to think about Lucian. I hate to think what will happen when he finds out. What if he tries taking my baby from me?"

Daniel pulls me across the seat and tucks my head into his shoulder the way he's always done when I'm in need of comfort. I let myself relax into him for a moment.

"He can't do that. You two will be married, and you know he can't leave you. Same as you can't leave him."

The words do not bring me any comfort. Instead, I mumble the family vows, which suddenly sound like a death keel to my ears. "Till death us do part."

Daniel chuckles darkly, and I wince, grateful he can't see my expression. "Exactly. It's easier to leave if you're dead, Mel. And Xander will never let any harm come to you. He'd rather die."

For some reason, I doubt that. The Xander I knew is nothing like the one who dressed me in solid red for a wedding I don't want. Xander still exists, but he's not mine.

That Xander knew I don't like the color red, not since I'd seen it spill out of my mother's side before she'd keeled over to her death. Not since every flower at her funeral had been the red roses she'd loved so much.

Father had made sure all of it had been arranged around her casket, and then he'd torn down her rose garden and went on a vengeful spree of killing that had lasted an entire month.

No, this wouldn't be anything like when we'd both been younger and thought ourselves in love.

2

XANDER

I TIP MY HEAD UP AND DOWN HALF OF THE DRINK. MY brother Alec hitches his brow and smirks like he's seen something funny.

"Mel really won't love it if you're drunk by the time she arrives."

I eye him out of the corner of my eye, then keeping my eye on his, down the rest of the drink. His lips twitch at the corner.

"Fucking asshole. They're here. Get the bottle away from him." Declan growls. Two years younger than Alec, he's the stiff one of the family, and he's always loved Mel.

Actually, all my siblings have always loved Mel. Of course, they don't want me drunk when she arrives.

They also do not understand that the only way I can face the woman who broke my heart six years ago is if I'm three sheets to the wind.

"I've barely had a sip of the drink. Get off my back, you two." I snap. I drop the tumbler to the table with a thump and shove my chair back. "Have father brought in."

Alec nods, and this time, his face is an expressionless mask of nothing.

I move out of the living room to the door, passing by the mantel with its many photos of our family that mother insists we put out.

When my father had fallen ill three years ago, I'd known this day was coming. His voice had been a still croak in his throat as he'd told me he'd brokered a deal with the Sedrics.

Marriage in exchange for a joint alliance and an end to the very feud that had birthed the end of my relationship with Mel.

I feel a bitter mask slip over my face. Six years later, I was back at the same place. Getting married to a woman I'd loved and lost.

Father's butler, Enzo, is standing by the door, an expectant look on his face. I nod and step out of the house when he opens it with a short bow. Right as she steps out of the car, her arm is tucked into Daniel, who sends me a glare as he leads his sister towards me.

The guards stationed outside have their faces turned away, their spines straight as always.

I feel the betraying hike of my heart. It racks its way into my throat, and I swallow. She's changed.

Her body looks titillating under the drape of her red dress to match the glint of the engagement ring I'd sent this morning.

Her hips are curvier, thrusting out of her waist like they wish to make a statement all their own.

"Might want to pick your jaw off the floor and go speak to your bride."

Declan is back beside me. I roll my eyes and walk down the steps towards them. She stops for a moment, her eyes freezing on her brother's shoulder before she inhales and takes a step forward.

I step forward and watch as Daniel lets her go without a word from me. I nod at him and offer her my arm.

She slips her arm into my elbow and looks up at me with those emerald green eyes, so deep and clear, like a forest with the sun breaking through its leaves.

"Xander." She murmurs, biting down on her lip. Her eyes snap away from mine and rove over Mother's garden surrounding us. A ghost of a smile flits across her face. "Looks like nothing changed."

It seems so because just the sound of her light voice has my cock jumping in my pants. Like it recognizes her. Like it craves her.

"We haven't had the time for much landscaping. Father's looking forward to seeing you."

She sweeps her dress around her and walks beside me to the door where my brothers are arranged, their faces blank as a clean slate. "My sister Gianna sends her greetings. She's been called away for an emergency. She'd been looking forward to the meeting."

I shake my head. Just like Mel to try smoothing things over. "Knowing Gianna, she's more likely to wish me a slow and painful death than to look forward to this meeting, but maybe she's changed."

Mel looks up at me, and a slow smile breaks out on her face. "She said something along the lines of she hopes someone sends a bullet through your ass. Maybe she'd been hoping to do that herself."

I nod, my throat too tight to let any words slip through. That sounded more like Gianna, and I could've said so, but watching Mel smile at me snatches the words away.

Her eyes are still light and airy. Like nothing had happened between us. I wonder how she can smile that way at me when what I want to do is wring her pretty little neck, then take her against my wall, wrap my hand around her, and hurl her into my chest so she burrows into me like she always did.

I blink the fantasy away to see her watching me, her brow creased. "What did you say?"

"Nothing. You stopped moving. I wondered if there was something wrong."

I shake my head no and ignore the tug towards her in the back of my mind.

My brothers take the steps towards us. Alec, as is customary, kisses her cheeks first, then Declan and my last born brother Knox.

"Welcome, Mel." Knox is the closest to her age and the only one of us who has kept up with her.

He offers her his arm, and she looks up at me first, asking my permission as a good wife should. My brow raises of its own accord, and I smile down at her without humor.

She pulls her arm from mine and slips it into Knox's.

I feel a flash of jealousy and stamp it down. She's to be mine. And mine alone.

The way it always should have been.

3

MEL

XANDER'S MOTHER SMILES AT ME, TAKES MY HAND IN hers, and presses a kiss to my cheeks. "Mel. It's so good to see you."

I let her hug me before pulling away. "It's good to see you too, Martha."

And it is. Whatever Xander and I had, whatever our past is like, Martha has always been kind to me. Six years later, there are streaks of gray in her dark hair and lines around her eyes, but it's obvious where Xander and his brothers get their charm.

"Come sit. I've had Asher make a feast. You'll like it."

She leads me to the table where a meal is spread out already. Xander pulls my chair for me before settling into his.

"Where is your father?" I ask, turning to him.

Silence greets my question, and I wonder if I've said something wrong. But how will a family alliance be forged without the man whose very business it is that Xander would be taking over?

I ignore the thought of just what it is that business is. The fact that we are who we are makes it all the weirder that Xander's father isn't here. It's not like we're in the grocery business or anything, but hey.

I can't sit and judge. It is, after all, the same thing that my father does. I can't afford to point fingers or throw stones from a glass house.

"He'll be down in a second. Alec will be with him." Martha replies. The table is silent, the ticking of the grandfather clock on the wall the only sound.

Father has probably gone ahead to speak to him. I don't understand how they can stand each other now after ruining their children's lives. But it is not my place to question the way the men run their business.

In truth, there's a maelstrom inside of me, zipping through my veins, and I find that I am tapping my hands on the table when Xander's hand covers mine.

I pull away and turn to him. "This will not be any different. All we need to do tonight is sign the contract." He says, his voice a caress that sends a shiver arrowing to my core, much to my distress.

Seems my body hasn't gotten the memo that this isn't the past.

I let my hair fall over my face to hide the rush of color to my cheeks.

"There's a contract?"

"Our families have not seen eye to eye in years. Of course, Amore mio, there's a contract." Xander says.

Amore mio? The use of the old name has my thighs clenching under the table, my hand almost fisting, too, except he's got his hands over them.

I lean into him, note Daniel has his eyes on me, and hiss my words. "Don't call me that. I can't take it. Please."

His lips tighten, and he fills my space. "You can take it, and I can't wait to have you begging for every inch mia mor." Then his hands leave mine as though he'd asked for the time of the day, as though he hadn't left me grateful I'm sitting because my knees are suddenly jelly.

I miss his warmth immediately, but it's better this way. Getting involved with Xander would be a terrible idea, especially as this time, we're signing a damned contract.

The rattle of a wheelchair fills the oppressive silence, and Xander shoves his chair back. I turn towards the sound, stifling a gasp when my eyes meet his father's.

Amory Vittoria has a blank look on his face like he has trained the rest of his children to be. I leave my chair, walk up to him, and bend to kiss him on the cheek as my sign of respect.

"Mel, never thought I'd clap eyes on you again. You've grown." His voice is half lost in his throat, no longer the deep timbre of a man who recognizes his own power.

He looks a step away from the grave, his eyes droopy, his hair as ashy as his complexion, and it comes to me finally: the reason Xander needs a wife. I lift my eyes to his, and I know he can read the look on my face.

He needs to take over the Famiglia, and he cannot do that without a wife.

"Come, let's sit. We can talk later. For now, food in the stomach as is our due." Amory says.

Alec rolls the wheelchair to the table and helps his father into his chair. My father comes down the hallway with Declan, murmuring to him words I cannot hear.

Everyone settles at the table, and soon, dinner is underway. Their chef, Asher, has outdone himself.

15

Chicken so tender it practically melts off the tongue, steak seasoned with herbs and spices.

I eat hungrily, having been too nervous all day to eat much. And finally, a dessert of my favorite chocolate cake, so decadent I go in for a second and third round.

We finish the meal off with wine, a Penfolds Grange that is still my favorite. I send a look to Xander, wondering if wine is his one concession to me. But he doesn't look my way.

With the meal done and the table cleared, Amory clears his throat, and I know we've finally meandered our way to the reason we're here.

"There's no need to pretend we're here to eat alone. The families have decided to merge their businesses. The contract will be signed by morning in the presence of our lawyers, but I thought it best that we spend time this way, together, without the animosity that always has brimmed between us two."

He addresses the words at Father, who nods and shifts forward on his chair. He holds his hand out to Amory, and the two men shake on it.

The marriage contract will be between Xander and me, but with their handshake, the marriage is basically sealed.

Father smiles at Amory, but it lacks humor. He's never gotten along with the man. And neither has Amory with him, and if it were not for the threats of the Russians, then they'd probably head to their graves fighting each other.

Xander places his hand on my thighs and squeezes. I look up at him, my heart in my throat. The imprint of his hand feels like a brand on my skin.

"You're as good as mine, Mel. Didn't think I'd ever see the day."

"I had no idea you were looking forward to this so very much. I'd have made some allowance for you." Much to my dismay, my thoughts wander off to just what sort of allowance he would've made. And just like that, it's warm in the room.

The rest of the table is watching us, and I wonder why he wants to start a fight here. With their eyes on us like a mother hen with its chicks when a hawk circles above.

Father bangs a hand on the table and glowers at the two of us. "Do not take the feud up between the two of you."

We jerk our gazes from each other, but there's a challenging glint in Xander's eyes that has my back up.

Amory breaks into the battle of wills. "Isn't this what you two have always wanted?" He turns to me first. "What do you think?"

I have no idea why he's asked my opinion. The Mafia have no use for their women. I know the marriage is a sham, and I am a figurehead.

I release a pent-up breath and shy away from an answer. "Xander is the head of the family. Perhaps he should do the speaking."

4

XANDER

I sink my teeth into my bottom lip and clench my fist beneath the table. I sure as hell didn't want to get hitched to Mel Sedric.

She knew it as certainly as I knew. The last thing she wanted to do was get married to me herself. And deflecting the question to me was just something she would do.

But calling me the head of the family was an admission, and I find myself hardening, my cock jerking in my pants. Whether the words are true or not, they stroke my ego. Being lord and king over a woman like Mel feels good.

But I pull up before I can fall too far into that misconception. When had Mel ever been subservient and meek? This Mel didn't sit well with the image of her I had carried around these last few years.

I snap my eyes to my father's and grit my teeth. This was none of their business. Their job here was done. "It's business father. Things have changed. Perhaps you two should not interfere any more than you both have already."

Father's eyes are like cold steel. "It is our business, Xander, we are trusting you with."

"And this is our lives. We'll take it from here. Once the contract is signed, it will be as good as mine. Do not interfere."

Mel's father breaks in before father can reply. "My business belongs to my daughter still until you both have been married five years. Do not think you will get away with treating her less than is due."

Anger washes over my skin, and I throw him a dark glare. "When have I ever treated your daughter less than she is due?"

Mel's voice breaks through the brick of anger in my chest and melts it like butter. "We do not need to fight right after our dinner."

My brothers are watching my face, theirs impassive. They have not said a word the entire time, and I wonder what they're thinking.

"Mel is right. Xander has proven himself more than once. He will be a man of the Famiglia after his marriage. There is no reason to rein him in." Alec says.

"And if war breaks out with the Russians, he'll need to make a decision. He can't keep asking for permission to run the business as he sees fit." Alec continues.

Father shoots Alex an irate look, but before he can counter, Mother's hand lands on his. "The engagement is still months away. Maybe we should make a decision after the wedding? Our alliance is fragile yet. There's no need to destroy it by bickering like children at dinner."

I hadn't considered I would have to answer to the older men even after my marriage to Mel. I didn't want to.

I wanted control over both businesses. And control meant that I had the final say on all decisions concerning the business.

I push my chair back and excuse myself from the table. I know Father and Sedric will spend the evening together, locked in his study.

Father will strain himself to prove he is still the Lord of the underworld who kept the business running and expanding all these years, and Sedric will let him.

I wish I could return to my own home, but while Mel and her family remain here, that will be impossible.

Daniel pushes his chair back and follows me out of the room.

"I need a break from your family. That includes you." I mutter to him. I sweep a hand to my hair and tip my head back to enjoy the faint breeze flowing through the air on the balcony. It smells of frangipanis and mother's tulips.

"So do I, from yours. It was getting rather stifling in there. I need to talk to you."

I spat out a chuckle. "If you're here to threaten me concerning your sister, forget it. I'm not interested in hearing one more word about her."

Daniel places his elbow on the rail and raises his brow. "Why would I do that? I'm not stupid. I know you're still nursing something for her. You'd rather die than let harm come to her."

I feel the squeeze of hate in my guts. He has no right to say that. "Things change. Maybe I hate her so much I'll do away with her myself when she's no longer useful."

Daniel looks at me like I'm stupid. His eyes are glowing like wood embers.

"You would never do that. But do not ever speak of my sister that way."

I shake my head and run a hand through my hair. He's right. I would never do that. He knows it too.

"What's the word on the streets?" He asks finally when I refuse to grace his words with a reply.

"Blood. The Russians sense weakness. They will sweep in as soon as they find a chink in our armor."

"And do you have one? You're the head now."

I bring my hand to my forehead and try rubbing away the headache brewing there. "Aren't you doing your best to stay away from this? Why question me?"

Daniel's face is an angry mask. "Because I worry for my sister. She's not like you. She's air and light, and you're the darkness of the night. You might very well ruin her."

I suck in a breath of air and flop back against the railing. "This is business, Daniel. I will protect her as much as I can, but there is only so much protecting I can do. Especially from myself."

Daniel rolls his eyes and continues like I'd never said anything. "And what will the fucking Russians do when they realize she's your weak link? Because fight it as much as you want, we both know you still want my sister and that she wants you too. You two will burn the world in your wake, but I worry that you will burn her too."

"She does?" I ask. I ignore the little tremble in my voice.

Daniel's brow creases with confusion. "Does what?"

"Wants me?"

5

MEL

"I'll be your secretary for the duration of your job here."

The lady takes my bag from me and points down the hallway to a door that already has my name and tag on it.

I smile grimly and follow the tap of her heels down the hallway. "The duration of my job here?"

"Yes. This is just until your wedding to Mr. Xander. It'll be great publicity for us if you work here."

No one had said there was a duration for my job with Amory Corp. The business, literally named after Xander's father, is most probably another money laundering joint, but I wince the thought away from my head.

I already miss the simplicity of my day, spending most of it with Lucian as I always did. Father would never let me work because he was worried about my safety, but his place is teeming with people, Xander's men stationed like statues at the door.

The real truth he would never say, but which I already know, is that women of the mob do not work. Their men keep them at home, like rich paintings, to be shown off when convenient.

Which is why I'm shocked Xander is fine with me working. I guess it makes sense though, since we haven't even signed the marriage contract yet, and I'm not his to control. Who knows what he'll do when we actually get married, especially if he has to convince his father.

I hope I'll still work, though. It gives me meaning.

Rosa pushes open the door and holds it for me to step in. Romero tries to step in, but she clicks it close behind us. I watch through the glass as he takes up station just outside the door, displeasure painted on his face.

The office is large and more rectangular than square. It's a corner office with a stunning view of the skyline outside. I settle into the chair behind the large antique desk and swivel the chair to the view.

"What will I be doing here?"

"Whatever you want to do."

I splay my hand over my dress and tug at a bit of bunched fabric, straightening it out. "What does that mean?"

Rosa drops my bag to the table finally as I turn to her. She has a look of perturbed curiosity on her face. "What do you want to spend your time on? There are projects you could indulge in. If not, we'll find what you like."

She really had meant it then when she'd said I was here more for the publicity than anything else. I consider if she knows what the business does, and I decide she probably does.

Xander wouldn't let anyone close to me who didn't understand the business.

Rosa scrolls through the tablet in her hands, then shifts her glasses to her nose and sniffs. "You could take over the charities. No one pays them much attention apart from pumping money into them, and I think that's a blinking shame. We could do so much with them."

She continues without waiting for a reply. "Or you could take over running the PR team. Your wedding would be a nice excuse to release a flurry of photos."

"Rosa. Take a seat." I wave my hand at the chair in front of mine and nod when she hesitates.

She blows a hank of her blonde fringe away from her eyes. "I can find you something else if none of the options appeal to you."

"Tell me about the charities."

Charities, as in there were more than one. How could the Amory family run charities? They're not exactly charitable people, if I'm being honest.

Rosa hitches her shoulder and shrugs. "Mr.. Xander's idea. That's all we know. He signs the checks himself too. Doesn't say much to anyone about anything. I only know about it because he asked my opinion once. Now, you could speak to him about it."

What is this about?

"I'm to make sure your transition to work is as smooth as possible. You have a need; I'm the person to ask. If you'd rather not deal with the charities like I said, you don't have to."

I nod. That all sounds reasonable. Rosa opens a folder and glances through it. Without looking back up at me, she holds out her hand. "I'll need your phone too."

I stiffen for a second. "Why?"

She pulls out something that looks like it's a shiny sticker, and gestures to it. "Mr. Xander requested a tracker be inserted in one of your phones. We could get you a new one if you'd rather have one. However, if you insist on keeping with your current phone, you'll need to put this in there."

"Why do I need one?"

Rosa casts me a glare with her eyebrow arched. "Miss Mel, you are aware the type of business your fiancé is in?"

"Of course," I mutter.

"So. Occasionally, the need arises to ensure that one's family is in the correct location."

"Right." I knew what she meant. If I went missing for any reason, they'd need to find me. But wasn't that the essence of having Romero? Father had assigned him to just me this morning, and I'd lived with some form of bodyguard for most of my life.

Romero, though, was something different. .

He was one of Father's most trusted men and having him assigned to me meant something really was brewing.

"I don't need a tracker. I'll be fine with the security detail," I clarified.

There was another reason that I didn't want to have a tracker in my phone. I had gotten used to using an untraceable burn phone while hiding from Xander out of the country with Gianna. I didn't need it or want it now.

Xander didn't need to know everything about me.

Rosa leans forward. "It's for your protection."

"I know what it is for."

"Then don't make it hard for him. Or us. We need to know you're safe. The Russians aren't joking around this time."

So, she does know a thing or two about this business. How the fuck had she, someone who works for the legitimate side of the business, found out? I only knew because the news had come up at dinner yesterday.

The fact that I was once again the last to know rankled me slightly.

I took a deep breath and willed myself not to care about that. However, I still didn't want a tracker on my phone. Getting a tracker on me meant Xander had access to my whereabouts at all hours of the day, every damned day. He'd find out about Lucian sooner than I could say 'Jack.'

I gave Rosa my iciest smile. "I'll handle this with Xander. Back to the charities, I'd like to take it on. Do I need his approval too?"

"Yes," she responded with that same dull sneer. "He will need to sign off."

Shit. It seems like he keeps a tight grip on everything. And considering the idea of the rest of Chicago finding out Xander had a charity. It would spell disaster for his name, his authority, his control over his routes, his drugs, and his guns.

Bloody hell!

Rosa smiles and pushes her chair back. "I'll let you know by tomorrow how everything runs around here concerning that. For today, you've got a photoshoot scheduled for after lunch. You're free until then."

With Rosa gone, I take a deep breath and do my best not to panic. I inhale again and again and decide I'm not about to let this pull me down.

Lucian is my priority, and keeping him away from Xander is becoming more impossible as the day slips away at sunset.

Xander

I arrive at Amory Corps a few minutes past six in the evening. The men at the door snap to attention, wide eyed as my car pulls up and my bodyguard Carl comes around to open my door.

I step out of the car and take the walk to the open lobby door. Rosa is standing beside Valerie, whispering something to her that has Valerie tipping her head back and scrunching her nose.

"Rosa," I call out. She turns towards me, picks a tablet off Valerie's desk, and walks over.

"Where's my wife?"

Rosa glares at me first. "You didn't say you hadn't told her about the trackers. I sounded like an asshole trying to convince her of something she didn't want."

Rosa is head of security here at Amory Corps. The extraordinarily tough woman is ex-military, and my father had paid a hefty price to get her to work for us.

I'd had her tagged to Mel immediately after Father had said he'd given her an office here. Once affiliated with the family openly, she would be the person with a target on her back, and Mel was too trusting and forgiving. She'd need Rosa to see through the bullshit.

Mel, on her own, was smart, sure. But she wouldn't have the same instincts as Rosa.

"What did she say?" If anyone could convince Mel she needed a tracker, then it would be Rosa.

She smirks. "No idea. She's stubborn. Like you. She's your wife, get her to agree."

I roll my shoulders and then my eyes. "I wouldn't need your help if I could've done that myself. Convince her."

Rosa steps into the elevator with me. "She's agreed on the charities, at least. She was very enthusiastic about it too. I've asked that she speak to you about the details."

I feel my gut twist. She really is an angel. Of course, she wanted to run the charities. That was just who Mel is. A piece of sunshine in my very dark world.

"She's in her office working. Romero is outside the door, so there's no need to worry about me being down there. I've got it covered."

I squeeze my forehead and exhale. "I wasn't worried."

"Your pants are on fire. I can see it." Rosa presses the button for the highest floor. The one where Mel is hidden away right now.

"How did she do today?" I ask, for lack of something better to say.

Mel is going to flourish, and I know she will because that's just who she is. She steps in and makes things better. And despite our break up, she'd still managed to have my siblings wrapped around her fingers.

"Really good. Most of the pictures came out pretty good. The media branch will have the news out before the weekend runs out."

"It's not to get out until we have that tracker on her."

"She's not a fucking dog Xander. You're not going to lose her to the Russians if she gets out of the gate. You're more likely to lose her from trying to smother her," Rosa snorts.

"I'm just saying that she needs to have someone on her. That's all," I snap.

Rosa rolls her eyes. "And you said you weren't worried."

I don't respond to that.

The elevator opens, and I step out of it ahead of Rosa. Romero's head jerks towards us, and he relaxes his shoulders slightly when he sees it's me.

"How's it been here?" I ask on my way to the door.

"Quiet. She made a few phone calls, but that's been all." Romero answers, his hand tucked away from sight, probably snug against the butt of his gun.

I nod and step through the door. Mel looks up from her desk and then away. She's bathed in the rays of the evening sun, her blonde hair glinting almost champagne, and I suck in a harsh inhale.

Will I ever not want this woman? I can't help the surge of lust in my blood or the strong desire I feel to pull her from that desk into my arms or splay her out like a sacrifice and gouge myself on her.

I turn back to the door and pull it closed behind me. No one will open it with both Rosa and Romero out there.

She flashes a small smile at me, and then her eyes flit away. "Good evening, Xander. I wasn't expecting you."

No one knows my whereabouts. Easier to be safe that way. The Amory family isn't lacking in enemies.

"I'm here now. Are you ready to leave?" I take the seat in front of the massive, ancient-looking desk and watch as her eyes move nervously away from me.

"Not yet. Rosa sent a list of charities that you support." Her eyes meet mine and hold. "I didn't know anything about these."

The appreciation in her gaze has me feeling a few sizes taller. I shrug nonchalantly. "I have a certain image to uphold. Started it after my father got sick, but owning charities sounds too cuddly for my world."

Her eyes cloud with something too close to pity for comfort. She leans across the table towards me. "How long has that been going on?"

"Three years. He seemed to suddenly waste away. It's cancer. The doctors give him a few more months."

I have no idea why the truth comes spilling out of my lips like I've been waiting this entire time to tell her.

No one but the family knows about my father's illness. He hasn't been seen by anyone outside of family either.

Her eyes grow large as saucers. "Oh, Xander. That must be so difficult for you. I certainly wasn't expecting to see him that way. It hit me like a blow, and he's never really liked my family."

"I've been trained since birth to take over from him. I'm ready."

"That's not what I meant. He's your father."

I know what she meant, and weakness like that in the Mafia got you killed. The Famiglia needed a man with a strong backbone.

If Father's time was here, then it was here. Soon, it would be mine too.

"Yes, he is. We should get you home. I have a meeting to get to."

Her tongue peeks out between her lips, and I feel it like a touch of sparking flames to my skin, pinpricks of heat and fire rushing over my body.

"Where is home?" She asks suspiciously.

That has my hackles rising. She doesn't have to make it sounds so fucking detestable. "Your father's house. I certainly wasn't referring to mine."

She makes me feel like a monster for trying to be good. Fucking hell.

"You don't have to. Romero's here with me," she waves at the bodyguard.

My insides twist. She prefers another man's company to mine. I clench my jaw and press my hands into a fist under the table. To think, Daniel had said she wanted me. Yeah right. He obviously didn't know his sister as much as he pretends to.

"I want to, Mel. Now let's go," I growl at her.

She's not going to get another man's attention.

She's going to have mine.

And damn it.

She's going to like it.

6

XANDER

THREE HOURS LATER, I WALK ACROSS THE BRIDGE AND into the basement. The table has been pushed up against the wall, and the men crowd around, most of them smoking, all suited and holstered, their firearms right in the open.

The room falls quiet with my entrance, and I take a chair at the head, placing my gun within easy reach.

"Good evening, boss." Ryder's voice has my gaze swinging to him.

"Evening, Ryder. What's the news today?"

"Not much happening. The streets have been quiet all evening. We're thinking something happened, or they've backed up."

Carl cuts in. "For now, boss. We can't believe they're gone for good."

And we can't be lulled into a false sense of security. It's impossible they're gone just like that. The Russians are sly, and they have the money to throw around.

"And the man we found?"

"Dead. Didn't survive the torture." Carl says blandly, obviously unbothered by the man's death, and considering the same man had been responsible for the death of at least one of our men, neither was I.

"Do we have anyone on the inside we can trust?" I look away from all of them, scratching at my itching scalp.

I'm hungry, but the Famiglia comes first. Always has and always will for a made man.

And remembering my conversation with Mel this evening parked in her father's driveway, I suddenly feel tired. She'd wanted to know why she needed a tracker.

I hadn't been able to tell her the darkness that existed in the world. The very one that I sowed with my existence.

I had told her the charity was because of my father, but truthfully, that sounded better than saying it was a replacement for everything that I ruined with the touch of my hands.

"Alec has someone he's paying, but I'm not certain how far we can trust him. He's not Capo, and he's not the underboss either." Ryder tilts his head back and takes a long inhale of the cigar between his lips.

The room breaks out in a loud murmur. It takes a harsh snap from me to bring any semblance of order back.

"Alec is not Capo, and neither is he underboss, but he is my brother. If he says we can trust this man, then I believe him." I bark.

There is no room for dissent. I am only underboss until my marriage to Mel, and that's still a few months away. With Capo's absence, his men are bound to get rowdy.

I can't afford a divide in my own ranks. Especially with the ever-looming threat of the fucking Russians clawing at my back.

"Yes, boss." Carl gives a little salute with his hand against his forehead and sits back against his chair.

"Things need to move forward fast. We need to have a plan of action. Some way to cut through the swatch of problems looming. Do we attack first?" Ryder asks. He sounds like the question has been on his mind for a while.

"We don't do anything to disturb the balance. Not yet."

Not when Mel is still so vulnerable. I remember her little smile today after I'd dropped her off. It had done strange things to my stomach, things she's always been the only one capable of.

Ryder's brow bears disapproval. A small knife appears in his hand, and he digs it into the table. The rest of the men watch. "We don't have time, boss. If they hit us first, even with Sedric's force, we might have a hard time bouncing back."

I tap the butt of my gun against the table and wait until I have all their attention. "Which is why we won't let them hit us. I need my wedding to go off hitch-free. After that, we'll discuss the rest of this."

The room breaks out in congratulations. Most of the men give half grins.

The rest of them look uncomfortable, like even the mention of a wedding is too much emotion.

"If anything disrupts the timeline, I'm going to be pissed. We keep the Famiglia secure until all this with Sedric's family is secure. Until I am married, and then we strike."

The thought of a fight breaking out has my chest filling with a sloven heaviness, like my limbs are weighed down with lead. This isn't like me.

Maybe war doesn't excite me anymore, but it shouldn't worry me either.

This is, after all, my life. It has been my life for all of my thirty-seven years. I've never known another existence, so why does my stomach feel like a hollow cave all of a sudden?

"It's a great plan, boss."

"Double security around both houses. And Amory Corp." I don't tell them why, but I'd rather be safe than sorry.

I shove my chair back and push my gun into the back of my pants and the shotgun into its holster around my arm. A few knives are tucked away in discreet places, all giving me a sense of security on my person.

I step out of the door, drained after the long day. I need a hot shower and a warm body. An image of Mel sneaks into my brain, and I chuckle bitterly.

Getting over her isn't going to be as easy as I am trying to convince myself it should be. Not when two minutes in her presence had me all wound up and needy for her.

Not when I hate the thought of danger coming to her so damned much I'm willing to risk my men to keep her safe.

Not when, for the first time in my entire dark days on earth, the Famiglia is not my priority. Keeping her safe is, even if it is safe from myself, until I can have her with no restraints.

7

MEL

"For God's sake, father, he's only six." I snap, my voice exasperated.

I've just stepped out of the car, and the first thing I see in the driveway is Lucian on a large dirt bike, his back glinting with sweat as he rolls the kid-sized bike around the garden while father watches with a fond expression on his face.

"Daniel had one just like it when he was six. I couldn't resist."

I roll my eyes and wait for Lucian to roll the bike down to me. He's smiling so wide it makes my heart ache. But he also shouldn't have a bike. They're dangerous as hell.

Or maybe I'm just being protective, as always.

Daniel is watching the scene from the balcony, his hair rustling in the breeze. "Damned near broke my shoulder twice on that thing. He needs the experience."

I glare at him before bending and sweeping my son into my arms. All sweaty and wiggling with joy. His blue eyes are bright like bluebells under the sun as he takes my hand and leads me over to the bike.

"Papi said it's a great way to learn how to drive without driving!" He explains enthusiastically as he tows the bike up and gets on it again.

I send my dad a look of indignation, and because I can't help myself, I tag a grim smile onto it. I ruffle Lucian's hair and step away from him, but he rides the bike behind me back to the door.

Romero watches the scene quietly, and I try my best, as always, to ignore him. He won't say a word to Xander, because he knows how important it is that Lucian stay secret.

He knows Lucian's existence is to be kept away from him for as long as we can till we can't anymore.

"Did you do anything fun today?" Lucian rolls the bike to me, drops it to the floor, and slips his hand into mine. He's warm, and it chases away the sudden cold I'd felt coming back to my son on that bike.

It was a dangerous gift for a six-year-old. Although not as dangerous as coming home to Daniel with his first knife set, which I was certain Lucian would get as well. But the bike had been a prelude to the knives, and I wanted to protect my son a little while longer.

"Uncle Daniel and I went to the zoo to see the penguins. Mommy did you know penguins give each other pebbles? We had ice cream," he chirps, and his voice tips even higher.

"Then, and then, we came home to play bikes!" His excited chatter trails me all the way to the kitchen, where I settle him into his chair at the table while I get a bottle of water from the fridge.

"Sounds like you had fun. A lot of it." I pour the water into a cup for him and place it right in front of him. He pouts, his eyes so like Xander's staring at me with a puppy dog look, and his lips thrust out at me. "No, you drink."

He drops his shoulder and picks up the cup, gulping down the water and then dropping the glass to the table with a thump. "Can we get pizza for dinner tonight?"

"No, Lucian. No pizza for dinner, but you can help me make some pasta."

I enjoy cooking with Lucian in the kitchen. Father has a chef, but cooking relaxes me, a way to unwind after a long day, and after the busy day I'd had, it was imperative that I did something I enjoyed.

As I cooked, I went through the events of the day. It certainly hadn't been a great one… more like, it had been a doozy.

For one, I'd finally crumbled and had Rosa get me a new phone. One with a tracker embedded in it. I'd held out for two days under her incessant questions until I just couldn't take it anymore.

She'd smiled and barreled right out to the hallway and yelled at someone to get a move on with getting the phone. An hour later, a new one had arrived.

As though he had been sure I would give in, Xander had called immediately after, his number already saved as "Marito."

I'd released a guttural rasp when he'd burst out laughing to my indignant question.

"Husband?"

I could hear his smirk through the phone, it was obvious in the throaty growl which graced my ear, streaking electric sparks over my skin.

"Soon enough."

The memory of that sent shivers skating up my spine.

The phone was sitting in my bag now, exactly where it was that I intended it to stay for the rest of its life.

I pushed the sauce around in the pan, still thinking through the events of today. To top off the long day, Xander hadn't shown up all day at the office.

And now, watching Lucian smiling up at me with a look so innocent in his eyes as blue as his father's but filled with light to Xander's bottomless pit of dark emotions, I don't enjoy the curl of slight worry in my stomach.

It's only been two days, but somehow, it feels like we already have a routine, and him breaking it is a betrayal.

I shake the crazy thought away and focus on Lucian, whose chestnut hair is almost falling into his eyes. I lean into his face and blow a raspberry at him. He does the same, and soon, we're giggling together.

"I'll change, and then we'll get on dinner. You go sit with Papi."

He wavers a minute between insisting on hanging with me before nodding and scrambling off the chair, his footsteps leading him outside to Daniel and my father.

I stand alone in the kitchen with my thoughts, then walk over to the window when I hear the ring of

Lucian's laughter. He's back on the bike, his grandfather right beside him, egging him on.

I watch them, letting my tired shoulders drop. I want to hold onto this moment for a few more years to come. I want to watch my son from this window as he grows, but I know that's impossible already.

The engagement to Xander means sooner or later, Father won't be able to protect Lucian anymore on this expansive estate. I will someday need to move in with my husband, and my son will do it with me—our son, because there will be no doubt to anyone who knows Xander whose son he is.

"You look so fucking sad, Mel. I promise it's not all that bad."

I startle and turn back to the door. Daniel steps into the room and joins me at the window.

"Gianna called today. She'll be here before the week runs out. You'll have your fighter back," Daniel says.

I wince and then laugh aloud. Well, he's literally right. Gianna has been known to get into more than one scuffle, a few of them physical. I can definitely see her standing up to Xander.

I lift my hand to my hair, and the ring flashes in the late light of the setting sun. My heart constricts in my chest as though someone's taken a piece of string and gone to work on the organ.

"It's like a brand, like a possession. He knows I hate red. Why get it for me?" The words dance in the air and dissipate like mountain smoke up in the hills.

"You'll go crazy questioning how the man's mind works, Mel. And we need to talk."

8

XANDER

THERE'S NOTHING I HATE MORE THAN WORKING WITH guys who are shady as hell.

The one in front of me? The shadiest I'm willing to work with.

I know how it seems. Being the leader of an organized crime family myself, I'm not exactly one to talk. However, I have to say, there's just something about a man who sticks to a moral code.

And, one who doesn't.

The man I'm waiting for?

He wouldn't know morals if they bit him in the ass.

Alec hitches his pants up and looks up at the cloudy sky. He rolls his eyes when a muffled clap of thunder rolls towards us. I tug my shirt away from my neck and wonder how long we'll need to stand around here before I lose my patience.

This is business, and I do not like to get involved with tawdry men.

"How much longer before you feel the need to hit something?" Alec grunts.

"Do not say a word to me, Alec."

Alec swivels towards me and drags his feet over to the fence. "Why do I have a feeling you're pissed about something entirely different?"

I puff out some air between my tight lips and keep my face turned up to the air that is slowly picking up. I feel it sift through my hair and bend my head gently forward so it sweeps across the back of my neck.

It doesn't offer me much of a relief.

I blink at the lack of space between us. "I have no idea what you mean, and take a step back Alec; you're not my fucking therapist."

Alec's face breaks into a wide grin. "You haven't got a therapist, Xander. And if you did manage to find one, you'd probably need to put a bullet in his ass after one session."

I laugh because, well, he's right.

A footstep sounds behind us, and I turn to watch Declan and Knox walk toward us. Declan's hair is gelled back against his scalp, his suit so stiff I wonder if he has the thing painted against his skin.

"You're late," I call to the two of them.

"And yet Mr. Sandro isn't here." He smirks. He doesn't smile, but Declan's lips tip up towards his nose like he might've in another life. Another reality that wasn't ours.

Knox is dressed just as badly. Except he's gone the opposite and is one step away from looking like he's just stepped out of bed with his latest fling.

I catch him with a harsh look.

"You could've made more of an effort, you know. This is business," I mutter.

His shoulders move up indifferently. "I still look better than all three of you combined."

With his windblown blonde curls and mother's green eyes, he's pretty, and I'll give him that. He's the only one among us who takes after her and, by virtue of this, has always been her favorite.

"I'll beg to differ on that, Knox. Any less effort, and you'll look like something the cat dragged in," Declan breaks in.

"And I'll still fare better."

Ryder clears his throat behind us. "Mr. Sandro has been led to the table."

We all turn together and head towards the room in the tiny house where we have all our business meetings. The place is teeming with our men.

Protection has been drummed tighter with the way things are up in the air at the moment.

We step through the door and walk briskly down the short hallway to the last room. The door has been flung open, and seated in there is Sandro Botticelli. His head wiggles towards the door at our entrance.

"I've been waiting."

"You shut the fuck up, Sandro, or you might take a fucking punch to the throat."

Sandro runs the largest smuggling ring in Chicago, and we need him on our side. But I will punch him if I have to, and I'll be happy to do it. No one keeps the Amory waiting, not even Sandro Botticelli.

"Better than watching you gripe all evening."

I take the chair across from him, and my brothers settle in beside me. At the door, Ryder stands guard, along with who I'm certain is Sandro's right-hand man.

"We should get this over with fast. I haven't got all day," I start.

Sandro nods and spreads his hands out, as neither does he. "I've got the routes mapped out. And the men are ready."

"I'm not certain why we don't go in with our men and sweep up what we can." Alec shifts forward on his chair. "We've got the manpower, certainly the money. It's a better solution than trying to work our way in or look the other way. They'll never let anyone in that they can't do away with."

Sandro smirks and brings a flask to his lips. I'm certain it's raw vodka. The man doesn't drink anything else.

"They're not stupid. The Russians know we're coming for them. They're not worried. They're barricaded, and from the news I've heard on the fucking grapevine, they've got the support of the Cambodians. And that spells doom. It won't be a fair fight."

The Cambodians are stealthy and patient. They have a history as violent and colorful as a pirate's tongue.

The stakes would be considerably higher with them joining the fight. I run my hand over the hilt of the knife in my pocket contemplatively and nod.

"Can you get us eyes in there?" Knox asks. He pulls the bottle of whiskey on the table towards himself and pours a shot into one of the tumblers provided. I nod at him, and he prepares one for me.

Sandro shakes his head. "With the Russians, maybe. The Cambodians are a whole different story. They don't play by the same rules. I know a man who knows a man, but that's the best I can do."

"You need a safe route through the streets too. If the Russians start shooting, they'll get your men too." Declan's face is impassive.

"Why the fuck else do you think I'm here? Certainly not for you lot," Sandro growls. He tips the flask to his lips and takes another drink.

Ugh.

This is what I'm talking about when I say that you can be a criminal and have morals.

Sandro has none.

I step in before it gets out of hand. This is our second meeting discussing the Russians, and I'm ready to come to some more final solutions. They're important, sure, but they're certainly not the only ones I need to keep a lookout for.

Time to be done with this.

"We'll back you up on this. Split the profits fifty percent down the middle," I announce.

"Fifty percent? I'm risking my men and my name," Sandro's body nearly bristles with anger suddenly, as though he feels insulted by the very words.

Alec is smiling, as is Declan and Knox. We've got him where we need him.

Sandro is a perfect solution to keep the Russians occupied. Enough to buy me time to deal with them on my own, just after the wedding.

The wedding.

It holds a place in my mind, like a chapter. There's before the wedding, then there's after. I don't question why the wedding is suddenly a timeline for all my actions lately, since it's pretty clear to me where I'm coming from.

The wedding means a woman who has no idea what her insertion into my life is costing.

"As are we. You will, after all, be hoisting your flag in our name. And our authority will pave the way for your men."

Sandro licks his lips greedily. Fifty percent suddenly sounds good. He would be making almost double of his regular gain with an affiliation to the Amory name. It's a sweet deal on both ends. The money is good, sure. But the endorsement of my name?

That's even better.

Amory is, after all, synonymous with control and authority. It could keep alive and kill just as easily. It had before. It always would.

"And for how long does this last?" His beady gaze eyes me.

"Until we get rid of the Russians," Alec replies in my stead.

"And you aren't even the Capo. Yet. Can't wait to see what you do with that position." Sandro sucks air between his teeth and shoves his hand through the air towards me. I watch him with a threat in my eyes, then slap my hand into his.

He and his men leave the room, and I pick up my glass finally, hurl the whole drink down my throat, and groan when it burns like fire down my chest.

"You're buying time you don't need," Knox says.

"I'm preventing a war I can't afford," I grunt.

"Is this about Mel?" Declan is watching me with a careful appraisal in his steely grey eyes.

"Why the fuck would this be about her?" But I don't meet his eyes either.

Alec's tone is withering, and he smirks. "You're hedging your bets. Not giving your best. And for once, business wasn't the first on your mind. Fifty-fifty? When have the Amorys ever done that? You're selling Sandro to the Russians for a flat fee."

A twinge of disgust at myself sizzles over me. Scraping my insides raw. I'm back to the man I was while I was with her. Already making her a priority when she's done nothing herself to prove she's worth the trouble.

I have to do something to stabilize. "He's a greedy fucker. And he kept me waiting. He'll survive."

"And after the wedding, how bad will this get?" Knox drags his glass across the table, drawing patterns with his fingers on it.

"Are you doubting me?" I question, my voice sleek and dangerous. He's my brother, but he's not above the law. And in my father's absence, I'm the law in this room.

He holds his hands up in the air. "Not a shred. Just worried. Last time, things with Mel didn't exactly go as planned. Don't get me wrong, I love her, but she's nothing like us. How certain are you that she'll stay put this time?"

Just the thought of her away from me has a growl building in my chest.

"She doesn't have a fucking choice. No one ever leaves a mafia marriage. Not without their body in a fucking bag."

Declan breaks in. "And will you be able to put her in it?"

I jerk my chair back suddenly and bang my hands against the table. "This conversation is over. No one is discussing my wife's death before I have her hitched to me in the first place. I'm fucking insulted. Does no one think I can take care of my fucking family?" I'm snarling at this point.

Fuck this. "I'm leaving."

I nearly jog out of the room, my head on fire, in a daze. I feel rubbery, and Ryder joins me at the door, following quietly like he's supposed to, unlike my dimwit brothers.

I ignore the greetings of my men on the property, heading over to the meandering stream of water that makes a small lake at the back of the property. I need a moment to myself before heading home.

Ryder takes a stand a few feet away from me, and I let myself sink to the floor, close my eyes, and let my thoughts wander.

The last time with Mel had been a roller coaster ride. We'd fallen in love clear-eyed and young. She'd been like a ray of bold sunshine lighting up and filling the cold, dank places of my heart.

I'd never felt so alive as when she'd been snuggled up to me or when she'd leaned into me when we were with company, seeking my warmth like a plant after light. Or sunk into her, riding wave after wave of pleasure with her wrapped tight like a vice around my cock.

And I'd been just as dead when she'd decided she just wasn't capable of watching my life as it was turning out to be. As it had been groomed from birth to be. It had been a spiral of drink and women after.

Even worse when she'd left the country with her sister Gianna. I'd done my best to keep track, but she'd seemed to disappear into thin air. And by then, the pressure of taking up after Father had dug in.

The very reason she'd left me had become the only way I could stay sane. That and the fucking feud between our families.

Sedric and Father haven't always seen eye to eye. In fact, it is much easier to say they hate each other.

And deep inside, I was frozen.

One cold, tender bit at a time, the darkness took over the light she'd planted until I was, again, the monster she had worried I would become.

And now, we are back down to where we had left off. And I don't know if I want her to thaw me again.

9

MEL

"Dinner has been slated for seven this evening. Rosa will send a few dresses to choose from. He'll pick you up. Be ready."

I scrunch my face up and turn from the mirror I've been staring into blindly for the last few minutes.

It sounded like a command, and it was. Xander calls, and I go. It is the terms of our engagement this time. My throat tightens, and I smile at myself, infuse some warmth into my voice, and answer.

"Of course, Ryder."

Ryder is Xander's underboss, second in command, and the person calling me to set up a date with my would-be husband.

I smile again and sink my teeth into my bottom lip.

"Are you okay?" Ryder asks. His voice is rough and hoarse. The way it has always been. Possibly the way it will always be until he stops smoking a thousand cigars a day.

I nod, though he cannot see it. Or me. "I am. I'm excited to get out of the house."

He gives a sardonic laugh. "You don't have to lie to me. I know this is difficult for you."

Ryder had been beside Xander during our first breakup, too. He'd gotten front-row tickets to the fights, and when I'd left the house, he'd been the one to call in the driver and send me on my way.

He probably knew how difficult it was being with Xander. He was smart enough to see it coming from the safe distance of his stoic mask.

"I'm fine." I'll be fine.

He doesn't push. "Alright. I'll call you when he's ready to leave. And send a driver with Romero to pick you up."

He hangs up, and I drop the phone on the dresser and get off my chair. It's already late afternoon, and the sun is doing a slow dance across the sky from east to west.

Xander won't like to be kept waiting, and I don't need to have him barking at me to get me on my way to dinner.

Lucian is out with Daniel somewhere. I didn't ask because neither of them seemed to want me to come along with them.

I slip into the bathroom to take a long bath, soaking in a lavender bubble bath that's supposed to be soothing. I don't feel any better when I step out of it thirty minutes later.

I have just finished moisturizing and stepped back from my nightstand dressed in a blue evening dress when the trill of the doorbell fills my ears. I know it's Rosa before I shove the door open and greet her barely peeking head.

She's holding about three bags already, a few more people trailing behind her with what appears to be more clothes in designer bags.

Nothing but the best for the Vittorios. I already feel tired.

"Do we really need this much?" I mumble, snapping the door closed behind him. Romero hefts the bags in his hands onto the couch and strides out of the room with a nod, probably back to the door where he's been standing guard.

"We do. You've got to look like a Vittorio." Rosa drops her own bags a lot more carefully onto the couch and points at one of the men who arrived with her to start unpacking.

There are designer clutches, a few more in the standard red, black, and white colors to match what I'm certain are simply luxurious dresses.

I trail my fingers over each one, feeling the quality of the fabric beneath my fingers.

They're gorgeous, for sure.

There are also some jewelry pieces when Rosa opens one of the smaller boxes; a delicate silver ring with an engraved sun cradling a small simmering opal.

A matching necklace features the same sun with a larger opal hanging gracefully from a silver chain.

The next box has a white gold ring with a beautiful aquamarine gemstone set right in the center. The band is crafted to look like waves. I have to admit it's stunning in it's simplicity. Like something he'd known I'd love.

Its necklace has a round aquamarine pendant on a white gold chain.

And there are a few boxes of shoes. But not just shoes. When I look at the labels, my eyes widen.

Some of these shoes would feed a family for a month.

Rosa coughs behind me. "Miss, your stylist."

She ushers to a slight man, who is dressed to the nines in a bespoke suit and designer sunglasses. He steps forward, and takes my hand. "Darling," he purrs. "Are you ready for your entrance?"

I snort. "I guess."

Rosa leans in. "What are you thinking? Something classic, or something striking?"

"Striking," the stylist murmurs. He leans forward. "She's got cheekbones and the face for it definitely." The man takes my face in his large hand and tilts my face to the evening light streaming in through the large windows.

I pull my face out of his grasp and turn to Rosa. She already has a glare on her face, and it's directed at him.

"You're better off not doing that when Xander is in range. You'll lose your hands and a family member just for that." She sweeps her head away without waiting for an answer when the man blanches.

I smile, but she's said exactly what I had in mind. Xander would never let him get away with putting his hand on me, as innocent as that was. He's so possessive sometimes it makes me feel safe; other times, I just feel crazy.

"Sorry. Part of the territory, I guess," I shrug.

The stylist nods. "I would expect no different."

"You have a few minutes. Get to work," Rosa snaps and waves her hand at me.

The man holds his hands out. "I'm sorry I did that." He grimaces, his nose wrinkling with distaste. "I get carried away, especially when I see a face with so much potential. I'm Mark."

I place my hand in his. "Well, very flattered to hear that I have potential I guess. She's right, though. Xander doesn't give a warning, Mark."

"Noted," he murmurs.

"Do we do this in your room?" Rosa's brow is tipped up, and she's not smiling. She's pissed at him, and she's making no effort to hide it.

I don't even understand why she's here. She runs security at Amory Corp. She shouldn't be here getting me ready for dinner. But no one tells Xander how to run his empire. It definitely wouldn't be me.

"Yes." I lead the way to my room, and the man files after me. The sound of the crackling bags behind me fills me with a dull sort of dread; my stomach is jittery, and I'm feeling nervous suddenly.

Maybe because it's dinner with Xander, and they're obviously all here to make sure I'm ready for it, like I need to be pruned and primed just for him.

I'm not sure how to feel about that.

Mark smiles. "So. Bold and striking work for you?"

"Yes, sure," I smile.

I'm definitely not going to say no to a makeover.

Mark agrees. "So," he says, "What brings you here, to be a mob wife?"

I snort as he rubs foundation over my skin, dabbing it in to blend with the other creams. "I don't think I had an option. I've got a mafia dad and mafia brothers as well."

"Look at you. A princess, one might say."

I wince. "Oh no. Please don't say that."

Mark laughs. He motions for me to close my eyes as he brushes makeup on my lids. "Don't ever turn down a crown that's offered to you, darling. Just my two cents."

"Even if the crown comes with thorns?"

"Especially then. Jesus is remembered just as much as anyone," Mark winks at me.

He continues to do my makeup, and I let the brushes and potions slide over my skin. Finally, he steps back. One of his manicured eyebrows raises. "Want to see?"

"Sure."

Mark spins the chair so I face the mirror. The woman looking back at me...

Well.

Bold is definitely the right word.

My eyes look smoky, a line of eyeliner and a bold shadow over my lids to highlight the shape of my eyes. My lips look plump and red. I lean into the mirror and watch as the woman in there moves with me.

I have no doubts about my self-esteem. I am a beautiful woman, and I know it. But I look even better today. The makeup is not subtle, but it still highlights my best features.

Rosa whistles softly, and she's back to smiling. "Let's do the dresses."

I roll my chair back and watch as she holds up a red Valentino dress, which I immediately reject . It's too glamorous, like something I'd wear to a red carpet than a dinner date.

The dress is sewn with silk, and It has been beaded subtly along the sleeves and bodice, with a figure-flattering silhouette framing the hips and flowing gently to the floor. It's beautiful, but it's not me.

"I see. Not a red girl?" Mark says, his voice light.

I shiver. "No. Not at all."

"In that case, what do you think of the black?" Mark asks. He's holding up a black dress that's a lot simpler but still doesn't look any less expensive.

The dress shimmers in the light, it's a classic boat neck inlaid with sequins and made of delicate lace. It moves fluidly even as Mark holds it up for me to see. The iconic interlocking GG logo has been subtly weaved into the fabric.

It's gorgeous.

I sigh. "No. Unfortunately I'm morally opposed to Gucci."

Mark's eyebrows gather in surprise. "No one is morally opposed to Gucci."

"Literally everyone in my world wears it. What else?"

He holds a hand to his chest. "Madam. I believe that I need time to recover from the dismissal of the greatest designers on earth."

I smile. "Come on, Mark. You're good at this, right?"

"The best," he says dryly.

"What else?"

Mark sighs. He turns and rifles through the clothing rack, muttering to himself. Rosa catches my eye. "Seriously?"

I arch an eyebrow at her. "I might be Xander's wife, but I'm my own person. I want him to know that. I want everyone to know that," I say, emphasizing *everyone* with intention.

Rosa shakes her head. "Your funeral."

"Maybe," I mutter. "Even more reason to wear whatever the hell I want."

She's quiet after that.

Mark finally turns. He holds out two options. "Okay. Pick," he says, clearly annoyed.

I stand to examine the dresses. One of them catches my eye, and I grin.

"That one."

Mark leaves the room. Rosa helps me into the dress, and when he returns, I'm all smiles in the mirror.

Mark whistles. "Wow. Okay, you called it."

I smile in the mirror. It's a champagne silk dress that's got a slit on it so high, there's no way I can wear underwear.

The bust is tight, pushing my breasts up so they're on display, and the waist nips in, emphasizing the curve of my waist.

It's borderline indecent.

And it's going to drive Xander absolutely nuts that everyone is looking at me in it.

Rosa stands behind me. "He's going to lose his shit."

"I'm counting on it."

She laughs, and for a second, I see the respect gleam in her eyes. "Good luck, Miss."

"Thanks, Rosa." I turn to Mark. "Alright. Accessories?"

"You got it, mafia queen."

By the time the driver arrives and Romero strides back in to inform me, I'm all decked out in so much expensive finery I'm certain I've got to be wearing a king's ransom.

He leads me outside, his eyes respectfully tilted to the side as he opens the door of the black limo and holds it as I slid into the car.

The leather beneath me is cool and I place my head against the headrest, close my eyes and let myself just breathe.

The car purrs and pulls away from the driveway. The drive is silent and long and I spend it sipping from the glass of Krug Champagne which has been provided for me.

I'm feeling a little calmer by the time Romero opens my car door and nods at the entrance where a maitré d is waiting to lead me into the restaurant.

I tap in my heels to the door and follow him to the table where Xander is already seated.

He lifted his head to meet my eyes, pulled his phone from his ears, hung up without taking his eyes off me and did a deliberate sweep of the bold Valentino gown I'd finally decided on.

I could almost feel him undressing the silky drape of the champagne dress off my hips, the sheer panels along the side allowing a glimpse of skin, which his eyes seemed to particularly enjoy.

Then, his eyes go dark. "Who saw you in this?"

"Oh, people. Anyone on the street. Rosa. Romero."

Xander's eyes flash. "Who on the street, Mel?"

"Literally anyone with eyes. I can't stop them from looking at me."

He looks at the wait staff, who look pretty nervous to see Xander glaring at them.

"Leave them alone, Xan," I say softly, my instincts kicking in. "I'm here with you."

He nods stiffly, then goes to pull out the chair. I walk over to him, my heels clicking on the floor. I sit, gently, and he pushes the chair in.

When he sits, his eyes darken again. As we sit, the bustier on my dress presses my breasts up.

If my calculations are correct, my nipples are almost hanging out of the fabric.

His face is flushed, and I can't tell if it's with rage or lust.

Internally, I smile.

Take that.

Xander gulps and grabs his wine glass, his fingers clutching the delicate stem a little too hard. "I'm glad you came. And doubly glad it's just us here, that dress. It's torture."

He slides his hand across the table and holds it out long enough that I place my hand in his and inhale shakily when he squeezes before turning my palm over and places an oddly sweet kiss in the center.

I'm glad you came, like there had been a choice. Ryder hadn't made the call like there had been one. When Xander Amory Vittorio called, you went.

"Are you?"

I look around the restaurant and give him a wry smile. It's just us minus the bustling staff who have made a show of the meal.

The restaurant aptly named Éclat de Saveurs, literally meaning "burst of flavors" according to the staff, seems to have lived up to its name.

I had ordered the Truffle-infused Wagyu Steak with Gold Leaf Garnish while Xander had gone with Lobster and Cavier.

It's a rich meal, but the man can afford to pay—said man is leaning across the table into me like he has something to say that isn't for anyone but me.

His musky smell of lethal energy and leather is so seductive it has me curbing the urge to strain forward for more of it.

The strict cut of his suit has him so mouth-wateringly good he looks like he came straight off from a model shoot. One for men of the mafia who look like they will devour you with one straight gaze.

"Very glad. Do you have doubts?" He inclines his head right, a strand of his hair flopping carelessly against his face. His eyes are the intense gaze of a hawk circling above.

I laugh, more to relieve the ache in my chest than because any of it is funny. I slant my head towards him, my favorite Stuller necklace moving with the motion; I had been shocked he'd still remembered. "None at all. You've never lied Xander. Not once."

He jerks away like he hasn't been expecting such blunt truth. My heart is thundering in my chest, and I'm holding on barely.

He looks handsome, almost delicious, with that heat in his gaze tracking my every move, sparking a blaze in my chest. One that just isn't letting go.

"I wasn't expecting that." He murmurs after a long moment of silence.

"I know. We can't all be predictable, can we?"

"Am I?"

I shrug. "We still haven't signed the contract." I nod to indicate the empty restaurant.

"You didn't call me to set up dinner. And you had Rosa bring the dresses. It's what you've always done."

His eyes glint with challenge down at me, and my nipples tighten beneath the cup of my dress.

Mark had insisted a bra would ruin the cut of the corset gown. Despite Rosa's protests, I had agreed with him, and that had been the end of it. Given the high slit, I'm actually wearing no underwear under this.

I hope Xander figures it out.

And I hope it drives him nuts..

"You never used to hate any of it." He lowers his voice and makes a tent out of our bent heads, his forehead almost grazing mine. "I remember quite distinctly you used to love being alone with me."

Damn him. He had no right to say that. It had been years ago. That had been another lifetime ago. We had changed.

"You're sprouting history, Xander."

His eyes darken when I roll my tongue over his name. His eyes linger on my lips for a second before he pulls away and straightens his suit. I miss his warmth immediately and almost regret my words.

Almost.

"My mistake. And if you keep staring at me that way, I won't be responsible for my actions. Or yours."

I know exactly what he means. But it's not like me to give an inch. Not when he's involved.

I wet my lip, hoping I don't ruin Mark's careful job on my face. "What actions?"

The meal on the table is almost done with. I'm tasting him. It would be just like Xander to lean across the table and take my lips with his. He hadn't cared before. I was his woman, and that's all that mattered to him. Then.

Now he moves his head from side to side ruefully and jabs a look at my phone on the table. I know what he's about to say before the words slip out of his tightly clenched lips.

"You're not using the phone Rosa provided."

I bristle. I have Romero and the safety of Amory Corp and my father's house. He doesn't need to keep me chained to him like a dog. "I have it with me. Isn't that all you need?"

"I also know you don't have your pretty little bags with you at all hours, not like this phone. Maybe we should have a tracker embedded here."

He takes my hand in his and rubs his thumb over my wrist gently back and forth.

"I'd feel so much better." He grumbles. He takes the fork and has a mouthful of his caviar.

I take a light sip of the red wine that had come with the meal and roll my eyes. "And how about how I feel? Doesn't it matter?"

"I have to guarantee your safety when you're not with me, Mel. Our history is very well known."

I fling a hank of my long hair behind my back and shiver slightly when his eyes track the movement. It's nothing sexual, but the look in his eyes is the piercing stare of a predator after prey.

I have nothing to say to that. He's right. There had been a time when he had meant we. When we had been so entwined with each other, there had been no space for anything else.

"I know. I understand you need to track me. But it's hard enough when I'm at Amory Corp and with Romero on my tail all day. Isn't that enough?"

He takes my hand and jerks me towards him. "Nothing will be enough, Mel, when you're my woman. Soon enough, you will be my wife, il mio raggio di sole."

His sunshine. I blink, my eyes closed a second before his lips mesh with mine.

I know then I'm not heading home after dinner. I know I'm not over this man.

Same way, he isn't nearly over me. It's a funny moment to realize we've really not changed as much as we thought we had.

Because despite everything, despite my bravado, despite our past, I really want to be his sunshine again, breathing light and heat into the dark places of his heart.

His lips crash over mine, his tongue probing and hungry. I melt under his touch, my chest heaving. Xander pulls back and looks down. "Did you not wear a bra?" he growls.

I peek down and notice that my nipples are pretty much out. I tuck them back in, then flash him a defiant gaze. "No."

"That dress has a slit on it," he says, his eyes narrowing.

"It does."

"A high one."

"Yep."

Finally, he puts two and two together. Xander abruptly steps close, and in one smooth gesture, lifts me over his shoulder. I squeak, desperately trying to keep my tits covered as he walks to the door.

One of his hands snakes up my skirt, and even though there could be witnesses, I feel his hands touch the skin between my legs.

"Fuck, Mel," he mutters, his fingers pressing inside me. I moan at the invasion, but I'm already so wet, it doesn't matter.

He pulls out abruptly, smacking my ass as the car comes into view. "You're going to pay for this," he growls.

It's not a threat, though.

It's a promise.

And I can't wait for him to fulfill it.

He tosses me in the car, walking around the backseat. I scramble to get myself together, pulling at the dress so that it could cover my breasts, trying to tug the fabric over the slit in my dress.

Xander comes into the car, and holds my hands. "No," he growls. "You put this on to tempt me."

I nod. "I did."

"Time to see what you wrought, then," he rumbles.

The car starts, but Xander doesn't move from where he's perched. One of his hands tugs the top of my dress down, and the other travels up the inside of my thigh.

"Xander," I breathe as he finds my slit.

He doesn't respond.

Two thick fingers press inside me. His other hand clutches at my breast, pulling my nipple as he pumps his fingers in and out of my wet entrance.

Fuck.

If I don't stop him, I'm going to come. I'm going to come much, much faster than I wanted to.

Xander knows. His eyes light up as he presses inside me. "Isn't this what you wanted? To feel my fingers on you? To see what this dress would let me do?"

I don't have a response for that. I'm so close, I just need...

Abruptly, Xander's fingers pull back.

I glare at him. "Why did you stop?"

He leans forward, kissing me until I'm moaning under him again.

When he pulls back, his eyes are dark. "You tortured me all night, Mel. Seems fair that I'd do the same to you."

The words make me shiver.

Soon, we're home and like a man possessed, he takes me by my lips the minute he ushers me down, kissing me all through the entrance.

His hand is all over me, pushing my dress to my waist, my hand desperate and hungry for the brand of his touch.

He lifts me into his arms and climbs up the stairs to his door. I don't argue with the display of possessiveness.

I don't think I want to be out of his arms ever again. Only Xander holds me this way, like he never wants to let me go.

By the time we make it to his room, I'm panting and gasping for breath, and when the door is shoved closed behind him, I know it's the start of a long, long night. .

10

XANDER

I'M RAVENOUSLY HUNGRY FOR HER.

When Mel showed up wearing a dress that looked like it would be more at home at an award show for adult entertainment, I knew that she was fucking with me.

All through dinner, the top of the champagne-colored silk moved, just barely revealing the dusky pink of her nipples, before she'd manage to tug it up again.

That, and the slit on her dress, showing all of her powerful thighs...

I knew the second I saw her, there was no way she had on any underwear. Nothing would fit under a dress like that.

I was rather proud of myself, actually, for not fucking her right on the table as soon as she got there.

Now, I am ready to fuck her. I'm ready to show her exactly what I can do for her.

And exactly how it could be between us.

Yet I take the time to pull the zipper as gently as possible down the back of her dress. Mel shivers and steps out of it when it pools around her legs.

I follow the curve of her shoulders with my fingers down to her hips, pulling the gold silk off of her inch by inch.

When I'm done, I lean back to admire my handiwork.

She looks fucking gorgeous in nothing but jewels and heels.

When my fingers graze the flesh, she turns towards me and twines her arms behind my neck. Her wide eyes look up at me, and my engorged cock presses painfully against the seam of my pants.

"Your sunshine? After all this time?" She nips a line of kisses down my chest, and I let her, thinking if she needs a conversation, this is the worst way to convince me of it. My chest is expanding, filling with air and lust and a flame of fire so hot it's scorching.

I hitch her legs up my body and drag her so close there is not a hair's breadth of space between us, and she melts into me. Her breasts smother my breath, the air stalling in my lungs.

I tip her head up to mine and let my lips lap over hers. She moans in the back of her throat and responds before pulling away.

Her hands stroke my skin, down the middle of my stomach, and straight to my girth, where she wraps her hands, her thumb skimming over my hard-on.

I groan into her lips and jerk my lips from hers. Her eyes are soft and watching, gliding over my face as pleasure bunches my stomach and I pull away from her grasp.

She gives a disappointed little mewl, and I suck at the line of her jaw, flicking my tongue from her neck to her collarbone, sucking the flesh into my mouth and soothing with the swipe of my tongue when she moans.

"You know you are." I heft her into my arms. "You know you have always been."

The pounding of my heart didn't let up, the singing of my blood didn't lessen, and I knew even then before I'd slipped into her that it never would. It would be just like the first time. Maybe better.

I could never be certain of anything with this woman.

The thought makes me harden even more, but there's a desperation in my chest that I also need to soothe.

I need to know that she's mine.

I need to know that *she knows* she's mine.

I press her back on the bed. She falls, her breasts bouncing, the diamonds around her neck twinkling in the light.

Her eyes look at me with a question. "Aren't you going to take off your clothes?"

I smirk at her. "Not yet."

With one hand, I pull my belt out. I lean over her, still dressed, and use the belt to bind her hands together.

Mel's eyes widen as I pull back. "Xander…"

I stop her with a kiss. "Do you trust me?" I whisper.

Her eyes widen, and there's a heartbeat when I don't know what she's going to say, but eventually she nods.

"Yes."

"Good," I grin.

I lean back then, and I pull apart her legs. I want to watch her as she comes, then I want to fuck her with my tongue. When she's wet and moaning, then, and only then, will I give her my cock.

I press my fingers into her, moaning at the wetness I find. She shivers, and the movement makes her breasts jiggle.

I watch as I slowly press my fingers in again, my thumb working her clit, as she pants.

"Xander," she moans.

"I know, baby," I murmur. "How about one, to take the edge off?"

She's close. I can feel it in the way she clenches around my fingers. I press on her clit again, and she gasps.

"Good girl," I murmur.

I don't let her recover. I move forward, throwing her legs over my shoulders. As she moans, I lap at her center.

"Xander, I can't," she pants.

I lean up and glare at her. "You will. You'll fucking come as many times as I tell you to. Understand?"

She moans in response.

I lap at her clit, moving down to press my tongue inside her. I reach up, gathering her breasts in my hands, pinching and kneading and tugging on her stiff nipples.

"Oh god. Xander…"

"Come for me, Mel," I murmur again. I punctuate my words with teeth on her clit, biting softly as I pinch her nipples.

She screams my name this time. I feel her clench around my tongue, licking every scrap of her orgasm as she comes.

When I feel her shuddering cease, I pull back.

Mel's chest is flushed red, and she's panting. Her eyes look glazed, and she's staring at me like she can't believe what just happened.

I grin at her. "Ready for another, baby?"

"No, I can't…"

"You can, Mel. And you will."

With that, I start to undress.

I let her take her own perusal, her eyes roving over my chest as I take my shirt off. I let her feed her eyes for a while on that which had been pressed insistently into her so many times before, letting her see my cock as I free it from my pants.

I'm so hard. Having her look at me like this, like I'm her own personal feast, makes me even harder.

Mel purses her lips. "You're handsome. Sometimes, I think I forget or maybe dull that memory of just how fine a specimen of manhood you are." She murmurs, her tongue darting over her lips. She leaves a line of wetness that I want to follow with my own tongue.

But I don't. Because her words have me engorging even more, an unapologetic bulge that's going nowhere straining at her.

She licks her lips again. There's no pretending I have no idea what she's referring to.

"Do you want it?" I ask, dragging her back into my arms, my thumb stroking her nipples, firing between us, heating the sheets and the air, and setting our skins aflame. I take her hands out of the belt, and she uses them to rake her nails down my chest.

She giggles, her eyes lighting up with mirth in a way I haven't seen directed at me in years. It makes me feel a million times bigger than I am. I like it.

I want to make her giggle that way again. It does things that are not strange but new to my insides. Things I never thought I'd feel again.

"Do I want it? He asks."

Before she can blink, my hands go straight to her thighs, spreading them wide enough to bury my head between them again. My lips meet the entrance of her vagina walls, and she gasps.

I feel her raise her upper body in reaction to the ecstasy she just felt, and instantly crumble back to the bed.

Her breathing stops and hitches in her throat, her hands clutching tightly to the sheets.

I dig my tongue into her again, rocking her walls over and over again, her eyes rolling into her head, her hands curving

and scratching my back as she wriggles in pleasure, burying my head deeper..

I pull away at intervals, tease her clit while stroking a finger over her folds. She's wet and getting wetter as I brush my fingers over her.

I thrust a finger into her, and her back arches off the bed, her chest heaving, her breasts wobbling with the movement.

Her pink nipples are taut and tight like little berries. And all I want to do is eat. I graze my tongue over one and then suckle it between my lips.

My fingers keep up their torture inside her, sinking and withdrawing, until her cry is a breathy rasp of moans and pants.

"Stop teasing Xander. You know what I want." She lifts her hips into my hands. "Fuck me, fuck me hard and fast. I've missed you inside me."

The words nearly send me over the edge, and she must feel the same way because the scent of her arousal wafts up between us, and I know I just have to taste her. I need to have her on my tongue; I crave the tangy taste of her on my lips, like an addict with their drug of choice.

She's mine, and there's no weaning me off her. Or her off me, because this is the cry, the wetness, the abandon of a woman who needs a man, who's willing to take as much as she gives.

I take my lips off her nipple and blow a warm stream of air over the flesh.

She blinks her long lashes open and watches me as I kiss my way down her body again, stopping at her navel to shower a flurry of deep kisses there.

She cups my head and allows her fingers to anchor into my hair as I continue blazing a torch of heat over her skin, down to the apex of her thighs, where I kiss around my fingers.

The little dark dot beside the neat trim of hair, her clit that seems to be pulsing, the weeping lips that let me know she's enjoying this as much as I am. And then, finally, I pull my fingers from her and sink my tongue inside her, again.

I bring her there, right to the edge, then I pull back.

The woman before me is exactly as I want her. Needy. Panting.

Desperate for me.

This is the woman that I could never forget. This is Mel, *my* Mel, the person that I've had a thousand fantasies about. The woman who keeps me going.

My sunshine.

I want her sun to steal over my skin and bring back the light that she is. I want her warmth to remind me of all the things I had forgotten. To remind me why I'd risk my men for her.

Why I wanted her enough to beg that she stay, and I want to remind her of all she'd missed by running away from me.

"Do you want me to use a condom?" I growl, barely coherent, already tipping my hand to the bedside table.

Her hand falls over mine, and I stop. She shakes her head, her eyes gleaming like jades in her face. "It's useless, isn't it? We'll need an heir to appease our fathers. Best to start now."

I hate the words. I don't need to get my wife pregnant to please a pair of men, whether they are the two most powerful men I know or not.

Whether they're our parents or not. But what I do want to do is take Mel without any restrictions between us.

And her reasoning might be flawed, but this is not the time to try convincing her.

I shake her hands off mine, bristling with anger.

I keep my jaw tight as I take off my trousers rapidly, my chest rising and falling from more than anger as my eyes track her flushed body.

I drag her hips towards mine, and ram into her without warning, all the way to the hilt, her body parting around me, wet and tight and snug like a glove.

"Il mio raggio di sole."

She clenches around me, harder and harder, tighter and wetter, as I snap my hips into hers, taking her like I've always wanted to. Her cries are exhaled from parted lips, her legs hitching up my ass, digging in and encouraging me.

She pulls me into her, raking her fingers across my back hard enough that I feel the bite of pain, and finally, her insides clench tight around me. She bends her head into my shoulder, sinking her teeth in hard as she shatters around me, splitting open as the force of her orgasms drags her under.

My breathing is ragged, and the sound of our sharp, fast breathing fills the room, the smell of sex biting and baiting my senses, sending me into a spiral that has my hips slapping against her, pulling away from her, and then sinking back in, forcing my way through the slick wetness of her body in the grasp of an orgasm.

Soon enough, my balls tighten, and a tingling begins from the tips of my fingers and sweeps its way over my body like waves over the ocean, drenching pleasure so sharp and hard that a scream unlocks in my throat and tears its way out of my tightly secured lips.

I roar, coming inside her. Her body, still cinched around mine, goes taut when the first spill of my seeds coats her insides.

And even as I jerk into her, I hope this very seed sprouts the heir she so desperately wants to provide.

"Possa il tuo grembo germogliare il meglio di noi, Mio Sole."

May your womb sprout the best of us, My Sunshine. It is a fervent prayer and a plea.

———

I JERK AWAKE SUDDENLY. There's a bang at the door, and I freeze, listening, my heart constricting in my chest. It's oddly silent after the bang and my first reaction is making sure Mel is safe.

She isn't in bed, but there's the sound of water rushing in the bathroom to let me know where she is. The sheets are slightly warm when I pat around, which means she's just been out of bed.

I groan and decide the flush of anger I'm feeling really isn't her fault, but after our night together, I'd at least expected to wake up to her in my arms. Not already washing away evidence of the night in the cold light of the morning.

I push my feet out of bed and ignore the voices at the door. I can hear Alec's husky baritone already. Ryder won't let them up here, not with Mel up here with me.

I pull a robe off the bedpost and slip my arms into the holes. I pad over to the bathroom door and push it open as slowly as possible. Mel is in the shower stall, her hair wet as she washes her scalp, her back turned towards me.

My cock responds as it always does when she's in close proximity, lengthening against the front of my robe, a solid tent, my blood revving like a Harley in my ears, and my heart beating, thumping, and strong.

Her hair is streaming behind her, steam from the warm water coating the glass of the stall.

All I can see is the outline of her body, but my body remembers her, tight and panting around me, her body needing mine as much as I need hers. Chasing her release, her legs tight around my ass.

Almost as though she can sense my presence, her back goes stiff, and she swivels towards me. I step towards her and open the bathroom door, stepping in there with her.

"You didn't think I'd want you this morning?" I let my eyes drop to her wet lips, watch as she catches a drop of water with her tongue, and follow the line of my eyes.

She swallows like she always does when she's nervous. Or needy. Or just before she mewls as she cums around me.

"I didn't think it was a good idea for us. For me."

The swell of anger clogs my throat. "You're not going to pull away like you always do, are you?"

"I don't want to. We hurt each other. We always do. We never stop. This was a bad idea. You know it, but you'll never agree." Her words are as angry as mine, and her stare is almost stern.

I tug her into my arms, washing the shampoo from her hair. Once the suds are completely gone, I take her lips with mine in an angry kiss.

She responds, the full globes of her breasts pressed into my chest and the taut points of her nipples poking into my chest.

When she's raking a hand through my hair, her mouth following the lead of my questing lips, I pull away from her and turn away without a word.

I know she's right. I don't agree with her, but I can't have an argument with a naked Mel. It's taking all of my self-control, just keeping my arms from sliding down her body. Just stopping my pulsing cock from sinking into her warmth.

I pull the robe off and drop it to the floor, thundering out of the bathroom. By the time I pull some clothes on and make it downstairs, Alec and Knox are gathered in my kitchen, warm cups of coffee in their hands.

I pour one for myself, grimacing the entire time, my teeth grounding down.

"Why the hell do I wake up to the both of you here?" I snap at Alec when he shifts a step closer to me. He doesn't seem to care about the rage in my voice.

He jabs a pointed look at Romero, who seems to have stood guard the entire time while Mel spent the night with me. "What's he doing here?"

"Isn't it obvious, Alec? Somewhere up there is Mel, and this early in the morning, we both know what that means." Knox breaks in.

I clench my jaw and take a drink of the coffee. There's the constant buzz of rage lurking somewhere in my body, spreading steadily through my body.

Maybe because finding she had slipped out so early out of my bed had brought back memories of the last time she had disappeared from my life.

Or maybe because I'd been looking forward to waking up with her snuggled into my arms, smelling of woman and the light zing of lavender that was Melissa Sedric.

And how the hell had I been so lost in sleep that she had slipped out of bed without me feeling anything? That kind of sleep got a man killed in his own home.

And the last time I'd had that kind of sleep had been exactly the last day she'd been in my bed. Six fucking long years ago.

Alec is still watching, his eyes flitting between me and the clap of footsteps on the stairs. He strides over and drops the cup of coffee on the kitchen counter while my heart keeps beating with the sound of her on the stairs.

"I hope you know what you're doing, Xander. It's not just your heart on the line this time. There's more than an empire on your shoulders." His words are almost whispered, but they scissor their way under my skin in many ways.

I have responsibilities now. And Melissa will be part of them soon enough. It's time to see her as she really is.

Just business. One I want to bind to me at all hours of the fucking day, but still just business.

Besides, if I'm not careful, I might end up hurting her too, with my almost obsessive need for her.

11

MEL

FATHER'S OFFICE IS COLD DESPITE THE HEATWAVE THIS summer. The air conditioning is strong, regardless of his doctor's order to tune it down. The cold is bad for his heart, and the pains rock his chest most nights.

He doesn't listen. Just as he isn't listening to me right now. He's a stubborn man, just like me.

"I can't move in with him, father. What about Lucian?" I flick a look at my watch and frown. I should be at Amory Corp right now.

But I'm here at my father's house, in his home office. This seems like a meeting more than a conversation. And I know it's no mistake that he's chosen this room to inform me I'm moving into Xander's house in two days.

Father shrugs but doesn't hold my eyes. He peers at the bust of himself on his table, a gift from my brother Daniel on his birthday three years ago.

"He's bound to find out soon. He's not stupid. And you'll never let Lucian stay here."

How can he ask that? Lucian goes with me. I haven't severed myself from society for almost six years, only to let him go now.

I glower at him, trying to stop the rampant tremble of my hands, winding one around the other on my lap. "Father! This is a contract. We don't even need to live together."

"And what kind of marriage is that? What image does it send of the unity in our ranks if the very head of the Famiglias live in separate homes?"

I squeeze my eyes closed and relax into the seat. He's right. The marriage is to resolve the feud between our family. Living in separate homes sort of defeats the purpose of the entire thing.

But after last night, the last thing I want to do is be stuck in the same house with Xander. We'll never be able to keep our hands off each other. And it would be an insane idea, especially with Lucian in that house.

"What do I do? I can't help worrying. His family can't protect me against the extent of his anger. He's liable to crush them too."

As he would crush me too.

Xander is a possessive man. Learning I had kept his son and heir away from him this entire time would send him into a blind rage. I open my eyes and latch onto my father's hard eyes.

He gives me a slight smile of assurance. "He won't. He can't."

"He can. He'll be wielding control of the Famiglia. He will be able to do all he wants. There will be nothing to stop him this time. And there will be no shade of earth to hide in. Not with us in the same house." My heart speeds up, and I swipe a wet palm across the length of my dress.

"He won't hurt you, Mel. I would hunt him. Besides, we both know he's not over you." A quick smile tugs at the corner of his lips. "Romero says you spent the night at his home."

There is no reason for the flutter in my stomach or the heat creeping from the corner of my ears to the apples of my cheeks. I splay my hand on the desk and keep my eyes from his.

"So it's that way, huh? And you worry? You'll be fine, Amor." He pats my hand on the table.

"I'm not worried about me, Father. I worry he'll use Lucian as a chip. Some way to control me. He's a madman. I refuse to put anything past him."

The beat in my chest is rising higher and higher, until I feel it would choke me, until I feel I can't breathe beyond the boulder of fear lurking like a monster in my stomach.

Father waits a moment, dragging in a measure inhale of air so his chest rises and falls. "He's not a monster. He doesn't need to control you. Have you ever thought me a monster?"

"Mother didn't hide your children from you. It might have been a different tale if she had. Imagine the story when everyone finds out."

I don't know all the particulars of what goes on when he goes away to "work." But I am not foolish enough to believe this wouldn't spin out in some bad press for him.

God. I am just tired of thinking. I want to spend time with my child. I want to hug him good night and have him fall asleep in the safety of my arms. He's my priority. Anything else is debris in rushing water. It'll pass.

Even Xander. It doesn't matter how my body aches for him. How much I seek the caress of his fingers over my skin. It doesn't matter how he's already making me feel.

He chuckles, the sound dark and throaty. "She didn't. She wasn't in your situation. But knowing her, she would've done this too."

I bite my lip and hike my eyebrows. I don't believe a word he's saying. "Would she? We both know Mother was fearless."

I wish I had half her strength. Half of the fire of herself. She'd always kept father in line. Had him wound so tight around her finger, she'd become the center of his existence.

"She was. But so are you."

My lips are already parting to answer when he holds his hand up in the air and silences me with the spark of anger in them.

"No arguments Melissa. You go in and get Lucian ready. Amory has already had Rosa pack your bags. You'll move this evening."

I tremble, worry, anger and helplessness blooming and spreading like fire in my tight chest.

"You said I had two days."

His face is a clean slate. He's no longer my father. He's a businessman, telling me as it will be. I'd known there was a reason we were holding this conversation in his study instead of at dinner, where he discussed most family business that concerned his children.

"Well, you don't anymore. You'll keep putting it off. Amory will let Xander know he'll be expecting you. Go speak to Lucian."

How do I tell him he will be moving into a house with a man who is his father? How do I explain why I'd left in the first place?

He is a child, but he isn't stupid. He'll have questions. He is a person in his own right. He deserves answers.

I nod at Father and yank my hand away from his when he goes to comfort me with what I'm certain is a squeeze.

I can feel the spear of his gaze on my back my entire walk to the door. I feel jittery. Like I can't think. Caught in a state of limbo.

The walk to Lucian's room is long, almost as though I'm buying myself time for Father to change his mind, for Xander's father to decide the Russians weren't enough of a threat, as though that would help me either way.

When I arrive in Lucian's room, Hailey is already packing his clothes. Most of it is upended on the bed, large pills of soft cushiony fabrics. He's jumping on the bed, more interrupting than helping.

I smile when he spies me by the door and comes jumping off the bed.

"Papi says we're heading to another house. Do you think it'll be fun?" He loops his arms around my neck when I sweep him into my arms.

He smells of baby lotion and his shampoo. Hailey is watching me, her eyes half on the clothes she's folding carefully into boxes.

I inject a suitable dose of enthusiasm into my voice. I press a long kiss to his forehead, and my arm coils him deeper into my chest.

He's warm, and his wet hair from a shower tickles my nose. My heart thuds faster. "it's going to be a lot of fun. You'll love it."

I hope he does. I plan on protecting him however I can from the tension between Xander and me. He'll never physically hurt Lucian, but I will never allow him to teach my lovely boy to be as hard and emotionless as his own father has taught him and his siblings to be.

"Will Uncle Daniel visit?"

"He better."

"And Aunty Gianna?" He pronounces the name with a slight lisp, his voice producing it as "Gi Ana."

I smile and swing him in my arms, the sound of his laughter calming my heart. Hailey is still watching, folding the clothes faster now without the distraction of Lucian to divide her attention.

"You're coming with us, Hailey. Do you mind?" I watch her face, trying to see if she has any objections in her eyes.

Not everyone is comfortable around Xander. Anyone who has lived here for more than a month knows the Amory family.

I have known the man for years, and yet I still fear his rage.

"I don't mind." Her words are simple, but the tone she delivers them has me turning away from her, my son tucked into the arch of my hips.

There's a forlornness to her tone, as though she senses trouble in the air but is choosing to wade through the heat for me. She's always been that way.

I look down at Lucian in my arms. "How about you go let Hailey dress you up? We'll need to leave soon."

If Father is right about Rosa being in my room, and I have no doubt that he is, then I want a moment alone with her. Something is obviously happening that he isn't being completely honest with.

He'd given me two days to move into Xander's house, then changed his mind at a moment's notice. How then had Rosa been informed to show up here?

It wasn't possible. Which meant she'd already been here. Which was either a mistake on his part, or there was never any two days. And just what was the rush?

I let Lucian slide down my hips, watching as he runs back down the hallway, and then I take four slow, deep breaths, attempting box breathing to still myself. I have a feeling I'll need it.

When I step into my room, there is a flurry of action. Rosa seems to be directing three women who are packing up box after box of my clothes. One of them is sifting through my jewelry and placing them in separate velvet boxes.

"I could've done this myself, you know." I move across the room to her, ignoring the jab of fear that seems to be crushing my rib cage. I fear I will have no control over my life.

Perhaps this will be the last moment in which I will ever have a choice, and this in itself isn't even one.

"You don't have to. Xander sent the women."

The mention of his name has me clenching my fist at my sides. Rosa sends a look to my tight fingers, and I open them, splaying them against my side.

"So he knows I'm coming? Was this his idea?" I would understand it better if it had been. Just one more piece in his empire to move as he saw fit.

Except I wasn't even his wife yet.

And you've already fucked him once.

A pulse throbs all over my body at the thought. I ignore it.

Rosa shakes her head. "Both your parents decided. He's been driven home to await your arrival. Is there anything you'd like to take with you? This might be one of the last times you'll be here."

I grit my teeth and flash her a look of anger, my eyes gleaming like gems.

"I'm not allowed to visit my father?"

"Not to stay. This will no longer be your home."

12

XANDER

My gut clenches. One clean drop like a roller coaster, making the tough drop with humans in its bowels. She'll be here in a few minutes.

Knox is standing by the window, a reflective stoop to the drop of his shoulders. I pace my way across the length of the house, grateful it's just the both of us here.

My heart thunders like a stallion in my chest, and I tighten my jaw. This isn't the first time Mel will be spending the night here.

But this feels different. This time, there will be no leaving and no running away when things get tough. I wonder if she knows what that means.

Knox walks over to me, dressed as always a little better than a juvenile.

"You can stop pacing. It's not a good look."

"Why the fuck are you here, Knox?"

"Mel needs a certain level of familiarity. I'm here to provide that."

I glower at him, turning away so he doesn't see the way my guts twist, and I grimace. If he's going to be some sort of familiarity, then what the fuck does that make me? And I don't argue because I know he is right too. "More accurately, what you mean is Father made you come."

"No. I chose to." He watches me like a hawk, his lips tasting words he doesn't let slip out of his mouth.

I ignore him. "How much longer?"

Ryder takes a look at his watch, where he's standing at the door. "About five? They should be here soon."

I stride out of the house, Ryder ahead of me. He has the door open by the time I make it to the front door. I fold my arms across my stomach and note that Father has sent a few more men over than necessary.

She's just moving into the house. There is no harm coming to us. But then, father had always been oddly protective of her even after she had left.

My stomach twists.

I twist my head to Knox. "What's with the men? Why are they here?"

He looks away and mumbles his way through a reply. "Father had them arrive with me. I have no idea."

He definitely knows what's going on. I take a step towards him, already deciding I'll get the truth from him some way, when the large gate rolls open, and her car comes crawling up the driveway. Another car follows behind hers.

My heart stills. "You're lying to me, Knox. And you know I have a hatred for liars."

Knox stares back at me evenly, but there's fear and an emotion akin to anger in his eyes. "What would you have me say? It isn't my truth to speak."

Before I can decode the cryptic words, the car pulls to a stop. Romero pushes open the front door and steps out. He nods, a brief jerk of his head, before he pulls her door open and steps back.

My hands curl into hard fists when her leg drops first to the ground. She's wearing flats. It's not anything sexy, but it has a zing sparking my nerve endings and has me stepping towards her.

I stop with another step when her head comes peeking out of the car. She lifts her face first to the house in front of her and swallows. Then her eyes find mine, and fear flits across them.

It's gone in a second, but I can see it. I wait and let her come to me, as it should be, as it has always been.

I ignore the hard thud of my heart and wait. I'm still waiting when she bends into the car and comes out with a child in her arms.

I think nothing of it. I have no idea why she has a sleeping child in her arms, but knowing Mel, it could quite literally belong to anyone. It piques my interest, but it is not the center of my attention.

She is.

She's trembling, her shoulders hunched in on herself. In her eyes, a spark ignites, vivid and captivating, akin to the vibrant leaves of an untouched woodland.

But when she steps into my orbit, my eye drops to the sleeping child in her arms, and I freeze.

Breathe stolen away.

The fury inside me shimmers with volcanic force, ready to erupt.

There is nothing moving. Not a muscle, not a hair. Even the trees seem to obey the rage in the air.

My anger is rising, and as much as I want to control it, it's boiling, and could rage like wild fire at this pace. "What the fuck, Mel?"

The boy looks about five years old or six. His arms are curled on his stomach, one finger linked protectively to Mel's index finger. His hair is chestnut, an almost exact shade of mine. I have no doubt he is mine. None at all.

"He's sleeping? Can I at least put him down? Then we can talk?"

What is there to talk about? What is there to say? And how is she going to explain this away?

Knox steps forth, slipping his hand around her shoulders and taking the baby from her. There is a dare in his eyes, and I am not a monster.

I take a step back, frustration beating at me.

Was this why she'd disappeared?

Why I hadn't been able to find her after she'd left my eyes, taking with her my light. How, in fact, was it possible that she had hidden him from me this entire time?

I stalk my way up the stairs to my study, allowing the door to bang its way closed after me. I'm shaking.

There's a line of sweat breaking on my forehead, my hands fisted at my sides, and a red haze over my eyes.

I want to punch something, a wall, a man, anything to relieve this rage. At this point, even Knox will do.

I watch the men gathered outside. There's a tenseness to my shoulder as they bunch together. It makes sense now why Father had the guards stationed.

Not that any of them would've been able to stop me if I'd decided to wring her little neck for lying to me this entire time. And most of my anger is directed at myself.

Because despite everything, I could feel, even as I scowled at her, the surge of heat, powerful as a wildfire spreading through dry grass.

I still want her. There is a big tent in my pants that isn't leaving. She deserves to be disciplined for making me this person, this being with no control when it came to her. I will certainly think of something.

The door behind me creaks open with a faint premonition, and I turn towards it, the words already scalding on my tongue.

It's Knox. And I realize he hadn't been surprised. And he hadn't really been here for her. The betrayer!

"How long have you known?"

He'd always been the closest to her. But I've also always believed he and I were close too. It doesn't sit well that he seems to have chosen her in some way over me.

His lips twist. "A while."

He pours a shot of whiskey at the low bar beside my desk, bringing me a glass of it.

"You didn't think maybe I deserve to know? That he was my son? That I even had a son?"

"It's complicated, Xander. Do I apologize?"

I want to roar, sweep the books off the table to the floor, and watch as they flutter away. Maybe they will take with them this burn in my chest, this fire that makes me want to hurt my own brother.

Instead, I sweep the drink from his grasp when he holds it out to me. I knock it back in one smooth swallow. "What the fuck is your apology to me, Knox?"

The burn of the drink helps, but it doesn't erode the bitter taste in my throat. I wonder why I had thought it would.

A tentative knock comes at the door, and I swing my head at it. I bite down hard on the flesh inside my mouth, teeth gnashing. "Get out. Let her in and lock the door behind you."

Knox stays put, a defiant glower on his face. "You can't hurt her."

I let a sickly, sweet smile trickle like water off my face. "You mean like you hurt me? What? You won't help me hide the body?" I point a hand at the door and roar with anger, finally finding some outlet for the void in my head. "Get out!"

He doesn't move for a second. Then he swivels stiffly like a puppet on a string and lopes out of the room.

A sweep of air later, and Mel walks in. Her shoulders are high now, and there's as much fire as an apology in her jade-green eyes.

She licks her lips and sends tongues of fire lapping at the edges of my consciousness. I refuse to let it control me. "I didn't know how to tell you."

"About what Sole?" I've always called her my sunshine, but today, she's pushing shards of darkness, crowding anger and rage into my chest. The things she has always rid me of. I revel in it.

"About Lucian."

She'd named him. My son. With no input from me. But the name Lucian has always been ours. She had always loved it. Her mother's father had been named Lucas.

And we had decided Lucian was a better variation for us, for our child, when we had one. The feeling was rising again, the rage, only this time, it was piercing, like salt on open wounds.

"You named him Lucian?"

"I did." She inhaled a shaky breath. "I'm sorry."

"You're sorry? You're fucking sorry, Mel? What the fuck does that even mean? Does he know me? I've missed years of his life. How the fuck old is he?"

She's shaking, tears swimming in her large eyes, sparking outrage in mine. She had no right to make me feel guilty for raging about her betrayal because keeping my son from me is one. But when have I ever reacted as I should to her?

"Five years."

A startling truth finally pierces the veil of anger, clouding my consciousness. "You'd been pregnant when you left? That's why you disappeared, wasn't it?"

She nods, and I fall into the chair behind my desk. She bites her lips and takes a step towards me. My eyes flash, a snark curling my lips.

"You don't get to take a step closer to me, or I swear to God, Mel..." I stop and let her complete that sentence as she will.

She shivers, and a line of sweat makes its way across her neck, disappearing into the swell of her heaving cleavage, and I groan.

Stupid. That's what I am.

"Can we talk? Please? I didn't know what to do. You were just beginning to take a more active role in the business; your attention couldn't be divided. Not with a son on the way. It was never the right time." She pleaded, her voice catching in her throat.

I clench my fists under the desk. "And if this had never happened. If our parents hadn't forced us together. Would you have ever found the right time? Would I have been good enough to know my son?"

She jerks her head up, and her eyes track mine. "It was never that. I wanted to protect him, just for a little longer. I wanted him to have a childhood. There was none for him here."

My heart seizes. "Did he?"

She nods, her hands balled into fists at her sides. "With father's help."

Of course. It made sense. Sedric knew. He'd kept his grandchild a heavily guarded secret. I wonder how they'd done it, how it had been possible. And then I think of my inability to track her after she'd left the country with Gianna.

It would've been easy enough to keep her stowed away in some little countryside far away from me and the dangers of my existence.

I snap up in my chair. "I want him. He's my son. My heir."

Her eyes tighten. "That's rather fortunate, Xander. We're to be married. I'm sure you'll have enough time to be with him. But he is our son, and you do not get to hold him over me."

Oh, is he now?

I feel fury unfurl in my chest, and I fight a losing battle to leash it. "And you just had that epiphany now? Not six years ago when you stole my son from me?"

Her face creases and crumbles, and I bite back the urge to go to her, to pull her into my arms and tell her it'll be fine.

She doesn't deserve it.

13

MEL

I CAN STILL HEAR XANDER ON THE PHONE RAGING. HE'S mighty angry. I have a feeling it's going to stay that way since he can't take out his rage on the subject that had caused it.

NAMELY ME.

Knox is beside me on the balcony. He's watching me, his green eyes glittering, flicking between me and his brother inside his house.

"HE'S GOING to tear the world to shreds. He's going to find out you all knew about Lucian, and then he'll hate me even more for turning his family against him."

· · ·

I swallow an empty swirl of air and fold my arms across my chest. I feel cold. There's no way to relieve the anxious thoughts fogging my brain.

But I feel relieved too. He finally knows. It's now time to deal with the repercussions. Six years too late.

Knox looks away from me, staring into the neatly landscaped grounds surrounding Xander's home. "He already knows I knew about Lucian."

Shit.

"What did he say?"

Knox winces and runs a restless hand through his hair. It's already styled to look windblown and in no particular direction. Now he's sporting the sexy look of an angry man who's just stepped out of bed.

And I still don't react to him with the blinding hunger that had swept over me, resonating like the hum of a hummingbird's wings in the quiet.

. . .

EVEN WITH HIS pores practically releasing anger fumes, I'd wanted to cup the back of his head in my hand and to take those tight lips with mine. I'd known he would've responded too.

THEN HE PROBABLY WOULD'VE KILLED ME in my sleep later.

"HE LOOKED HURT. For the first time. He looked like I'd kicked him in the balls."

A GENTLE BREEZE ruffles my hair, and I wonder how I'll survive the next week. The sound of his footsteps tearing towards us has us turning towards the door.

HIS FACE IS blank when the door crashes against the wall, and he comes thundering out like a herd of buffalo.

HIS EYES AVOID MINE, and my stomach sinks. His jaw is bunched so hard I know it has to hurt. "Alec knew? Father knew? Declan too? Did mother too?"

. . .

KNOX REFUSES to hold his eyes. "Yes." He states simply.

XANDER NODS. Just a simple nod that says more than an entire essay would have.

"XANDER..."

HE CUTS his hand through the air at me. "You're not a part of this conversation. There is not an apology you can provide that will make this better. You stay out of it."

HE SWINGS his head to Knox and takes a steadying breath, his chest expanding and releasing under the fabric of his harsh white shirt.

HIS MUSCLES BUNCH, and I jerk my eyes away, refusing to undress him. Refusing to recognize the flare of something in my chest.

"AND WHEN DID you all think it would be a great idea to let me in on this secret?"

·   ·   ·

Knox turns to glare in turn at his brother. "Whenever we were certain you wouldn't react this way. Guess we were right, huh?"

I curl a hand into his arm and squeeze. Xander's eyes land with a crushing intensity on my grip on his brother. His eyes glint dangerously, and he looks away, the strong profile of his jaw hard like diamonds.

His fists curl once and open. A hard smile glides across his face like water off a rock. "So I'm to blame for not knowing him? It's my fucking fault he doesn't know me either." He turns to me. "Does he?"

My throat constricts, and I can't bring in enough air to say no. I shake my head instead.

His eyes glaze over. And finally, it's like a heavy veil drops over his being. He stills, only the sharp rise and fall of his chest an indication that he is human and not, in fact, a bronze statue.

"Get out of my house, Knox. I do not want to find you here when I get home. I do not want to see you here, ever!"

. . .

HE DOESN'T WAIT for an answer or confirmation. He just turns around and leaves. A tense silence settles in between Knox and me until the sound of his car rolling out of the gate out front filters into my ears.

"WE'RE FUCKED. I can't be here to protect you." Knox sounds pained. Tottering between staying and leaving.

I PLACE a hand on his arms like I've always done and lean my head against his shoulder.

"I'LL BE FINE. Xander won't hurt me." I whisper into the gentle breeze blowing off the trees lining the large property.

"YOU SOUND CERTAIN. I know Xander. He's going over to Alec's club. He's going to give him a beating, then he'll rage at home, and he'll be cold for a few days. But this time? I have no idea what will happen after all that. I've never seen him this angry with me. There's a fire in him that needs to burn something to subside."

. . .

AND I'D CAUSED THAT. My fault. I feel shame and a potent dose of guilt. But regret isn't there. And that makes me feel a lot worse.

I HOLD his eyes and tune my voice as convincingly as I can make it. "It might be me. But this is my bed. Let me lie on it. Don't get scalded trying to protect me."

"YOU DON'T UNDERSTAND. Hiding Lucian wasn't about you. Father was using you as much as you were using us. He wanted Xander to take over the Famiglia. He never would've done that with a child on the way. Not the way you two were then. So in love, it was beautiful to see. We're greedy. Don't ever forget that."

He vomits the words between us like that should make me care less about him. Like I haven't always known it, or at least suspected it.

"OF COURSE, I know. I didn't think his protection was for free. My father is powerful, but he never would've been able to keep me away from Xander alone. I knew I needed him then. I know I need him now. Why the hell else am I here?"

I snap, my body vibrating.

· · ·

I PULL my arms from his and walk away, gulping down air, my chest burning from holding off my tears, my eyes smarting.

EVERYTHING FUCKING HURTS. I'd betrayed the man I loved to save a child I loved even more.

AND NOW I worry he will use that very child against me. There is no hope for us.

ROSA HAD ARRIVED on Xander's estate with us, but she's gone now. The room I've taken is Xander's largest guest room. It's painted a soft pastel and navy blue, and the view from the open window where air is streaming in is stunning.

A BACKDROP of water meandering gently in a tiny pond and green grace sheltering in the shade of the evening sun.

LUCIAN IS STILL asleep in the large king-sized bed, his body tucked in like a fetus, his long lashes crafting shadows on his cheeks.

. . .

I TRAIL a hand over his face, needing his warmth to remind me why I'd left here. Why I'd decided the violence and the drugs and the death just weren't going to be a part of his childhood.

I NEED it to remind me why I'd run away with a broken heart, crying as I'd told Xander I just couldn't do it anymore. Jerking away from the hard slant of his lips on mine, only the reminder of the pregnancy test burning in my purse enough to get me to slap his hands from my skin and amble away.

I PRESS a soft kiss on his cheeks and stand up, wiping the tears that have finally made their way down my face. So long as he's safe. I'll be fine.

He's the center of my world. The sun around which I orbit. He gives me light to send to the world.

I HOPE I'm able to convince Xander of all this. To make him understand why I had to do what I'd done, why I'd run away only a month pregnant with his baby.

WHY HE'D FOUND me in the shower crying and threatened to shatter the globe for me, willing to tear to shreds any mountain with his bare hands to keep me safe, and now, he was going to shred me.

I TAKE my phone from my bag and call Gianna. I haven't spoken to her in two days. I need someone to talk to, and only she will understand.

SHE'D BEEN the one person who had followed me out of the country when Father, with Amory's help, had found us a safe house out in the coastal region of Montenegro, right on the edge of Serbia, so we could slip away safely if there was ever a need.

THERE HAD NEVER BEEN A NEED, but we had been careful. No calls and definitely not a lot of communication with the local folks. Father had flown in with Daniel and Knox every few weeks with supplies.

AND WHEN IT had been time to leave, a few years later, Gianna had fallen in love with the water and the people and had decided to stay put. With my safety guaranteed back here, she could exist freely.

. . .

HER VOICE CRACKLES over the phone, and I inhale a steadying gasp of air. "Hello, Mel?"

"HE KNOWS." It's simple. I breathe, she breathes, the air heavy between us.

"HOW?" Worry threads through her voice, echoing the storm brewing in my stomach.

"I MOVED into his house today. Father said it was time. He was going to find out either way." I mutter, closing the door behind me as I step out of my room.

"I'LL BE FLYING HOME VERY SOON. When is the wedding?" Gianna probes. "And have you been in his bed yet?" .

"I HAVE NO IDEA. It'll be whenever the men decide it should be." I drag in a ragged breath and tell her my fears. "Xander is so angry I feel he'll do something we're both going to regret. You should've seen him. He was a beast. He asked that Knox never visit the house." My voices becomes a quiet confession. "I have been in his bed."

. . .

Gianna's tone is reassuring, her voice certain and centering. "He'll come around. His pride has been wounded. And he finds out his family knew the entire time? He's bound to react since he can't act. Give him time." She purses and inhales. "And stay out of his bed. It's another layer of complication you don't need."

It's the first time ever that Gianna isn't raving and raging against the man. She hates him. To her, letting me leave had been Xander choosing the Famiglia over us. She didn't understand that he hadn't had a choice. Not one since his birth.

He had been groomed to take over what was already a large empire at his birth. He had the weight of it all pressing on him. I didn't ask him to choose. It would've hurt too much if he hadn't picked me.

I'd told him I was done, and then I had left.

"And if he takes Lucian from me? Or hurts him in his anger?" I let my eyes rake over the men stationed all over the property. They're just as bad as the phone in my bag, tracking my movements.

THEY'LL NEVER LET me leave this gilded cage without a call to him. Asking if I was allowed.

I SMILE BITTERLY and repress the urge to hurl the phone or the contents of my stomach.

GIANNA SNIFFS. "He won't. And if he did, to where? You'll always have your son. Marriage in the mafia is forever. He's going nowhere. And unfortunately, neither are you. Buckle in."

14

XANDER

THE DRIVE OVER TO THE HOUSE WAS LONG. BY THE TIME I arrive, Enzo is standing by the door, starched and straight as always.

He opens the door and places his folded hands behind his back again.

"Good evening, Xander." He greets.

I nod and pass him by. He follows behind me. "Where's Father?'

"In his study. Although your mother has asked that you stop by the garden to speak to her."

I stop and glare at him, my head buzzing with something more than anger. I know it's pain, but I refuse to give it voice. "What did you say?"

"Your father's worried. He knows you're angry, and you know his condition. Therefore, your mother has asked that you speak to her first."

Enzo has his hand behind his back, as I've always seen him, but today is the first time that there's been a challenge in his voice when speaking to me.

"Tell her I'll speak to her after speaking to Father. Do you understand?" I bark at him, then turn and walk away, taking the steps up to my father's bedroom, where I find him sitting at his table, a glacial look of anger on his face.

What did he have to be angry about? I bang the door on my way in, and I settle into the chair in front of him.

"You had no right, Father. None at all."

He twists his lips, the dark look on his face softening for a second before it snaps on again. "I know, but let's talk. I had to."

"He was my child. He is my child. When were you going to let me know?"

"It was always a deal, Xander. You were always going to know. You just had to settle into your duties first." Father croaks out.

He coughs gently, and I tip forward, worried yet wishing I didn't care. He didn't deserve it, neither did she, and yet I'd wanted to wrap my arm around her and hold her close too.

"And if the Russians had never started fighting us? If they'd never gotten so strong, would I have ever found out?"

"I'm sure you would have. You know Mel. She wouldn't have been able to take it for too long." He takes a drink from the glass on his table, and I look away, trying to understand.

He's getting old, sick with a cancer that's been eating away at him. He'd been unable to declare himself sick; the competition would've swept his empire away from him soon after. I did sort of understand.

But it didn't help the thud of anger inside me. It didn't help that today was the first day in six years since I'd had a look at my son. It didn't help the shame that I had no reason to feel.

I squeeze my forehead with my thumb to release the gathering cloud there. "I'll never be able to forgive you this father. I promise you."

He hunches his shoulder and leans forward, a wry smile on his face. His hand sweeps out to his side, and he bows his head towards me. "I'm a bag full of dying bones, Xander. I'm not the one you need to forgive."

Before I can reply, mother's snappy footsteps fill the room. Another heavier one follows behind her, which I attribute to Enzo before Alec's voice breaks into the furrow.

"I'm sorry, brother."

I swing my head towards him and fist my hands at my side. "Are you really? You have been my brother for years. And yet you have hidden this one thing from me. Do you expect I'll be able to call you brother again?"

He walks forward to settle a hand behind Father's chair, showing his stance. "Yes. Because we did it for your good."

I shove my chair back and bark my words, barely holding back from relieving my anger in a way I know how. I need to get away from these people. "You have no idea what is good for me, Alec. It seems you do not know me as much as you thought."

"And yet, you almost gave up the Famiglia for her. You never would've stayed put with a child in her. And the violence would've trailed you right to them."

Alec looks as though he wishes he could convince me of the truth, a crease between his brows.

I stop and sink back into my chair. He's right. Damn him and the rest of them, Mel included. Being the underboss had been violent. But what has changed now? Why was she here now?

"Then why the hell is she here now? Why the fuck did you bring her back into this if you're so worried about her?" I question my father, slanting my head up at my mother because she's been quiet this entire time, and that's not like her.

She has tears in her eyes that I do not acknowledge. She holds her hand out to me, and I shrink away from it. There is no way in hell that she deserves to be forgiven so easily for this betrayal.

"Because there is no more time. The Russians are getting too strong. They will ruin us, and we need Sedric's power and his men. This is no longer just about us."

So it's greed. I chuckle with a bland attempt at humor that sounds flat even to my angry ears. "I'm leaving. I do not want any of you coming close for quite a few days. I'm going to talk to Mel."

Father straightens up, as does my mother. "You can't take this out on her."

I glower at him. "She is to be my wife. I will decide how to punish her for this, Father. I think you'll find you've done enough harm already."

I turn away from them and walk away. Out in the hallway, I exhale a deep, chagrined breath. I hate them. I love them. I don't know what to settle on.

I clench my fist and head toward the door, deciding spending the day torturing someone would be a great way to get this anger out of my system.

But I can't, so I decide to head to the gym. One look at Mel and our son will have me up in arms. More than that, this hunger to work through this pain by pounding into her needy body means it would be a terrible idea to be in the same space as that crazy woman.

And I can't be this mad around my son. Never. I'd seen the way it had been with my father. My son would never have to witness that. Not if I had a choice.

A hand lands on my arm and tugs at me. I growl, the words barely legible. "If you put a hand on me again, I'll fucking kill you, Alec, and I won't give two fucks about the fact that you're my brother."

"I know you hate me. But none of this was Mel's fault. She did what she had to do." His voice is soft and certain. Not at all the Alec I know.

And why did all of them keep defending her?

"And what she had to do was declare me a monster and hide my son from me? I never hurt that woman. Not once!" I hiss through tightly clenched lips, my eyes hazy with anger.

Even at my worst, I'd always reserved my best for her. Always. Never once had I come back from a bad day to her with blood on my hands.

I'd always made sure to keep her shielded from the worst of the Famiglia. Always!

"You didn't have to. She saw through the mask that you wore. You knew it was getting worse. Father was asking that you take over. He never would've let you be."

"So it's my fault I don't know my child?" I snap at him, wringing my head around to him so fast I feel a crank in the muscle. "It's my damned fault I've never heard Lucian call me father?"

"No. But..."

I cut a sharp hand through the air to wave him off. "Save it. I'm leaving. Do not follow me."

I walk away from him, striding to the car where Ryder has the door open without question. I slide into the warm leather and close my eyes, press them very tightly closed, and then I relax the entirety of my face.

"Did you know about Lucian?" I ask him.

Ryder goes quiet for a very long time, and for some reason, I begin to pray he didn't. I'm angry enough, and Ryder is right there.

He's close but not close enough that I won't have to fight the urge to shoot him in the back of the head.

"No. No one told me this had happened. I knew she was sad, but not that the child was the reason." He murmurs, taking turns that lead me away from the rambling mansion.

I sit up and run a hand through my already scattered hair. This is something I haven't heard before. "She was sad?"

He lifts his eyes to the mirror and watches me quietly for a moment. I wave my hand to tell him he's safe to speak to me as he will. "Trust me, if I was going to kill anyone today, I'd much rather it was Mel. You would barely move the pendulum on my anger."

"You wouldn't kill her. You never would be able to." He says, his deep voice certain in a way the rest of the family seem to be when it comes to Mel.

And because I'd rather not deal with that thought, I ask what I want an answer to. "Mel was sad? For how long?"

"Maybe three months before she left. You were busier. Away more often. She was alone a lot and you never did explain. She had to learn all she did during that period from your siblings or whatever scrap her father would let her glean. I promise I didn't know about the pregnancy, but it would explain a lot."

Fuck. I close my eyes again. How the hell was I to explain to a woman I love—loved, that I was drenched in something that was such an utter opposite of her? I was lucky enough to have her light in my darkness; I had no wish to ruin her.

I had no plans to make her hate me for things I couldn't help. And it was starting to look like I'd pushed her away.

"Get me home."

Ryder whistles a dull tune the entire drive back to the house while I keep my eyes closed and massage my forehead. I'm still angry, but I'm willing to talk. I'm willing to listen to her.

Let her explain, make me feel less at fault or the worst man for driving her away.

When we arrive home, it's already evening, and the guards stationed around the house snap to attention like they weren't expecting me back home. I wait for Ryder to open my door, then I step out of the car and walk into the house.

It's oddly quiet. Not a sound. And Romero is absent at the door, which should've been my first sign that something wasn't right—isn't right still because I do a rotation of the down floor before walking up the stairs, a strange buzzing disquiet in my stomach.

The sound of rushing water meets my ears immediately I step into my room, and I rush to the bathroom, worried, just not giving voice to all the thoughts rushing through my head.

I swing the door open and pull to a stop. Literally frozen in my tracks, my throat dry, my hands itching, and my eyes feasting on the woman showering.

I'm fucked. I know it now as certainly as the first time I'd laid eyes on her during my first visit to Sedric's home. I was hooked then, as surely as I'm hooked now.

15

MEL

Xander is in the room with me.

I stiffen, my shoulders relaxing the next second. The water is still pounding down over my bare body, but it barely disguises the way my heart is pounding in my chest, the way my stomach is suddenly queasy.

He's back. I can almost feel it. It's as though my body has an antenna, and right now, it's lifting towards and searching for him. And I can't find him because there's a dark cloud of anger between us.

I decide I'll ignore him; I don't have much of a choice anyway. I don't have anything to say to him that will make this anger between us vanish.

And I don't even blame him for it, which somehow makes it worse. Or better. I don't know which.

The shower door opens, and I do go rigid because the next second, his hips press into my bare ass, hard and insistent, and I shudder because though he's fully clothed, the imprint of his hard-on is so strong that I'm almost totally needy right away.

I try to turn towards him, but he presses his hand into my shoulder and keeps my face away from his. "Xander?"

"Stay just this way. Maybe I can pretend for a second longer that you didn't hurt me. That you're still the woman I thought you were," he growls at the nape of my neck, the words chasing a shiver down my body.

I push back against him, his cock digging at me. "Can we at least talk?" I'm not sure if I actually want to talk, though. The feel of him behind me is changing my body, and what I want is not words.

I want his thick cock inside me.

I can practically feel him vibrate with frustration. "I want you. I need to take you. If you don't want this, here's the time to say no."

I feel his hands all over my body, which makes his words null and void, saying I have any right to say no.

Because how can I? I'm already shaky and quivering and wanting him, aching for him. My heart is beating for something else just as my body pulses for him.

"I want you. But not like this, Xander, please."

"Too bad. This is the only way you get me," he grits out. He cups my breasts into the large spread of his calloused palm, then coasts his head close to my neck and exhales his next words there. "For now, at least."

Which sort of gives me hope and makes me feel as though there is a slim chance in hell that we will be able to work through this.

So I push my ass into his cock and ground back against him. "Then I want this. Badly."

He groans, and his hand slips and slides down my body, running slowly across the wet flesh of my stomach, bringing pleasure pouring through me along with the water, which he immediately slaps shut as though he senses my thoughts

"Where's Lucian?" He asks, his tongue sweeping along my neck, licking at the flesh, which he then sucks into his mouth, biting down hard on it.

I shudder, and my knees buckle a little. I gasp when he repeats the action. "I asked you a question, Mel. Where's my son."

I close my eyes to center myself. "Daniel picked him up. Hailey went with him. As did Romero."

He stops, and I moan in disappointment. "Why the fuck did you let him do that?"

"I didn't know you'd be home. I wasn't expecting you. And Daniel picks him up regularly. It gives me a bit of time to myself, and I felt really teary today." I stop and exhale raggedly. "I'm so sorry."

He's right. Maybe I shouldn't have let Lucian go with Daniel, but I had been teary and broken somehow, and I didn't want my son to see me that way. So when Daniel had offered to drop by and pick him up, I'd let him.

Hailey had gone along with them, so it had given me the house to be in alone. Stewing in my fears, pain, and tears, which I hadn't been able to hold back on.

His hand digs into my waist, almost painfully. "You've apologized a fucking lot today, Mel, yet you always go back to doing the wrong thing."

I go rigid in his arms and pull away. "Don't speak to me that way."

His hand tightens, and he pulls me into him again, this time his hand between us, running over my ass.

"I'll damned well speak to you how I want. You're my wife."

"Your wife-to-be Xander. And that still gives you no right to speak to me however you want!" I snap at him, even as I enjoy yearning for the bite of his nails digging into me. I'm hungry for the very man whom I am angry at, who is angry at me, whom I have hurt—who is hurting me. It's an insane cycle.

"Do you want me to fuck you or not?" He asks, pulling away slightly.

"Do you want to fuck me or not?" I challenge him right back. I know Xander. There has never been a time when he hasn't wanted me. There will never be a time when I do not want him myself.

He doesn't reply with words, but his hands slide between my ass cheeks which he spreads and then slips just the tip of his finger into me. I moan and cry out, my body needing more.

"Please. More Xander."

"Impatient at all times, Sole. The sun doesn't beg to shine, Amor."

I try to still the rampant beat of my heart at his words, but there is no stopping it. I want this man. I've hurt him.

And he's punishing me by withholding the very thing he is tempting me with. But if this is his entire punishment, then I can take it.

He presses the finger into me slowly, bending me so my breasts flatten against the wall of the shower stall. The cool tile feels like a shock after the grazing heat of his skin. Even wet and drenched, his skin against mine will always feel that way.

He groans and clicks his tongue. "Sole. You're so damned wet and tight. How long has it been without me? How long before I took you again?"

I see no need to lie. "Six years. There was never anyone beside you. There never will be. I never once betrayed you that way."

He growls again, his voice haunted. "And that feels good. So fucking good, I'm ready to forgive you for what you did but I can't, not yet. You drive me mad, Mel. You're not good for me."

I push my ass back into him, and he slides the finger into me, adding another so that I can't hold back the gathering cry. "Oh. That feels so good, Xander."

"There's more where it came from." Then he starts fucking me in earnest, his fingers running in and out of me, slow and steady, then fast and hard, and all the time, he croons how angry he is at me.

How much he wishes he could wring my neck for what I'd done. And just how much it is that he wants me, that he wishes he could stay angry at me but just can't.

I accept all of it as my due, squealing and squeezing around his fingers, crying out again and again as he rubs his thumb against my clit, curving his fingers inside me at that same moment so that my knees go rubbery and I relax against the wall.

His fingers pinch at my nipple, tight and almost painful, and all those things combined have me rocking back into his fingers, exhaling as my orgasm finally blows over me like a wave at sea, dragging me into its dark, starry depth.

Xander bends at once and sweeps his tongue over my folds, drawing out my orgasm as his tongue sucks at my clit, his fingers pumping in and out of me as his hand cups my breasts.

I'm shaking, crying, wet, teary-eyed, shuddering, and pulsing around his fingers, my stomach fluttering with sharp swirls of pleasure that leave me feeling wrung out and yet so oddly full.

Xander pulls away, but not before giving my sensitive body one final lick that has me feeling like a second orgasm might not be too far away. Then he turns and walks away from me. Just like that.

His footsteps thud dully as he strides out. I catch his tense shoulders only as the door closes almost gently behind him.

By the time I finish washing up and make it to the bedroom, he's calmly on the bed, his phone in his hands as he makes a call to someone I can't hear.

"Tomorrow will be too late. Have it moved tonight. Right away if you can." He barks at the person on the other end of the phone.

I pull the robe tighter around my shivering body and pad on the bed beside him. The time says it's nine at night on my phone, and I know sleeping with Xander beside me will be impossible.

He gets off the phone and gets out of bed on his way to the bathroom.

"Why didn't you?" I ask softly, tears biting at my lids again. This time, because I feel sorry for us. This is no way to make a family, especially with my son hanging in the balance.

His jaw ticks, his hand, the one I can see flexing at his side. "Because you don't deserve it, Mel. I'm allowed to hold onto this anger as long as I can. It's the only thing I have left."

Then he stalks out of the room, and I wonder how mad he'll be if I tell him I'd like to sleep in a different room tonight. Just one day.

When he returns, my stomach does a free fall. He's so decadently handsome he makes me hungry just by looking like chocolate on fat red strawberries. The V of his narrow hips tapering away to the junction of his thighs, which he doesn't bother hiding.

He towels his hair calmly as he walks towards me, where he stops at the bedpost and smirks. "You look hurt. Like you've been denied your favorite dessert."

"I'm just glad you're smiling at me. I had a feeling this afternoon you'd much rather have me dead."

"I still do. Don't tempt me, Sole."

But he does slip into bed beside me without bothering for anything between us. And his guns are in the bathroom too, which makes me wonder if he has another beneath the bed. He slides his hand around my shoulders and brings me to him.

"Ryder said you were sad for months before you left." He murmurs softly into my hair, almost as though the words hurt on their way out of his lips.

I think about it, not knowing what to say. First, I'm surprised he's asking; second, I'm even more surprised that Ryder noticed that about me.

"Why are we talking about that? It's the past."

One I'd much rather leave behind me. One I didn't want to think about. One that would forever be triggering for the two of us. My heart stutters a beat, and nervous butterflies flit through my stomach.

"Because I'm wondering if it's part of the reason I don't know my son. Didn't know he even existed until this morning. Had you been planning for months to leave me? Was it not just about Lucian?"

I press my eyes closed and exhale shakily. "I wasn't. I was worried. I was angry with you for cutting me out of this thing that was obviously a huge part of who you were. And part of it was worrying about how you'd be with our child with the Famiglia demanding most of your attention, but never was I sad with you. You were my light as much as I was your sunshine."

I flip my body around so I'm staring straight into his eyes.

"I loved you. Fiercely. I never wanted to hurt you, but you hurt me. And I didn't want that pain getting to my child in any way."

By the time I've spilled all the words, I am breathless. And all Xander does is kiss me. Hard and strong. And I know without doubt he still hates me but that there's also hope for us.

16

XANDER

THE MORNING DAWN'S CLEAR AND NEW, AND WHEN I wake up, my chest isn't tight and I don't feel immediately angry at the world. The light streaming in through the open windows feels warm across my face, and I shade my eyes and sit up with a stretch.

The window is never open. It's too much of a hazard. But I find Mel at the vanity, dressed in a gown made of a soft blue fabric that has me thinking of clear days.

My head must really still be hazy with sleep because I don't immediately feel like slipping my hands around her neck.

She turns to me with a smile. "I've called Daniel. He's on his way here with Lucian. I thought you might like to meet him finally."

And without warning, a nervous sweep of emotions makes its way through me. He's my son, and I shouldn't be worried about meeting him. But I am. "What does he know about me?"

I swing my feet out of bed and feel a surge of lust when Mel slides her eyes slowly over my skin. I take a step towards her and then stop when I remember I'm supposed to be mad at her.

I grind my molars and run a hand through my hair in frustration.

"Nothing much. He's been too young to really ask. And Daniel and your brothers had taken much of a rather active role in his life."

So my son doesn't know about me. But more than that… every damned person in my life does, minus me.

My heart wrenches painfully, and I swivel from her to the bathroom, where I shower fast, muttering all the time about how I want to meet my son.

I smile in the mirror, making a caricature of what I think a disarming smile should look like. I shake my head and then step out of the bathroom into the room where Mel is missing.

I take a long time dressing, discarding my usual black for more colors, all the while thinking of my son, praying he likes me, hoping he doesn't hate me at first sight. I step into a pair of soft home sandals and call Ryder finally.

He picks up immediately, almost as though he'd been waiting for my call. "Cancel all the meetings I have today. I'll be unavailable."

Ryder is silent for a second. "Sandro already called. He's in trouble. He might need help."

"I don't fucking care if all the world burns to the ground. Cancel everything."

I hang up the phone and drop it to the bed before walking out of the room. I can already hear voices as I walk down the stairs. I stop and raggedly exhale. Then I stride into the kitchen where the voices are coming from.

The boy is the first person I see because he's sitting on the island, his head bent towards Mel, who looks up at me with a nervous smile. He turns to me with an almost smile; then he holds his hands out to his mother, who lifts him from the island.

Immediately his feet touch the ground, he walks over to me in a strong parody of my own confident stalk that has me almost smiling too. He stops in front of me and holds his hand out in a handshake.

"My mom says you're my dad."

And I'm floored, just like that. He has my heart and all of me too.

Everything there is to give has been given. I bend a knee before him, an action I never have taken even once in the entirety of my life.

"Yes, I am. My name's Xander Amory."

Then I shake his hands before pulling him snug into me and promising to never let him go. There is no doubt he's mine. None at all. He smells of Mel's hug and the slight breezy smell of a warm bath.

Lucian pulls away and smiles. "My mom says this is your house. Which makes it my house, and I have my own room too."

I nod and smile right back. "And any other room you could need."

Mel sniffles, and I look at her, just at the same time Lucian does too, tilting his head as though he doesn't understand why. "Mommy's crying." He states factually.

Mel wipes a quick hand across her face. "I'm not. Really, Lucian, mommy has happy tears."

I feel my guts squeeze painfully tight. And I know keeping the child from me must have hurt her as much as it hurt me because she's crying.

With joy, her eyes are alight, and though they're swimming in what is definitely tears, I know that she's happy.

Lucian lets me go and runs to Mel, who lifts him into her arms and sinks her head into his hair, hugging him tight. And finally, I look away from them because I feel weird. A way I've never felt since she left my house six years ago.

She lifts her head to smile at me, and though I don't return the smile, I do not look away. Someone sighs, and I startle, turning to clock another woman by the stove.

I almost swear before remembering my son in the room. But my voice is still tight when I address her. "Who are you?"

"She's Hailey. Lucian's nanny."

I exhale harshly and relax marginally. I pat my body and jerk to a rigid freeze of my entire muscles when I realize I do not have my guns on me.

I'd left them upstairs last night. I clench my fists, fucking mistakes like this are how people end up dead on the cold ground.

"Can I go see my room?" Lucian's voice breaks into my thoughts, and I wonder suddenly if I really want a gun around that innocence.

It's a question I do not have a quick answer for, which makes me feel a mess of emotions—makes me think Mel was right to keep him away from me.

The silent woman takes a look at my face, throws another look at Mel, and holds her arms out to Lucian. "Come on, I'll take you. Then maybe we can paint a bit?"

Lucian nods and wiggles down from Mel's arms, and then he's gone with Hailey. It's quiet for a long second with a pregnant silence.

"He doesn't hate me," I say.

Mel walks towards me. "I didn't train him to. I swear I never would've done that to us. It would've hurt me as much as you."

"And I'm thinking he's better off without me, because you're right. He deserves the childhood you can give that I never had."

Mel knits her brows like she doesn't understand where it's coming from. I shake my head because I don't want to think about it but I know it feels like the truth. Now that I have a son, now that I've met him.

I know without a doubt I never want any harm coming to him, and the fact that said harm might, in fact, come from me is downright more worrying than staring into the barrel of a gun aimed at my head.

"Stop, Xander. Let's take this a moment at a time." She slips into my arms and lays her head against my chest. Her chest expands on a deep inhale. "I'm so glad you've finally met him."

I lift her head with my fingers and press a hot kiss to her lips. She responds, running a hand through the hair at my nape to graze my scalp with her nails.

I probe at her parted lips and slide my tongue over hers slowly, and she creeps even closer as though she wants to climb into me.

I tug at the neck of her dress and slip a hand into the neck of the bodice to cup her breasts as she makes a sexy little needy moan that has me going rock hard in my pants.

"Fuck. You taste like heaven and a side of something sweet."

"Can't imagine what that tastes like, but I could say you taste even better." She puffs at me, tugging at my shirt.

I nip at her jaw, grazing my teeth along the soft, warm flesh to the corner of her lips, then to her ears, which I suck into my mouth and bite down on hard, leaving a mark and the ring of my teeth.

I lift her into my arms, and I'm about to deposit her on the kitchen island when the sound of footsteps breaks in between us.

I inhale hard and exhale a rush of hungry air, then straighten the bodice of her dress because anyone who gets a look at my wife will die a very torturously long death.

Ryder comes into the kitchen the next moment. His eyes are hard, and his lips are curled in a hard smile, which he directs at Mel first.

"Good morning, Melissa."

Mel pulls away and nods at him before throwing me a long look and folding a hand across her breasts. I know that look, and I recognize the look of desperation on Ryder's face.

Something's wrong with work, and he's wondering if he should spill with her here. And Mel's look either means she's not going anywhere or she desperately wants to go elsewhere.

I turn and walk away from her. Ryder follows me out of the kitchen. Because whether Mel wants to listen or not, I'm not discussing this shit anywhere close to where my son might hear.

I walk to the door and step outside. I nod sharply at the door, and Ryder pulls it shut behind me. Romero is standing guard outside this morning and sends me a greeting. I reply and then fold my hands across my chest.

"Before you say a word. You're not to let even a whiff of business around my son. If he's in the house, then we do not discuss business in the house. Understand?"

Ryder tilts his head to the side, and I slant mine the same way. "Do you or do you not fucking understand me, Ryder?" I grate out.

"I understand."

"And no swearing around him. Not a slip. Tell that to the rest of the men."

"Yes, boss. I understand."

"Now what's wrong?"

"Sandro's men were ambushed by the fucking Russians. Three men dead. Four captured, which is a fate worse than death."

I jerk and still. "How long ago was this?" I ask.

"Last night. Just after I dropped you off, I received Intel from him this morning. He's asking for a meeting. He wants to pull out."

I won't have a meeting. "Have the Russian routes shut down. Two should be enough to show we're serious."

Ryder bares his teeth in a humorless smile, then hacks a harsh cough from his lungs. "We can't afford to shut down the routes. We'll lose as well."

"No, we won't. Have the men stay armed at all times. Shut down the drugs for two days. Everything. Their entire livelihood is drugs and the women. Shut down the drugs."

Ryder sighs and stretches his body out. "Alec called."

"Fuck him," I growl at him. "If we're done here, I'll be spending time with my son the rest of the day."

"Xander..."

"I'm the boss, Ryder, and I say this conversation is fucking over. Do not push me."

He nods and walks away, already pulling his phone from his pocket. Fucking Russians always messing things up at the worst moments.

I'll need to speak to Sandro soon, but for now, I step back into the house. I follow the stairs and then the long hallway till the sound of giggles leads me to Lucian's room, where Mel is blowing raspberries into his stomach. His giggles sound like peace.

I screw my eyes shut.

The wife I wanted. The son I wanted. Both of them are right here. Right next to me.

So why does it all feel so wrong?

17

MEL

GIANNA'S RETURN IS AS UNEXPECTED AS IT IS WELCOME. I mean, I've been expecting her to call any day now to meet her at the airport.

But when I wake up from a small nap to the sound of voices coming from the living room as I head downstairs, I'm not expecting to see her sitting on the sofa with Lucian giggling in her arms.

They both scream, "Surprise!" Then she walks over to me and hugs me so tight, and I sink into her arms.

"Oh, my goodness. What is this?" I whisper-scream against her neck. I pull away and stare into her eyes to assure myself she really is here, hair tied up in a whimsy little bun, clad in a blazer and pants that are way bigger than her.

"A surprise. I know you're surprised. Daniel dropped me off." I pull her into my arms again and smother her and myself with how tight we're hugging.

"I'm shocked. I love it. Come sit." I usher her into a sofa and swing Lucian into my lap, where he wraps his hand around my neck.

"Where's Xander?" She asks. I shuffle uncomfortably on my seat, and she clocks the movement. He'd gone to work. And he hadn't said it, but I'd known something was wrong.

Something he wasn't telling me.

"He's at Amory Corps. He'll be home before dinner. He'll be so glad to see you." I lie through gritted teeth.

Gianna rolls her eyes, and even I can hear her suck at her teeth. "I know Xander, Mel. The last person he'll be glad to sit at dinner with is me."

"Not true." I laugh. "I'm sure there are worse companions for dinner than a beautiful woman like yourself."

"Which he won't notice because you'll be at that table yourself." She teases.

I wave my hand, but my heart trips in my chest. "Oh, let's not talk about him. How's Montenegro been? Papi?'

Papi was the man who lived on the compound with us. He ran security for us and dealt with most of the locals that we couldn't deal with. I've missed him.

"He's fine. Sends his regards along with his recriminations. Why haven't you called?"

I shrug. "I'm heart sick. If that makes sense."

She nods and sighs, relaxing into the chair. "I didn't want to leave." She swings a finger in the air back and forth. "Be glad I love you."

I place my hand against my chest and smile at a bouncing Lucian before turning to her. "Trust me. I'm ever grateful for that. Where's Daniel?"

"Went in for a meeting with dad, and then on to work. I've really missed you, Sissy. It's so good to be back."

"I've missed you too. Lots and lots." Lucian snuggles into me, and I sniffle gently.

"Now let's talk. How are things with Xander?"

I take a look at Hailey and place Lucian on the ground. "Do you want to go get chocolate with Hailey?"

He nods and runs over to her. She leads him out of the room and I wonder how she can stay so silent most of the time.

It's worrying because I have no idea how she feels about being here. But Gianna is here, so I return my attention to her.

I walk the distance to her and sink onto her own couch, my eyes on the view outside. It's a picture of nature with trees stationary in the heat outside.

"Better than I thought it could be." I bring my eyes back to hers and zero in on the probe in hers.

"Are you hiding the bruises? You can be honest with me, you know.".

I shake my head no and chuckle. "I swear he hasn't hit me, and I can't believe I have to say that to begin with. Xander would never hurt me."

"I know."

"He's taken it better than I expected he would. We're down to a few angry looks, at least. He's been open, and we've talked."

Gianna's eyes widen. "Xander talked? He's not mad? He didn't bring down the roof? I'm shocked."

I am too. And it had been my experience. Since the night when he'd returned and refused to take me in the shower, he hadn't been with me since. Not even a touch.

Three days later, I was yearning for even a touch, and he hadn't given me that. He comes home these days early enough to have time with Lucian, and then he would be in bed immediately.

I lead Lucian up to bed unless he takes him up himself. Then he would shower and fall into bed, either to read or lie awake, just staring at the ceiling.

Last night, he'd pulled me into his arms and taken the kiss I offered, but when my hand had started wandering down his body, he'd stopped and groaned, then put me away and slipped out of bed.

I found him twenty minutes later in Lucian's room, just staring at his son.

So no, I don't believe he's angry, but there's definitely something rattling around in his head. And while I don't want to probe, I'm dying to know what it is.

I snap back into the conversation when my sister blows her minty breath in my face. "What were you thinking of? I mean, do you need a penny or a dollar for your thoughts?"

"How about a million? Xander's not mad. Or maybe he is. I don't know, but he's been cool. Really fine with all this and taking it in his stride. If I'd known this was possible, I never would've kept Lucian away from him that long."

"I'm glad to hear that I have your stamp of approval, Melissa." His cold voice breaks in.

Goosebumps break out on my skin, and I snap off the couch, but I only get his back. Gianna has a hand over her mouth and a cool look in her eyes that belies the whole hand over her mouth.

I hurry after Xander into the kitchen, where he's dropping off the bags in his hands.

"That was nothing like what it sounded like." I stutter from behind him.

"What did it sound like?" He asks calmly, his back to me. He sounds like he doesn't care. But I know this man. I've been in his bed a million times; I've skimmed my fingers over his skin; I know all the groves and creases of his flesh.

He's angry. And holding a tight leash over it. His back is tense, his shoulder tight, and he isn't looking at me.

"As though I never meant to tell you about Lucian. I was going to."

"Stupendo. I believe you. Okay."

I stop, wary about his easy acceptance. I don't understand it.

"I realize you'll never trust me again, Xander. But I swear that was all. It was just a conversation with my sister."

"Then come prove it to me." He turns to me finally, and I see the redness of his eyes. He's angry, but the tight clench of his lips has nothing to do with me.

"What happened?" I hurry to him and let myself relax into him the way he's always liked to have me. I can make him feel he is my protector. That he owns my body and soul and no one else but him will do.

"Bad day at work. Lost some of my men." His hands tighten painfully around me, and his chest expands with a deep sigh. "Fucking Russians fucked us over with Sandro."

"Who's Sandro? Actually, don't answer that. Come have a shower with me." He hesitates when I leave his arms and hold my hand out to him. "Please."

He looks around uncertainly. "I wanted to spend time with Lucian, so I brought us some lunch. I'm fucking barking with anger, but I wanted to hold him."

"Come shower first. Maybe later we'll have dinner together. "

He nods and follows beside me, his hand on my waist. When we slip into the room, I lock the door behind me and undress first. He watches me, hunger and rage playing across his face, his brow taut.

"What are you doing?" He asks warily. I ignore him, instead stepping out of the black dress and stepping towards him in the little scraps of lingerie I'm wearing. I hide a smile at the answering bulge winking at me from his pants.

I cup him through his pants and stroke my hand over him. "Getting you ready for a shower. It'll be a long one."

The intensity of his eyes is as warm as a sunbeam, but he doesn't pull away when I bend to kiss my way to his zipper. He doesn't protest as I unzip it gently, my eyes on his the entire time.

I pull his pants off slowly, very slowly, the thump as his belt hits the floor somehow very satisfying. I grin up at him, and he steps out of the pants, his eyes flashing like a predator's after prey.

I kiss his thighs slowly, tenderly on my way up to his cock, and wrap my hand around his thick girth, licking my lips gently.

I glide my hand from his base up to the tip, tracing my thumb over his slit, which finally elicits his first groan.

He tips his head back, and the sound vibrates his body, which leads to me placing a hand on his stomach before repeating the action to feel the vibrations.

"Do you want me to suck you off Mi'lord?" I whimper up even as my tongue sweeps out over my lips, my mouth salivating at the thought of it.

He lengthens in my hand, and I stare up at him, offering everything he wants. All the distraction there is to give in the world.

He shakes his head, and I feel a twinge of disappointment that feels embarrassingly close to uselessness and failure. "No. But I do want that shower. Then I need you to hold me." He looks away as the words slip between his tight, full, luscious, giving-me-everything-I've-always-wanted lips.

I kiss his tip and then push to my feet. "Then let's do that."

I spend nearly twenty minutes in the shower with him. Focusing all of my attention on him, letting the water glide between my fingers as I wash him, allowing him to feel all of me against his back.

All the while stroking at his hard length and then coursing my fingers through his hair to massage his scalp. He sinks against the tile of the bathroom like I had and starts talking.

"I've missed this. Remember those nights you used to do this?" He asks.

Did I remember? Had I ever forgotten? Could I ever forget? Every time he'd had a bad day, or I'd had a bad day, all I had to do was request a shower, and he would be there, talking me through it and holding me afterward. It always worked with no exceptions.

MAFIA HEIR'S SECRET BABY

"Yes. I never forgot. It got me through many long nights. And quite frankly, days."

"Did you ever touch yourself to the thought of me?"

"I never had a choice. No other man would've done. Therefore, your memory had to be enough."

"I want to fuck you so hard right now." He swears. "Fuck Melissa. I'm scared you'll get caught in the crossfires of whatever's about to happen. And you're not even my wife yet."

"What's about to happen?" I ask. "And if you want to take me. Then I'm willing. Right now."

"I can't. I'm punishing myself, I know. But for some reason, I just don't want to. Even though I need to."

My brows crease with questions I couldn't wait to voice. "Why?"

"Because I'm fucking scared I'll fuck all this anger out, and it's all I have, Mel. This anger is everything protecting me from you."

The hurt comes whittling at me, sharp and stabbing at my chest and my stomach and my heart and anything else it could find.

18

XANDER

I FEEL HER BODY CHANGE. HER HANDS LEAVE ME FIRST, and I feel the withdrawal like a body part gone, as though she's already an extension of me.

"Why do you need protection from me?"

I point at my side. "Did you see this?" I rumble out of my too-tight chest.

"The tattoos?" She asks, confusion leaking into her voice. Her fingers land on the tattoo of a black light with the sun shading it.

The larger the dark light, the smaller the sun until it dims away almost completely at the other side of my back in just a small sliver of light and a very dark light.

She's the sunlight. I'm the darkness. And all six tattoos represent all six years she was gone.

The first year, I hoped she'd return. Hoped it was a joke. Until by last year, I'd nearly given up. And now she's back, I'm not certain if I'll need more tattoos or not.

Now the fucking Russians are encroaching on my territory, war is certain to break out, and she's making me entirely too unstable.

Worrying about my child and my wife. Because when I'd heard the Russians had invaded my territory, I'd immediately made a call to Romero to make sure she was home.

Then I'd had Ryder drive me down here to make certain because she was my weakness. She'd asked why I couldn't have her.

Well, I could just be honest and say you didn't indulge in dessert you knew would rot your teeth. At least, I shouldn't. But when had I ever listened to myself when it came to this woman?

"Yes, Mel. The tattoos. Six of them for all the years you've been gone. That's how much I missed you. That's how much I kept a reminder of you on me. You drive me to extremes."

"Oh. Oh, my goodness. That's so beautiful." She whispers, her fingers gentle as she whisks them over the tattoo, stroking over the inky skin.

"I would've never known, and I never would've asked. Thank you for telling me." She plants a gentle kiss on my back.

"I thought about you every day too. And after I had Lucian, it became everyday. There was no escape."

Her voice is so filled to the brim with a joyous sort of disbelief, and I find it gratifying that I've given in to that. I turn to her and heft her into my arms, slide my hands to cup her ass, and steal a strong kiss from her surprised lips.

She kisses me back, then spreads her legs and curves them over my ass so that her folds are right over my cock, and I throb for her.

I need to have her. She grinds into me, and that's the last string holding my restraint together gone. I bite down on her lip and swallow her cry of pleasure when I slide my cock into her tight sheath.

"Fuck Xander." She wails, her cries like beauty and life and everything in between to me.

"You want that?" I grit out, pulling all the way out to the tip and holding myself there even though it feels as though I'll drive myself mad doing that.

"I need this." She whimpers, bearing herself down on me. Her body pulses around me, the tight sheath of her body dragging me into the depths of my soul where an orgasm is already tearing at me.

I drive into her slowly, pushing and stroking inside the tight-as-glove wetness of her wet body. She grinds down to meet me halfway, and I fight her vice grip to pull out again and repeat the action.

I bend my head and suck her nipple into my mouth, first one and then another, my fingers tracing restlessly over her skin, little sharp swells of pleasure exploding like fireworks over my body.

She arches her breasts into my sucking tongue, and I allow my tongue to saw over her. Then I kiss my way to the other breast and lavish the same attention on it, all the time thrusting my thickness into her.

All the while groaning every time she tightens around me as her body prepares to rock over the ridge of her orgasm into another realm.

She flutters around me more and more, her moans acquiring a lighter edge to it as she crests and then spills, shuddering and shaking so hard she tips me over too.

My balls tighten, my fingers tingle, my body rears back and slams into her with no rhythm or rhyme or an attempt at control.

I sink my teeth into her neck, right into the curve where her neck meets her shoulders, and bite down hard on the flesh. Her body jerks, and her core tightens as the pain draws a pant from her.

She grinds into me harder, her body growing almost limp in my arms, and I drag my teeth along her body to give her a respite, then return it to the bite mark I'd left and sink my teeth in again.

She shudders this time and moans a loud moan that's a symphony I want to hear my entire life. I cum into her, spilling my seeds into her willing body, wondering why I'd waited this long to have her again.

Wondering why it still felt this good all these years later. Wondering why I feel the need to have her again even as I spill the evidence of my need for her inside her warmth.

It's insanity. A warm, wet, lovely insanity with heaving breasts that hold my attention, with hips that will cradle my child—has already cradled my child.

I kiss her lips and then let her slide down me after however long it takes for us to have our breathing under control. She smiles at me with her trembling lips, and I kiss her again; this time, it's soft and gentle, and when I pull away, I blow a gentle breeze of air across the mark on her shoulder.

"Did I hurt you?" I ask. She shakes her head and darts her eyes up to mine.

"Not at all. I liked it. I'll wear it like a brand."

I chuckle softly and pull out of her. Then, slap on the shower, which has somehow ended up off. I don't know how.

"How come you always slap it that way?" She asks, snickering at me.

I look at the knob. "I do?"

She swings her hand through the air in a bad imitation of me. "Exactly like this. All the time."

I smirk, then glare playfully at her. "I don't do that." Yes, I do.

"Yes, you do." She says. "Seen it at least three times. I like it. It's very inherently you. I don't think I'll ever see anyone do it quite like you."

"You better not. Another man has you like this; he'll lose more than his balls."

She licks her lips and sighs happily, which makes me ridiculously happy. "Possessive. You really know how to turn a woman on."

She lifts her wet hair off her shoulder, then looks towards the door.

"We should probably get out there, though and devour that lunch. I'm hungry. Someone drained me."

She takes a step away, but I shoot my hand out. "Do not go anywhere without Romero. Or the phone. That's a command, Mel."

"A command?"

"Will it sound any better now if I say 'please'?"

"Xander. I understand. I'll try my best. I don't want to worry you unnecessarily. But sometimes, it gets tiring."

I understand. But I was worried about her. Daniel had been right even before we'd gotten here.

She's my weakness.

Like dessert I couldn't stop gorging myself on. Didn't even want to stop at this point.

Which means I need to keep her safe. The war is on the horizon, and I haven't forgotten how it was when she'd left me the first time, either. I could feel it hurtling towards us again.

"I'll be gone very often in the next few weeks. I'll need more than your best."

Her eyes darken, and she stares at me for a long moment. "Fine. I'll always keep him with me." She leans on me and plants a soft kiss on my lips. "Now let's go.

Your son is waiting, and I'm certain my sister's just about ready to break down this door."

We find Gianna and Lucian in the kitchen, already halfway through the lunch I'd brought back. Lucian lifts his head, and for the first time, he runs straight into my arms. I lift him and swing him into the air, and walk with him towards the table.

Gianna watches suspiciously, like she's not certain what's taken over me. "It's nice to see you," I say as I pass her on the way to the fridge to get myself a bottle of water.

"I'd say the same thing, but it really ain't Xander Amory."

"I'm Lucian Sedric Amory," Lucian announces into the gap before I can find a suitably good comeback for Gianna, which has me lifting my eyes to Mel's.

She smiles slowly, the smile spreading over her face like fire in a range. Which in turn burns inside me a heat that I do not want to extinguish. And just like that, I know I'm at risk of falling for her all over again.

Fuck.

"That you are my boy. How about we watch some TV together, buddy?" I ask, pressing a kiss to the side of his head when he agrees with a very exuberant nod.

Hand in hand we walk to the living room and settle onto the couch. "So what's your favorite show, bud? Who is your favorite character?"

His eyes light up and he yells "Orf Orf Officers! I want to be just like Ripper the German Shepard! He's a police and he makes sure everyone stays safe," he proclaims proudly.

I HAVE no idea what this show is. I do not make it my business to know children's television, but I suppose I will now.

I ruffle his hair and chuckle. "Maybe someday you'll be a hero like Ripper." I make a mental note to find this... Orf Orf Officers and figure out what it is. If my son likes it, then so shall I.

With Lucian engrossed in his beloved show, I wonder if I'd ever seen this future for myself. Even with Mel, I never pictured playful nights on the couch, seeing the world anew through a child's eyes.

Yet with Lucian by my side, the future seems brighter, open even for a dark world like mine. I could get used to this, the two of us laughing and learning together.

A boy like Lucian who looks so like me I see a reflection of myself staring at me every day now in his gaze.

I don't understand how I've slipped so perfectly into this. When my phone rings five minutes later, and I find Ryder's name flashing on the screen, I know reality is about to intrude heavily. I leave Lucian on the couch and walk to my study.

"You're sliding." Are the first words out of his mouth. "And the men will notice."

"Am I now?"

"You are. Your men are dead, and you worry about her first."

"Men are replaceable. Lucian isn't." I snap at him. I recline into my chair, pushing it back from the desk. "Besides, I have everything covered before leaving."

"Yes, but you never would've left before." He says.

"What's the point of this conversation?" I set my eyes blearily on the trees waving outside and decide I'm not going to like whatever he's about to say.

"The point is, I've noticed. Your siblings know. Your men will see it soon enough. And then so will the rest of the world. If they know your weakness, Xander, you damned well be certain they'll use it against you."

I exhale a deep, tired breath and sit up straight. "You're not saying anything I don't know."

"Which is why I have to repeat it. If you don't do it for you, do it for her. They'll kill her if they know it'll kill you."

"I thought we were talking about Lucian?"

Ryder had never been known to pull his punches, and he doesn't pull it now. "I'm not fucking stupid boss. And neither are you."

And because I trust him to tell me as it is really, I ask a question that grates its way roughly out of my throat like sandpaper. "How bad is it?"

He pauses, and I can almost hear him thinking in the silence. "Bad enough, but love is love, I guess."

Who had said a word about love?

"You're going too far, Ryder." I bark. Then I hung up the phone.

MEL

"I NEED YOUR HELP WITH THIS." I POINT A FINGER AT THE screen and turn my chair around to make space for Rosa to step closer. She pushes her chair back and walks toward me.

"The charities basically run themselves. If you'd rather not concern yourself with them, then I repeat, you don't have to." She blinks down at me from her perch on my desk and then swings her gaze to the computer.

"Why do you feel the need to repeat that?" I angle my head and peer at her until she lifts her face from the screen.

I'm at Amory Corp with Romero. We'd dropped Lucian off at school and then driven straight down here. It has been a few days since I've been here, with my move-in with Lucian and the entire struggle of settling in. But this morning has been a lot calmer, less jarring, and I've felt a lot more useful.

And just as I said, I'm taking an avid interest in running the charities. Except I don't understand why Rosa seems to think I shouldn't. Or maybe that I don't. I can't seem to decide which it is.

Rosa shrugs and pushes her glasses up her nose as she always does when she doesn't know what to say, or maybe in this situation, doesn't know what to say that won't offend me. Her blond hair is styled in a bun with the fringe a lot longer than it usually is.

It's almost unkempt, which rings a bell. Something's wrong. It's not just her hair; her eyes are dark, bags are already pumping under them, and her body is stiff under the already stiff cut of her two-piece tailored pantsuit.

"No one paid any attention to it. You shouldn't feel the need to pay it any attention. Xander doesn't want any attention drawn to it. It'll be one more weakness on his long line of weaknesses."

I tilt my head to fix her with a glare. "It's a fucking charity, Rosa. I'm not planning on splashing the news on the TV screens." I inhale, and my shoulders deflate.

I lower my voice and swing my head around the office, even though it's just the two of us. "I want to help. I need to have something of my own. Something I can do. And this is it."

Rosa twists her lips in a wry smile. "Fine. We can arrange a day for you to visit the hospitals, maybe one of the charity homes. Maybe you can talk to the kids too."

She still doesn't understand. I snap a hand into the desk and watch as she startles. I curl my fingers into a fist. "No maybes. We're doing this. We've held off on it long enough. I'd also like to make some more money for the charities."

Her jaw bunches, and suddenly, I don't understand her reluctance. This had been her idea. She'd wanted me to do this. Why the sudden change of mind?

The threat of the world finding out Xander had a few charities had been there when she'd first asked if I'd be interested in taking over. "Xander has enough money to run the charities. You don't need to do that."

I lean towards her, and though I know I shouldn't, I place a hand on her thighs. She jerks away from me but doesn't get off the table. "What's wrong, Rosa." I wave a hand between us when she goes to reply. "Don't you dare fucking lie to me either. Something's wrong. What is it?"

She grimaces, and her voice rumbles out of clenched teeth as a rumble. "Shouldn't you ask Xander? He's your husband."

I give her a cold glower and fold my hands across my stomach. "And you're here. Right in front of me, worried about me. Why the hell shouldn't I ask you?"

She inhales and exhales, her chest rising and falling. She tilts her head to the door and leans into me like I had. "I can't say much. Xander doesn't want you worried or in fear. But things aren't as they should be."

My heart quakes and flips like an obstacle in a hurricane. I bite my lip to hold back the cry on my tongue.

Then, I ask the question that I'm most worried about. "Is he in danger?" Even the thought of it has my stomach queasy and cold.

Rosa's eyes are flinty. "È solo di questo che ti preoccupi?" Do you not understand what I've just said?"

What else was there to worry about? Xander would never let any harm come to his son. And by extension, that meant no harm would come to me. He would lay down his life to protect his child. So why wouldn't I worry about him? I sure as hell knew he wouldn't worry about himself.

"I do understand. But if this is war, who does he have on his side?"

"An entire army of men who will lay their lives on the line for him. Who do you have on your side, Melissa? The Mafia is no joke. How many deaths have you seen?"

I back away from her. This was getting gory. And I had thought I wanted to know, but now I'm not certain.

Do I really want the gory details? The death? The guns? The violence? The darkness embedded in these men like diamonds in dust?

I heave, and a surge of air streams out of my nose. "Let's come back to the Charities. Tell me what I need to know."

Rosa cranks her neck, and then she stretches. "There's three. Two contributing towards a cancer cause. If you've seen his father, you'll understand why. The last provides support for children who grew up in abusive homes. If you know his family, then you'll understand why too."

God. How much worse can it get? It makes total sense why he keeps his involvement hidden. Possibly under layers of businesses and corporations that will ensure any contribution from him can never be traced back to him.

I nod sharply and turn to the screen. "Arrange the meetings. I'll meet the leaders and directors of these charities."

"What do you mean directors?" Rosa returns to the chair opposite.

I look up at her. "Isn't there someone running these places?"

"I think you'll understand when you visit." She places her head against the chair and blows her fringe off her forehead.

"Then hasten the arrangements," I say, my voice as commanding as I can make it. I need her to understand she can't weasel out of this. "And I'm visiting my father from here. Just in case *my husband* wants to know."

She nods and pushes to her feet, straightening her suit over her shoulders so the fabric drops into place like armor. "I'll call him. Or you could do it yourself, Melissa. You have an authority I don't think you understand yet."

With those cryptic words, she turns on her heels and marches out of the room. She holds the door open and exchanges a few words with Romero who sticks his head into the room and gives me a hard stare.

I ignore them. The screen on the computer already shows a long list of people who have in some way benefitted from the charities.

Rosa had sent it to me this morning when I arrived, along with the list of people who need help and how much money I'd need to sign for.

My heart squeezes. The money is illegal. It's the fucking Mafia. I know that much, but it's for a good cause.

I look up. I don't know how much later when the door opens, and Romero steps in. I watch as he strides to the desk and stops with his hand folded respectfully behind his back.

"It's lunch break. What shall I order?"

I smile up at him. "What time is it?"

"A few minutes past noon. The entire building should be emptying in a few minutes."

Who knew hardened men ate lunch? I'd have thought they inhaled torture and pain for sustenance. Jesus Mel! Get a grip.

"I'll have a salad. Maybe a green tea to go along with it."

My phone trills on the table, and Romero's eyes swing towards it. "Marito" is written across the screen. I smile as I swipe the phone up and answer.

Romero nods and turns away, shutting the door behind him. I relax into the chair and giggle finally.

"I expect I'm not the one who's being funny without saying a word, am I?" Xander's crispy baritone meets my seeking ears.

I giggle some more and succumb to the light floating through my chest. It feels so good to be in this state where we're just fine. No animosity, no pain, no anger. Just us.

"Why would you think that mio marito?" I purr at him, my core tightening deliciously when a rigid pause greets my ears. I exhale a rush of shaky air and graze a finger over my breasts.

Then I pull my hand away sharply. I want his touch; mine that had always sufficed just doesn't feel the same anymore.

"What did you say?" His voice is tight with lust. And I can almost imagine his blue eyes feasting on me. My skin tightens, tensing, pounding in the air between us.

"Which? My husband?"

His raspy exhale is rushed and sexy as hell. A pant escapes my lips. It's ridiculously apparent how much he wants me. It's palpable how much it is that I want him right back.

"You tease! Say it the other way. Now."

A breathy little moan slips into the air. I press the phone close to my lips so he can imbibe every word. "Mio marito. My own. My husband."

"I'm calling Romero. He's bringing you down here right now. Pack your things."

I laugh finally, the sound bursting out like fairy dust to shower joy over us. "I can't. I'm working."

"Fuck work." He stops, the pause short but conscious. "I need you."

"How about you come down here?"

"I can't. There's something here that I can't leave." The words are like a stream of cold water over my warm flesh. I press my eyes closed and wiggle uncomfortably. But he doesn't allow me to lose him. "But I will be home early. And I swear, I'll take you in so many different ways walking will be a chore. It's a promise."

My nipples bud up against the soft, lacy fabric of my bra. "I look forward to it, Mi'lord."

"Goodbye. I really just wanted to hear your voice. Now I have a raging hard-on for my troubles. You're a distraction, Sole."

He hangs up abruptly, and I spend a few good minutes imagining him in his office, maybe touching himself to the thought of me, craving me as much as I want him, need him.

Submitting to him somehow feels good. It's better than fighting him. And him putting me on an even keel feels even better.

It makes me drip, makes me itch for his touch, makes me needy in a way he alone can satisfy. And without warning, I want to be home.

It's almost six, and I've worked myself into a lather thinking about him. So I'm definitely not expecting Romero to stalk into the room after a single knock, his brow jumping, his face dark with a forceful glare.

"We need to go." He packs my large black Birkin without asking my permission as usual, and I don't question him despite my almost desperate need to ask what's wrong. There will be enough time to probe in the car.

Rosa is at the door, her face drained of color, so she looks almost ashen. She swivels and walks ahead of us, already barking words into the wire clipped into her ear.

"Bring the car around. No stops until she's home. I repeat, no stops."

I walk faster till I'm beside her. Immediately she's done talking, I break into the minute silence. "What's going on?"

Her chest expands on a deep exhale, and I realize her glasses are foggy. "Someone found out about Xander's dad. There's a fucking uprising. We need to make sure you're safe. You're heading to his father's where security is max."

Damnit. Then I freeze and tug her to a stop, my chest too tight, my vision wobbling. "Where's my son? Where's Lucian?"

She stops and tips her head to Romero and I know without doubt none of them had even thought about him.

20

XANDER

IT'S A FUCKING UPHEAVAL. RYDER HAS HIS HAND FISTED so hard I'm certain the nails are biting grooves into his palm.

His guilt is clear, as is the fact that it's unnecessary. He's blaming himself for something that really isn't his fault.

It's no one's but mine. The walls around us are the grotesque gray of an underground building, which we currently are. A man hangs upside down from a chain hitched to a pole, his face about as colorful as a bleached bone in a desert.

Well. I guess it would be, considering how much blood has been taken from him. The floor is coated with it, a vicious dark pool that seems far too long.

"How much longer does he have?" I snap at Ryder.

"About an hour. Should be dead in less than that if his weak lungs don't hold up." Ryder walks over to the man and sinks a solid punch into his stomach, his shoulders snapping back under his leather jacket.

The crunch of bones and the loud wail that opens the man's lips do nothing for the anger boiling through me.

I pull a gun from the hostler that swings across my torso and walk over to him. There's no need to waste my time on scum like him.

Ryder hears my footsteps and turns his head to me. He stops and then lopes towards me fast, his footsteps biting the ground between us. He places a hand on my arm and hisses at me. "What are you doing?"

"Killing him off. He's useless to me."

"We don't have the information we need from him," Ryder turns to glare at the man who is crying, the tears dripping out of fat black eyelids. He's been tortured for hours, and yet, still no information from him.

He won't say a word if we beat him all day. He is, after all, a man of the Mafia. It is after all one of the reasons he had been ours.

He understands this is the end of every traitor. And he deserves every second of the pain we have given him as punishment.

Because he sold us out. To the fucking Russians, no less. And now the news of my father's Illness is in the streets, in everyone's mouth. There will be hell to pay, and I will start with him

"You," I spit. "Talk."

The man's eyes flutters open. He wheezes slightly. "No."

"Then you'll die."

"I'm dead anyway," he whispers.

"There's time. Ryder can call a doctor. Talk, and I'll save you," I grunt at him.

The man shakes his head. "Doesn't matter. If you don't kill me, they will."

"Who are they?"

He lapses into silence. I can see it, then, in the shape of his jaw.

He's resigned himself to die.

There's no reason for me to keep going. I turn and look back at Ryder.

"We won't have the information we need from him. So better we use him to inform the rest." I growl, the words tumbling like dry weed past my lips.

He deserves to die. Things are going to be so much worse now. I need to get to my father. I need to protect my men. I need to nip the uprising of my very own men in the bud. I need to get my family to safety. And I need to make sure I have a tight grasp on things.

"Let me do it." He takes a gun from his thighs, and the click as he pulls the hammer echoes through the dim room. "You go to your family."

I turn away from him, walk a few steps, then turn fast and click at the hammer of my gun. A few seconds later, the man slumps forward on his chains, his shoulders relaxing in death.

I still feel nothing. Nothing but anger. Rage. Wrath. Fury. I want to rip something apart. I want to kick and rage, but all that is tucked away inside. Beneath the layers of control I've been taught since my tender years to express.

I swivel to bear down on the men who line the doors and space around us. "Let that be a warning to anyone who even bears the thought. Before you think it, I know you. I will find you." I point at the broken man, bloodiest, streaks of red essence flowing down his skin. My voice is an angry roar. "That will be your fate. Yours and your family's."

The room is silent enough to hear a pin drop. Ryder walks up to me, and together, we leave the room. I return the gun to its place and nod at Ryder, who makes a call to bring the cars to the bar doors. We take the steps up to the ground floor of Alec's club, where we have a bunker underneath.

Alec meets my angry face and looks away. He takes a long look at Ryder and walks over, avoiding my right side. He knows that's my most powerful hook. I hide my grin, my shoulder loosening marginally. "Is he dead?"

"Yes. Xander dealt with him."

I point a finger at Alec. "Come to father's. We need to be there with him. Mother will need us with the news everywhere and on every bastard's lips."

I walk away, striding through the club with music so loud it rattles my bones. And this is still the middle of the fucking day, but it's so dark inside the path to the door is illuminated by strobes of dark light that sizzle red and blue and purple across the velvet of the club. These idiots would never believe what it is that they help hide.

When Ryder and I step outside, one of my men rushes to the door and has it open. Ryder rides gunshot, and I slip into the back seat, close my eyes, and exhale the rage out of my pores.

Men do not bring the rage to the house. Especially because my wife will be there. "Where's Mel?"

"Rosa has had her transported to the house," Ryder says.

"And where's my son?"

He has no ready answer.

The silence begins to stretch, and I snap out of my seat. "Where the fu..." I stop and swallow the swear. I will not dirty his name like that. "Where is my son?"

Ryder pulls his phone from his jacket pocket and calls Rosa. He barks out the question, then listens for a few seconds. His shoulders relax, and mine do too.

Ryder tips his head back to speak to me. "Daniel is picking him up at school."

"Send some more men," I growl. I look outside the window at the people going back and forth. They have no idea the danger that floats, digs, and swirls around them, among them. All they think is that life glitters, and they only worry about trivial things like bad coffee.

I almost wish I had their life. That the very scent of danger doesn't mean my son must be pulled out of school, that he was still safely back with his mother, that I can protect him from the damp twirl of fire that is his father.

But I also love having him around. I'm greedy enough that his snuggling in my arms manages to still me. To bring peace in much the same way that holding Mel makes me someone else.

Someone who is hers. Not the monster with a fiery chest full of fire that combusts and burns, dragging along enemies that kill. That torture and maim.

We arrive at Father's thirty minutes later, and I'm relieved to see Romero at the door, his face tight. He nods inside and then greets.

"Where is she?"

"With your mother." He replies, then looks away.

I step through the open door, and Enzo closes the door behind me. "Good afternoon, Boss."

I spare him a nod and take the hallway, curving a single corner into the living room where Declan and Knox are seated on two separate sofas.

Knox watches me warily. "Everything's okay."

A mask flits across my face to hide the tug of pain and hurt I carry. It makes no sense how I can forgive Mel but not these men. "I never asked."

Declan smiles wryly and pushes to his feet. He's dressed as always in a three-piece suit, this one a light blue that somehow manages to look masculine on his bulky frame. He walks over, and I sink my feet into the Persian rug beneath us. "I'm sorry."

I tilt my head, then squeeze my fists at my side. "Are you now? What does that have to do with me?"

Knox walks over too, and they step closer in sync, crowding my space. "This really ain't the time for us to fight."

I inhale and exhale. Then I hurl off and punch Declan right in the stomach with my left fist. An "oof" of air escapes his lips, and his hand covers his stomach, but he doesn't show any reaction apart from that. Knox opens himself up to receive his, but I grin at him.

He blinks, as does Declan. They had done wrong by not telling me about my son but they were my brothers, it's no good to hold it over their heads forever. "I'm done. You two hurt me. I understand you didn't mean to, but you did."

Declan softens, then smiles too, a slight curl of his lips that looks painful. Knox leans into me and curves his arms around my back in a big bear hug. Declan does the same, and I hear a sniff that seems to come from Knox.

"Are you crying?" Declan asks softly.

"Don't be an asshole," Knox murmurs. But when he pulls away, his quiet eyes are suspiciously bright.

"Oh." The words come from the stairs, and I turn to find Melissa gleaming down at me. She traces her fingers over her lips. "I really thought you three idiots would kill yourselves. That was really sweet."

My stomach flares with fire, an inferno raging that flickers and bites. "Come here," I grunt at her.

I need her.

I don't know how, exactly, but I need the solace that only her body can provide.

"That was our warning to get out," Declan mutters. I don't spare them a glance as their footsteps shuffle out of the room. My eyes are entirely on the woman coming towards me.

It doesn't matter if the hounds of hell are licking outside, if the fire is getting hotter, if the bastard Russians are creeping near like vines up a building.

I will never not want this woman. I will never not need her to smile at me this way, rush down the stairs and into my arms, sink into me like she is mine, and she knows this as a fact.

I press a kiss to her hair, tighten my arms like a band around her, and then another kiss to my mark, which is just dying away on her skin. "Are you okay?"

She tips her head up to press a kiss to the throbbing vein right on my neck and grins up at me. "I'm fine. You don't need to worry. I listened to Romero. I followed him here like you wanted. I've been a good girl."

Gesù Cristo.

She floors me, just like that. I cup the back of her head and tip her lips into mine. My tongue sweeps immediately between her lips, and I curl it over hers.

She moans and gives me a hard kiss back. Her teeth grind down on my tongue, and I groan.

"Fuck. Fuck. Fuck. Come upstairs."

She nods and kisses me harder, letting her hands roll over my skin, the pad of her thumb pressing into my stomach.

She sighs and smiles. Her eyes open. "What happened?"

I sigh just as softly and tug her into my side. "Gabriele ratted us out to the Russians. The men were being antsy. I didn't know how fast they would strike. I need you safe."

She gazes up at me and nods. "Who's Gabriele?"

My finger tightens around her waist, and I snort angrily. "A dead man."

She stops and looks up at me. "Will this always happen? Will his life always be disrupted like this?"

My guts want to spill. But I know the truth. I've lived it for years. "Yes. Until things die down."

She's quiet the rest of the way inside the house. I have nothing to say either, but the silence isn't the sort that needs breaking into.

It's the silence of two people who understand each other enough that words are not necessary.

When we enter the dining room, Mother and Father are already seated. Father looks dead already, a skeleton with breathing skin.

I walk to him and bend my head to receive his kiss. He waves at a chair for me. "We knew it was going to happen soon. This is nothing to worry about. The wedding will go on, the contract will be signed, and you will take over. As we always planned."

Mother closes her eyes and then pats the chair beside her for Mel. Mel gives me a look, and I nod. She takes the chair beside my mother, and I take the one beside Father.

Mother doesn't have a female in the family. I sort of understand why she needs Mel.

"I know, Father. I understand my duty." But today, the words taste sour, sliding like slough off my tongue.

21

MEL

Dinner with his father had been a stressful affair.

The tension in the room is so thick, you could cut it with a knife. His brothers were worried about his father's health and how the news of escaping the family would make him fare.

Amory, as usual, had been staunch, a frown on his face that only lifted when the food had arrived and he'd said the grace. Then he'd proceeded to take only a taste of it and asked to be taken to his study, where Xander had soon joined him, and then his brothers after a few minutes.

So it's just his mother and I, the two women of the family left together to pass the time.

"Are you happy?" She asks, a kind smile on her face.

I smile back at Xander's mom, the slight breeze in the air carrying the earthy smell of the frangipanis that border her garden. We're seated on the porch, the sun waning above us, the trees waving listlessly to and fro. "I think so. Are you?"

She smiles back, tipping her head back to take a gulp of the wine in the glass with the twisted stem she favors. "What is happiness Melissa? I take my joy as I see it."

I nod. Isn't she just right? "So do I. I'm as happy as it is possible for a human to be."

She leaves her seat and I do the same, thinking we're returning to the men inside. Xander and his father have been locked away together for about an hour now in his study. She comes towards me though, her arms stretched out and I lean into her just as she locks her arms around me.

It reminds me for a poignant second of my mother. She'd always hugged me this way, sharp and there, her arms locked tight like a vice around my small body. I sniff and drop my head into her shoulders but her head moves too fast and she pulls away.

The stamp of footsteps reaches my ears and I turn to find Xander watching us, his eyes heavy. His mother smiles and walks towards him, offering him the same hug.

He fuses his arms around her but his eyes remain on mine and my eyes, they fill up just like that. I stand up and pick my bag off the table, throwing back the rest of my wine.

He holds his hand out to me when his mother pulls away. "Are you ready to leave?"

"Yes."

A few minutes later, I place my bag in the space between Xander and me and slide as far away as I can go.

I smile sadly out of the window, and Xander's fingers cover mine. "What are you thinking about amore mio?"

I shift my head to him, and he lifts the bag, dropping it to the floor with no regard for the thousands of dollars that went into getting it.

He drags me across the seat into his arms, and I relax my head into the crook of his shoulders. "I'm thinking about my mother. Your mother reminds me of her. Or at least she did today."

"What does she remind you of?" He slides his hand through my hair, gentle swoops that have my body wanting more.

I shake my head. "I don't know exactly. Just the way she asked if I was fine. It's much the same voice and the way my mother would. And the hug? I don't think I've had one quite like it in a while."

He nods and plants a soft, almost tender kiss on my forehead. I like it. I enjoy it.

"Where's Romero?" I ask, looking up at him for a second.

"Ahead of us. I need to know the house is safe."

I sit up, sliding on the leather of the car seats before hitching myself to him. "Lucian is there. Father wouldn't let anything harm him."

Xander nods again. "I know. But I needed to make sure."

I smile and incline my head towards his. He bends towards me too but stops just before he claims my lips.

He waits, as though he's waiting for me to kiss him, like he wants me to finish what I started. I look out of the window for a quick second to gauge where we are.

We're too close to the house. I don't want anyone to see, especially not with what I have in mind. I shudder a deep breath out and sway towards him before biting my lip and slanting my head away to hide in his shoulders.

He chuckles, the sound reverberating inside my core. He nips at my ear and pats gently at me. "Sometimes I forget how innocent you are. I wouldn't care, you know."

I kiss a trail of wet smooches across his neck, to his collar, where his shirt hinders my path. "I will. Lucian's home."

His hand tightens on my skin; he digs into my waist and then sighs. "Then you should stop. This hard-on won't go away otherwise."

I snicker, but I do lean away from him. Except he rolls his eyes and tugs me back into the cave of his arms. And I go willingly enough. I'm still caught against him when the car pulls into the driveway of our home, and we pull to the door.

He pushes his door open, glides out like a fucking lion hunting, and then holds his hand out to me, one hand on the door to hold it away from me.

I lift my bag off the floor where it had fallen and give him a playful glare. "This cost a lot of money, you know."

He smirks. "Get thirty more, Sole. I don't fucking care."

Why his response sends a rush of wetness to pool in my thighs doesn't make sense, but what makes total sense is the way I bend to the floor and sweep up Lucian in my arms when I take a step away, and he comes hurtling out of the house like a rocket into my arms.

"Mommy!" His cry is all I need. All I want at this moment. I hug him. Wondering how Xander's assurance was more than enough to assure me he was safe.

I'm happy to have him in my arms, but when he wiggles to get down and holds his arms out to his father, I let him go just as willingly.

There's a weird feeling in my chest. One that is stranger, but it feels new. It feels like magic. It feels like home. My son in his father's arms spikes tears as always in my eyes.

I wonder if it'll take a year more before the sight feels usual—feels normal.

I wonder if it will ever feel normal.

"How was your day?" Xander asks Lucian.

The boy lifts his shoulders up and down. "Uncle Daniel picked me up from school. We had ice cream at his house." He smiles. "That was nice."

Of course, it was. Uncle Daniel seems to be laying on the ice cream pretty thick these days, and I'll probably have to talk to him about it. I turn to walk into the house.

Romero is at the door, his hand tucked away as always. I smile at him because, well, I'm in a cheery mood. It only gets better when I step into the house to find Gianna.

She hugs me tight and then sniffles. "I was so worried about you."

I place my arms around her and hug her tight too. "It was nothing really. I promise."

She frowns. "I know, but still. I realize this will be my fate now."

I nod at her sagely. I'd realized that truth this afternoon too. Any sign of a threat will have Xander hurtling us away from wherever we are to a place he deems safe.

Gianna tips her head to the door. "Where are the men? Lucian was about to head to bed. You should take a rest. I was hoping he'd be in bed before you return."

I shake my head. "It's just as well he wasn't. I'd have needed his warmth to remind me he's totally fine."

Gianna's smile is warm and understanding. "I understand. I'll take him up. Dinner's in the fridge. I'll be going up with Lucian."

Xander's voice precedes his padding footsteps into the room. He's holding Lucian into the air while he blows air into his stomach.

Lucian struggles to get back, but Xander won't give an inch. Lucian's legs are swinging in the air, and I hope one doesn't knock into his father's head.

Gianna watches me watch them, then she steps towards me. "He's good with the boy," she mutters. She turns and walks towards them and holds out her arms for him.

Xander's arms tighten around his son for a second, then he lets him go. "I'll come give you a kiss goodnight soon."

Lucian nods and drops from his father's arms to the floor. He runs up the stairs when Gianna points out that's where they're headed. She follows him up and I walk over to Xander.

He tips my head up, and the small smile at the corner of his lips nearly melts my heart like ice cream in the heat. "Thank you for giving me him."

His voice is quiet, almost too low to be heard, but I hear him. I understand all the other things that he can't say—won't say.

I turn and lead the way up the stairs to our room. Once he pushes the door closed behind him, I drag him to the bed. He lets himself go.

His hand grips my waist almost painfully tight. I skim my finger over the front of his pants, and he hisses. I lift my head to his and smirk. "Looks like it didn't let up at all."

"And even if it had, you're a minx. It wouldn't lie low for long," he growls into my hair.

I unzip him, my hand wrapping around his thick cock. I don't know if it's the day we've had, the tension, or the fact that I just seem to crave him, but my fingers are urgent around him.

I need him now. He just has to take me. I don't want to wait; I don't need foreplay. He's safe, and he's here. We're all here together.

And I need him.

I stroke him, one long caress that has his fingers pinching my nipples painfully tight. I shudder and cry out. He racks the skirt of my dress up to my waist, almost as though he understands the thoughts in my head.

He shoves my panties to the side and sinks a finger into me. It's not gentle, but a sharp thrust that has my back aching towards him, my hips pressing my wetness into his fingers. He joins another finger to thrust in and out twice.

Then he pulls the fingers out of me, already coated with my essence. Keeping his blue eyes firmly on mine, he takes a slow, sexy lick at his fingers. Then, he closes his eyes and groans. "You are ambrosia. I'd eat you all up, but I've been holding back all morning. I need you."

He lifts me onto the bed, tugs my dress up my legs to my waist, and then strokes a fast caress at his cock before shoving my lace panties out of the way and sheathing himself inside me with one hard thrust.

"Ohh. *Oh*," the cry slips out of my open mouth, and he anchors himself in my dress to hold me to him. His hand fists the dress so hard I know I'm not going anywhere until he wants me to. I like it.

I pant at him. "Hard. I can take it, Xander. And I need you to give it to me," I tilt my head to look up at him.

His blue eyes are the color of a rough sea, dark and luminous, and he slams into me, his hips tight, my legs pressing down against his ass, my screams echoing his grunts of pleasure. I accept the fast thrust of his hips, the way his hands just hold on as he rams into me over and over again.

Sweat dots my forehead, pleasure singes my senses, dragging me into a cave of pleasure where my body doesn't belong to me but to him, to strum and touch and bring heat to.

"I'm close." I gasp, pant, cry, shudder, clench around him.

His face creases as though he's in pain. "Good. You're such a good girl for me, Mel. You take me so well, and I want to fuck this pussy until you know that you're mine. Mine," he grunts.

His rhythm is long, punctuated by short strokes into my warm body. He sinks in deep, and then finally, his fingers leave my dress to slide over my clitoris. I lift into him with a loud cry, and I fall back into the bed, too far gone.

My entire body is racked by blinding flashes of pleasure so intense it sweeps me away. My cries are loud and choked.

I feel ragged, but his thrusts keep me right on the edge, holding on as he sinks in and pulls out until he tightens and comes inside me. I feel the heat of him like a brand, scathing my inner walls, and I like it.

God help me, I like it a lot.

He falls over me, and because I know soon he'll roll over to put me on top, I press my fingers into his back. "Stay this way a moment. Please, Xander."

He holds still, his muscles tense under my fingers. Then they unfurl and relax. "Let me know when I get heavy. I don't want to burden you."

He still doesn't understand. I sweep my tongue along his lips, and he opens his eyes. "You could never be a burden to me, Xander. Never. Do you understand?"

I press a kiss to him so that he knows I'm serious.

Xander's weight is a welcome anchor. It keeps me grounded, pulls me down.

I want him inside me.

I want him always.

I don't know how to tell him, but I need him to know.

For me, it was always Xander. Only Xander.

And it will always be him.

22

XANDER

"Jesus. Can you please sit down?" I grumble from across the room.

Alec rolls his eyes and clambers over my feet to stride over to Knox, who is standing by the windows, watching the men outside.

It's a cloudy day, which is perfect, really. It matches my mood perfectly. Because enough has quite literally become enough. We're having a meeting with Sandro, and he's running late as usual.

"Let's bet he arrives an hour late." Declan holds out his hand, thumb facing me. I run a hand through my hair and glare at him.

I glower at him. "Is this a fucking joke to you, Declan? You choose this one moment to fucking laugh?"

It's not his fault I'm pissed. It's Sandro's, and today, I'll teach him a lesson. I've been waiting twenty minutes already.

"I'm interested in the bet." Knox turns towards us and walks to the table where he takes his seat and, as always, pours me a glass of whiskey along with his.

"Good. Five hundred dollars says he's an hour late."

Knox leans over and clasps his thumb to Declan's. "An hour thirty minutes for a thousand dollars."

I run a frustrated hand through my hair and lean into my chair. I hope it rains. The lake in the back will be teeming with water. Maybe I'll go for a swim with the thunder rumbling above, the lightning flashing in my eyes.

"You two just lost. He's here."

Good. I sit up and flip my gun from my waist, blow at its cylinder, and place it squarely on the table. I want it to be the first thing he sees when he steps into the room.

He's coming along with most of the Masters. The men who do the grassroots work, so they say.

They dispense the drugs, get my money, and make sure it's complete. They're my men. And today, I'm making sure they will continue to be.

"Take a seat, Alec."

Alec returns to the table and sits. Ryder sticks his head into the door and nods in our signal. The men are complete. Perfect.

"Make sure Sandro comes in first."

I have a feeling there's something off about him. It's either the Russians have bought him out, or he's weaker than I thought. Either way, the Russians are still too fucking close for comfort.

The old saying applies: if you want something done, do it yourself.

The sound of multiple footsteps comes thundering down the hallway, and then the sound of Sandro's voice on a harsh laugh. I make sure he's the one who steps into the room first, then I pick the gun off the table and blow his kneecap out.

The sound of the bullet ripping out is a loud, startling clap of thunder, just as I intended, and it has all their attention, though it is too late for the one whom it was intended to escape.

He falls to the floor with a hoarse cry, holding onto his leg where red is already spurting from. He lifts hate-filled eyes to me, and I stare down at him blankly before lifting my eyes to point the gun at the men who are still staring down at him, various degrees of shock in their equally blank eyes.

I smile somberly. "Come sit." I turn a glare at Sandro. "You too, Sandro."

The men settle around the table, away from my brothers, who have taken their seats around me. Alec is on my right, and Declan and Knox are both on my left.

Sandro wails again as he tries to place force on his legs to push up. His face is dotted with sweat, pain, and anger smeared across the red expense of flesh.

I nod at Ryder, who helps him to his feet and leads him to that table, handing him a batch of bandages to tie across the seeping wound. "That was rather unnecessary, Xander Amory."

I smile again. Not at him but at the men ranged around me. "I understand. But a lesson needed to be taught. And you're the scapegoat." I point the gun at Enzo, his ragged red hair falling around his face. "Tomorrow it might be you." I point across the table. "Or you."

None of them blink. None look away. None say a word.

"Good. Pour the drinks, Knox. Let's discuss business. I've been eager to hear from all of you."

MAFIA HEIR'S SECRET BABY

Knox pours the drinks, but no one takes the glasses until Alec has a gulp of his, as though we couldn't poison ourselves and have the antidote as backup.

"I know what the news says. My father is sick. There is no longer need to hide this. The Russians have made sure Chicago knows this."

"And what does this mean for the Famiglia?" Antonio asks. Antonio ensures our guns get to the points where they need to be. He's straight-tongued and doesn't deviate from the truth.

"It means things continue as usual. There will be nothing changing."

The silence is long and winding. Enzo breaks it. "The Capo..."

I stop him with a blunt cut through his words. "I will be Capo in less than three weeks. Trust me, the issue of the Capo has nothing to do with this. It will be as I say."

Matthew Benjamin, who has the most American name I've ever heard and also the most dangerous swing with a knife I've ever seen, lifts his hand in the air. I nod at him, though I don't know why he bothers. "Shouldn't we hear this from the present Capo?"

I frown at him, lifting the gun to check its heft in my hand. His eyes roll to the gun just like I want it to. "Are my words not enough for you, Benny?"

He jerks and stills. "Very well. But I do need your assurance that nothing changes. The Russians are parading the streets. Things are tight. I worry there will be trouble more than you can handle."

The group goes tight-lipped all at once. And I know this is the root of the problem. They doubt me.

"Do you have a solution for the Russians?" I ask. I pull the drink that Knox had poured for me and take a large gulp, pretending the burn from the whiskey is all I feel.

"I think we should wipe them out." Sandro barks. He takes a swing from his flask and glares across the table at me.

Declan drags the drink across the scratched mahogany table to pour himself a shot. "You don't deserve a voice in the gathering of men, Sandro. We gave you a task. You failed at it. If you ask me, Xander's bullet is not a fitting punishment for your failure."

Sandro bangs a large, hairy hand on the table. "They killed my men!"

"As we should kill you. Now shut up." I roar at him, fixing him with an intense stare that has him back into his chair in a few seconds.

Enzo wipes his lips with the back of his hand and cranes his neck to meet everyone's eyes one after the other. "There will be no reasoning with him. If these words don't slip out of this room, I will advise an extinction."

I tilt my head, my stomach curdling like bad cheese. "Do you have knowledge I don't? Is there a traitor in our midst?"

"None that I can think of. But loyalty is a commodity. I have no idea who will decide he can be bought." Enzo said.

"Let's talk about this... extinction. All the Russians gone. Is that what you mean?" Alec leans forward, his eyes gleaming in a way that says he is interested.

And I realize why, or at least part of the reason Father must have agreed to keep Lucian from me. Now, I have a child of my own, and I understand what Alec means. My guts squeeze uncomfortably.

There are innocents. I imagine someone coming after Lucian. Or after Melissa, and blood sings in my veins. Rage and the need to hurt anyone who comes even a step close to them wishing them harm.

The discussion is still swirling around me when I hit a fist into the table. All their eyes snap to mine. Good. I like to know all the authority is still mine.

If I don't hold onto it with a tight fist, I have no doubt it'll slip right out. "We'll wipe out the Russians. Very soon. But not the family."

"Then it is not an extinction." Matthew glares at the glass before him.

I nod. "Yes. But they will be too weak to fight back. That's what we need. It will be fun to watch them watch us win."

Smiles break out on their faces. Sick men.

I push my chair back and pick my gun off my table, waiting for my brothers to leave their seats, so we walk out of the meeting with a united front as we always do when outsiders are present.

"If anything changes. There will be another meeting. Until then, stay safe in the streets. Every man under one banner." I conclude the meeting and walk away, stopping at Sandro's chair to knock the gun against his knee. "Get that cleaned. An infection really isn't necessary in these hard times."

I stroll out of the room, already fishing my phone out of my pocket to check if Mel has called. She hasn't. I totter between calling her or not and decide not to.

I slip the phone back into my pocket and step out of the small house. The sky is still dark, hanging almost to the earth, swollen like a pregnant woman.

"You didn't have to be so harsh, Xander." My brothers have grouped around me. Alec stops beside me and watches the sky just as I am.

"Was I? The Famiglia is the priority."

"I worry about you," Knox says. He stops beside me, but unlike Alec, he keeps his eyes on mine.

I fix a harsh stare on him and lead them away from the door towards the back, where we will have more privacy. Ryder follows, "What is this? A blame party? I will do all I can to inspire confidence in myself. They will not look and find me wanting."

Declan heaves a sigh. "We should return to the house. Today has been a long day."

"You can leave. I will stay a bit longer." I haven't had any time to myself since the news spread. There were calls to field, men to placate, and fires to put out.

"Is that safe?" Knox worries at his bottom lip.

I shrug and walk further down. The trees lining both sides of the walkway sway gently in the breeze, whipping through the air. "Does it matter? Anyone who attacks me would have to be plenty stupid. And Ryder is here."

"We'll stay with you." They range around me, and together, we drop to the floor, sitting on the grass with the wind whirling around us, our shoulders pressed together. So long as I know I have them, I know it'll be fine.

My phone thrills in my pocket, and a slight smile curves my lips. I reach for the phone and find a message from Mel.

Coming?

It's simple and straightforward, and I jump to my feet. My brothers roll their eyes almost in unison.

"Guess we're leaving then." Knox drawls wryly.

23

MEL

I BLINK AT THE RAPIDLY NARROWING SHAPE IN FRONT OF my eyes. I sit up fast to find Xander half-dressed or undressed, depending on how you want to see it.

"What are you doing?" I whisper, blowing a puff of air into the room to check if my mouth has any bad smell.

Xander clocks the movement and gives me a smile. "I don't know really, but for once in a long while, I've got a free day." He stops and peers at me uncertainly. "Thought I'd take Lucian to the park. And maybe the gym later?"

For once, I'm glad it's the weekend, glad my mouth doesn't stink, and glad he's half undressed, I guess. I enjoy a leisurely stroll down his body with my eyes, land on his cock, and then trail my eyes back up. "Am I invited? Or is it just for the boys?"

"Could we leave you behind if we wanted to?" He prowls towards me, and I crawl slowly towards him on the bed, one knee after the other, till I'm close enough that my eye is level with his already awakening cock.

"If you really, really wanted to." I flick my tongue against his bare stomach, trace it across his torso, up to his navel, where I sink it in.

He holds my head still and then heaves out a heavy exhale and lets go. I kiss my way to his tattoo, letting my lips kiss every single sun, every dark light.

I love the way he turns to give me access to all of him. When he has his back to me, I twist my arms around his back and hold on. "Now let's see you leave without me."

He chortles, and I dig my hands into his side to tickle at him. He doesn't even twitch. "That doesn't work anymore."

I dig deeper, sinking my fingers in and out, swiping to the sides till his body quivers finally, and he lets a deep guffaw slip past his lips. "Gotcha."

He turns to face me and lifts me by my shoulder up to him. "What are you doing to me?"

I wiggle with pleasure at the slow playfulness of his voice. "Everything you want me to do to you."

He scoops me into his arms and swings me almost forcefully into the middle of the bed. He climbs over me and lifts my legs into the air, then drops it almost immediately and flops down himself. His eyes are pools of endless lust and wonder. "Ride me."

"Are you sure?" I bite my lip and bend to kiss him. He allows me, taking my kiss like it is his to devour as he wants.

He leans back and places a solid palm against my ass, hefts me up, and places me right over his face.

"Do we have the time?" He questions, right before he slurps at me through the cotton of my panties.

"I think not, but I want this."

He digs his tongue into me, sucking the panties into his mouth like he can already taste me through them. Xander lets it go, sniffs at me, and then groans. "Fuck. You smell divine, Mel."

"Make me feel it too." I anchor my hand into his hair and moan gently when he licks around me, his tongue sweeping over my thighs in a gentle caress, his hand on my ass, palming and squeezing a handful. I rock against his face, enjoying the way his finger probes at my wetness, sliding my panties to the side so he can slide his tongue into me.

His tongue is wet and yet somehow warm, and the feeling is indescribable in my euphoria. I slant my head back unconsciously, almost as though my neck can no longer bear its weight, and cry out over and over again.

His finger burrows between us, and he fucks me hard with them, withdrawing and stroking two of them into me fast in hard jabs that leave my lungs wanting for air.

I can feel my stomach clench, my nipples taut, and my body hurtling like a fast train towards that endpoint. "I'm close, Xander."

He exhales against me. "Good. Now ride me. I want to feel you come all over my cock."

He almost tears the clothes off me, then flings his off before grabbing my waist and letting me slide down his body over him. I settle slowly over his girth, allowing my body to acclimate to the size of him coming at me from this angle.

"Yes, baby. You're doing so well. Think you can take all of it?" He groans, the words dying away in his throat when my body tightens at his encouragement. And because he's asked, my body wants to take all of him, wants to let him feel the same pleasure he's giving to me.

I close my eyes, take his hand from around my waist, and place it on my breasts. "Touch me here. Right now."

His fingers pinch painfully tight around my nipples, and the pain pushes me through. I drop my hips over him and shudder with Xander through the belt of emotions, feelings, fire, and heat whipping through me.

"God, girl. You ruin me. Ride." One of his hands slaps across my butt, and I start riding him, gently at first, gentle drops that have us hissing, hard drops that have him groaning and grunting.

My orgasm spills over me with no warning, and he takes over without being asked. He cuffs both my hands to my back and bangs into me, hard thrusts that soon get him over the edge himself. He grunts and spills his seeds inside me, coating my womb with himself.

He relaxes into the bed and pulls me, so I snuggle into him, and we just fight to get our breath together, his fingers in my hair, sliding over my scalp. He kisses me on the forehead and gets up.

He steps out on the floor and lifts me into his arms, walks us into the bathroom, and slaps on the shower knob. When I lift my eyes briefly to meet his, he grins. "Not a word about it."

I zip my lips and spread my legs when his fingers wander there. "You're greedy, and I'm gonna be sore."

He nods like he expects nothing less. "I did promise you that, didn't I?"

But he doesn't bring me to another orgasm. Instead, he washes me, his soapy fingers skimming my breasts, brushing my hips, stroking my ass, sliding between my cheeks, washing my face gently.

"The men doubt me."

I lift my head fast to meet his eyes. "Your men?"

He looks away for a second, then back at me before nodding. "Yes. They worry I will not be able to see them through trouble. Maybe they think I'm weak."

I slap the water off and catch his jaw between my hands, an action I have never before taken. My eyes are fiery with truth.

"You're the strongest man I know, Xander. You would never let anyone hurt your men if you could help it. You would walk through fire for them. Literally. Anyone who doubts you does not deserve you to begin with."

His eyes are not convinced. I jerk his head to meet mine when he blinks away. "Tell that to my men."

I shake my head, my wet hair slapping my cheeks, the smell of shampoo hanging heavy in the air. "I can't tell them what you're not convinced of. You cannot live something you do not believe in, Xander."

His eyes shut, but I don't want to lose him. I feel almost panicky. This is new to him. He's always said he's ready, but actually taking over? That must worry him.

I let his jaw go and step fully into his arms because I need the covering of his body, the warmth of him, to get these next words out. "You asked why I didn't tell you before disappearing with Lucian."

His body goes rigid as a tack. "Do I really need to know?"

"No. But I want you to know. I had a feeling you didn't really believe me when I said it wasn't because I was sad with you."

"Go ahead. Say it."

I hide my face in his chest, running my hand over the tattoos across his back to remind myself none of what I am about to say is true.

"I was worried you'd choose The Famiglia over us. So, I took the choice away. It would've hurt too much if you'd picked them. Those men who never should doubt you. I wouldn't have been able to take it."

Xander pulls away fast, so fast he knocks into the wall behind him. He doesn't even seem to notice. "What do you mean?"

"Are you angry? I know you know exactly what it is that I mean." I mutter.

"There is not a word of truth in that. Not a smidgeon of fact. None!"

I nod solemnly. "I know that now. I didn't then. But this is why you are wrong to doubt yourself. There is no truth to your doubt. Just like there was no truth to my fears."

I look up to meet his eyes and spit the words to land like anchors unto him.

"You're handsome, you're smart, like the strongest person I know. I see the way you love our son, and I can never doubt it. You're the greatest man alive. How can you doubt the very evidence that you provide, mio marito."

He grits his teeth, his jaw tightening. He turns granite right before me. Then loosens up, and I can almost see the fear, the doubt leeching from him.

"I'm certain I'll get to the point where I totally believe that. But for now..." He leans in to capture my lips in a kiss that is more adoration than an action. "... thank you il mio raggio di sole."

I feel the tears slip out of my lids then. Tears for the young boy who could never be a child. Groomed, trained, and bred to take over what was larger than him. "Thank you too."

"For what?" His befuddlement is almost sweet.

"For being you. And for allowing me to be a part of you. For giving me Lucian."

He chuckles gently, air from his lips floating across my face. "I should thank you for him too. He's been an absolute breath of fresh air."

I nod and dart a look at the door. "We should get to him. He should be awake now."

"You stay here and take as long as you need. I'll take care of him." Xander kisses me on the cheeks, first one, then the other, and then slaps the shower on.

"You really could just say you plan on going to that park without me," I mumble to him.

He laughs, and I laugh, and then I hack up a loud cough, almost run out of the shower, and end up on the bathroom floor, the cold tile biting into my skin, spilling the contents of my stomach into the toilet bowl.

The splash as the vomit lands in the water inside the toilet bowl has me retching more, heaving, and gagging. I feel Xander's hand on my head, scraping my hair away from my face.

He pats my back, and by the time I lean away from the bowl with enough confidence that the contents of my stomach will stay where they belong, I'm ragged and breathless.

24

XANDER

MEL LOOKS AS WHITE AS A SHEET, HER CHEST RISING AND falling as she sags back against the floor, her eyes lifting to mine finally as she coughs one last time.

I let her hair go and watch almost with a certain level of fascination as it tumbles and falls around her face. There's fear in her eyes, in the way they widen slightly and then darken as though light has blinked from them but it is the tears that come springing up in their depths that finally push me into action.

I kneel beside her and slide my arms around her back to lift her off the floor. She sinks into me, and I tighten my arms around her. "Can you walk?"

She nods her "yes" against my bare chest, and I drag in air, flush the bathroom, and then fetch some water from the sink to clean her face off. She doesn't say a

MAFIA HEIR'S SECRET BABY

word, and neither do I, but there's a look that keeps sliding between us that says more than a thousand words.

I find a towel to wrap her in and heft her into my arms, walking out of the bathroom. I drop her gently to the bed and sit beside her. She closes her eyes and lies back against the sheets.

I watch her face as she inhales. "How long have you known?"

Her face tightens, but her eyes don't open. She licks at her lips. "Known what?"

I get off the bed and start pacing, my mind running through the motions, a hot blend of emotions I can't decipher spilling through me. She's pregnant. That's got to be it, right?

I fold my arms across my torso. "Can you at least look at me, Melissa?"

She pulls her legs into her body and curls up in a fetal position with her face away from mine. "I didn't know I was pregnant, Xander. That's what you're thinking, isn't it?"

"Is there any other possibility? When was the last time you saw your period?"

Her voice is a soft whisper in the breathing quiet of the room. "You don't think that's pretty personal?"

I grit my teeth to keep the snap from my voice. She's disappearing into herself. Her face is still turned away from mine. "You might very possibly be carrying my child, Mel; I don't see what could be more personal than that."

I stalk to the window, staring out blindly at the sight that greets my eyes and yet seeing nothing.

She's pregnant? She's pregnant. She's pregnant!

The thought runs through my head in many variations, and I walk back to the bed and crawl across the sheets until I can lift her face to meet mine. "I'll call the doctor, you'll go in for a test. If it's a yes, no one must know."

Her eyes open, a fiery fire light in their depths. She pulls away from me, her eyes shooting flames that burn in their intensity. "I wasn't planning on screaming the news from the fucking roofs, Xander."

She tugs her body from mine, but I haul her deeper into me. "What's the problem, Mel?"

She wiggles restlessly in my grasp, her body rubbing up against mine. "Why do you think there's a problem?"

"Because you're fighting me. You're pulling away, refusing to look at me. Is there something I should know?" I place my hand over her stomach, only now letting it sink into me that there might be a baby in there, already growing with life flowing in its veins. My heart is a wild stallion galloping in my chest. "Isn't this what you wanted?"

She licks her lips and swallows. "Is that what you want?"

My hands curl into fists, and I let her go. She scrambles away from me. "Does it matter? We're playing our parts perfectly well. I'm certain your father will be the happiest man when he hears."

She bares her teeth in a smile that comes out as more of a grimace. "As will yours, I'm certain." She shoots back. "We should do the tests today. Maybe I'm only coming down with a stomach bug."

I close my own eyes as she heads back into the shower. I lay back against the sheets, fold my arms over my eyes, and pull in a faint breath.

Mel's words don't make me feel good. Not any better than I had when she'd started spilling her guts into the toilet bowl.

I don't feel much of anything. Not fear, not anger, not happiness. Nothing. I feel as though I'm locked away in a bubble, and it's keeping away the emotions, preventing the fear lapping at the edges of my consciousness from making its way in.

The shower starts running, and I get off the bed, walking over to the closet where I find myself something to wear. My chest feels as though it's full. Tight and heavy.

I can feel the rope tightening around my neck. With Mel pregnant, we might need to marry faster.

The thought isn't as repulsive as it should be, and that's when I realize I'm in serious trouble because now the emotions I hadn't been feeling come to me. I still, my back tensing at the thought. My responsibilities will double—no triple, if there really is a baby nestled inside her.

And I have no doubt that there is. It's been more than a month since the first time I'd taken her here, with Alec and Knox finding us the next morning. We've been in bed a thousand times since.

And now I'm worried that when I officially marry her, she'll be in more danger, especially with me taking over as Capo. I worry I won't be able to protect her as much as I should, that she could be used as my weakness.

I unfurl my shoulders just as the bathroom door opens behind me, and I hear Mel's tread as she walks towards the closet. I turn to her. "You shouldn't go anywhere without Romero anymore. I'll have someone else for Lucian."

Her shoulders stiffen, and she goes rigid right in front of me. She glares up at me, but my eyes trail down her body, trying to find any evidence of my fear.

Her stomach is still flat, apart from the slight curve at the base. She still looks exactly the same as she always has.

She stamps her feet up to me, making no pretense of the fact that she's angry. "Why don't you just lock me up and throw the damned keys away if that makes you feel better." She blinks sharply. "It's not my fault I'm pregnant!"

My jaw ticks. "I wouldn't blame you for that."

She sucks her lips between her teeth, her eyes glittering dangerously. "Then what's that look in your eyes? I haven't been actively working to tie you down. Why the hell do you do this at the slightest sign of trouble?"

"Do what?"

"Self-sabotage." She walks away to the closet herself, where she finds something to wear. I watch as she dresses, no comeback in my head, and no words on my lips.

Is that what I'm doing? I don't believe so, but I'm uncertain how to feel with another baby on the way.

I stretch out an olive branch. "I'll get you a pregnancy test."

She throws me a long, angry look, the curve of her hips tucked away securely in the denim she's zipping up at her waist. I exhale a rush of stiff air.

It feels a hell of a lot better to be talking to her clothed. My cock doesn't seem to recognize the fact that we're having a fucking argument.

She finds a shirt and slips her hands through the sky-blue cotton of it. "I'm sure I'm capable enough to do that for myself."

"I want to do it for you."

She chuckles softly, but there's no humor in the hard words that slip from her lips. "Will you need to get me a DNA test when it turns out positive?"

I prowl towards her, her eyes widening the closer I get, her chest heaving with anger, mine with fear. "I know you haven't been with anyone else but me, Mel. There will be no need for that."

She exhales and the tears pooling in her eyes come spilling down her cheeks. My pulse spikes. I don't want to be the cause of her pain. I'm not worthy of it. "You hate me, don't you?"

I pull her into my arms. "I could never hate you, Melissa."

She glances at me and then away. "But this isn't what you want."

It isn't what I don't want either. Another baby means someone else to disappoint, to protect. Another human that I could hurt.

"I don't know Melissa. Can we take this a moment at a time? I'll get you the test kit from the store this evening."

I let her go, already feeling her loose and the chasm growing between us. It doesn't matter much if she'd gotten pregnant deliberately. It won't matter because we're to be married anyway.

But that budding fear that had grown back in the room becomes a tree as the day grows into the afternoon. My attention slides. I'm all over the place, unable to focus on anything for more than a few minutes at a time.

I end my meeting with my men, and Alec finds me at his club, nursing a drink a little bit past noon. He's probably been informed of my presence by one of his men.

He slides into the private booth beside me and pours himself a drink from the bottle. He swallows a loud gulp, winces, and drops the glass with a thud to the table. "You're drinking in the middle of the day."

I shrug. Maybe the drink will dull the spiral of my thoughts. I'd tried work, but it hadn't worked out much.

I'd even spent an hour at the gym, punching at the bag, hitting my fear for her into the bag, and the murky swirl of thoughts had somehow become worse. "So are you, Alec. What do you want?"

"Do you plan on finishing the entire bottle?"

"I'll pay for it. You don't need to worry about it."

He smiles and pours himself another drink, but his eyes are sharp. He shifts closer. "What's wrong?"

The music from the club pounds up at me, drifting through one ear and out the other. The sounds offer no distractions. "Why do you think something's wrong?"

He takes another drink from his glass. "Maybe because you're here in the middle of the day, gulping down my expensive whiskey like water."

He can be trusted. He's, after all, my brother. And I wonder how he'll feel about this. Maybe I'll know how to feel myself. "Mel's pregnant."

I don't tell him there's a slim possibility that it is, in fact, a stomach bug, or that she hadn't picked my calls when I'd called this afternoon, or that the thought that she might not be pregnant makes disappointment seep into my guts.

Alec finishes his drink and drops the glass gently to the table. "Congratulations are in order then. I'd expect you to look a whole lot happier than this, though."

I close my eyes, but I can feel the heat of his gaze. "You don't understand Alec. She's pregnant. She is carrying my baby."

"Yes. I realize that. That's what being pregnant means."

"She'll have a painted target on her back. The Russians and their damned Cambodian spies will take one look at her and know."

I open my eyes to find Alex nodding sagely. "Oh. I see where you might be inclined towards the drink."

I glare at him, my fingers flexing around my glass. "I'm not asking you to make any wisecracks right now, Alec."

He inclines his head and leans forward. "You're worried about her. You've always been. You'll always be. So long as you're never able to let her go, pregnant or not, she'll have a target on her back. You'll need to find a way to deal with that."

By the time I make it to the store with Ryder, where I wait in the car while he buys the test kit, I'm angry at my fucking self.

I needed to speak to her. Right away. When we pass by a florist's, I have Ryder stop the car, and I buy two dozen yellow roses.

It's an apology as much as it is a gift.

25

MEL

THE LOW STRAINS OF JAZZ PLAYING FROM MY PHONE LULL me into a false sense of security. Lucian runs around the kitchen beside me while I prepare him a meal. He's just returned from my father's with Gianna, who is rattling around somewhere upstairs.

Xander's chef could get him something to eat, but cooking the meal relaxes me even though it also tires me out. The aroma of pasta and meatballs hanging in the air makes my stomach queasy.

Bad enough that I am almost considering inviting Hailey in to continue the meal when he skids to a stop beside me and hugs himself to my waist.

I bend towards him to sink my nose into his hair. I inhale deeply, the smell of his shampoo calming me a bit. I nod at his chair. "Go sit."

He gives me a long look before sliding into the chair. "Can I have pizza today, Mom? Please?"

He always asks. I wonder if his brother or sister inside me will love the meal as much as he does.

My stomach squeezes almost painfully tight, and I jerk away from the thought. I have no idea if I'm pregnant yet. Xander still hasn't returned home since morning. I'm starting to worry he just might not come back for a few days.

I worry at my bottom lip, sinking my teeth into the soft flesh. I shake my head at Lucian, who sticks out his own lips. "Okay. Only if you eat all the pasta. Everything. How was school?"

"Fun. Can I watch Paw Patrol now?"

I nod and watch as he darts from the room, screaming on his way to the living room. I wince at the loud sound and finish his meal, alone with my thoughts.

I feel like an alien in my own body. Uncertain what to do or feel or be with myself. This morning hadn't ended the way I'd expected it to. Xander had left the house after our argument, and I'd considered going for the test myself and then decided against it.

He wanted to do it. Then he could do it. I turn off the stove and remove the pot from the heat, but I don't feel any better now than I had when I'd started boiling the pasta.

I splay my hand across my stomach, leaning against the kitchen counter for a second. This time feels different, maybe because he knows so early on, maybe because it's hurting even worse this time.

Gianna's footsteps sound beside me, and I lift my eyes to meet hers. I straighten and find a plate from the brown hardwood cabinet in the kitchen, putting together a meal for Lucian. I hold it out to her. "Can you take it to him?"

She nods and takes the plate from me. "You've been lost in thoughts for an entire minute. That's a block of time you can't get back, you know."

I pour a glass of orange juice from the fridge and find a tray to place it on. "Yeah. I don't want it either."

She takes the tray from me and is gone a few minutes. She finds me in the kitchen again, my hands kneading my stomach. "What's worrying you? You've sort of been lost all day."

The cold feeling tumbling through me is like a river of ice. I have a baby growing inside me and a reluctant father. I don't need the test to know. My periods are pretty consistent. That queasy, rubbery feeling in my stomach is all too familiar.

I'm pregnant and this time around, I don't know how to feel about it. The option of running away is not available. Xander would find me in any and all extremities of the earth. Not when he knows about his child this time around.

I stifle a laugh that tingles at my throat. "I'm fine, Gianna. I promise."

Gianna rolls her large eyes. "No you're not. Come on. What's wrong?"

She drags me to the kitchen island and pushes me into a chair there. I sit, tottering between tears and the maniacal laughter still scratching at my chest. "We had a fight."

She slants her head towards me. "I'm guessing we means you and Xander?"

"Yes."

Her concern filters into her voice. "What was it about?"

"I don't know. I have no idea why. I don't think he trusts me anymore, Gianna. I don't know how to convince him to forgive the past."

"He's Xander. Has there ever been a time when he trusted another human?"

I scratch at the table. He once trusted me. Back when I'd been deserving of it. What kind of home would I be creating for a baby if the very man whose baby I am carrying has no trust in me?

My answer is as simple as it is sharp. "There was."

"Then there will be again. Look, what's biting at you? Something obviously is."

I shake my head and back away from her, find my phone and make it to my room, our room, closing the door softly behind me. I crossed into the bathroom, undressing as I went, increasing the sound of the music pouring from my phone.

I don't want to talk about anything. Not right now. Not with the potent medley of anger and pain rocking through me. His words this morning had hurt. I could admit that much, at least. His anger had stoked mine. The short moment gone with the content of my stomach.

Our fathers would be pleased, at least. He had been right about that. But a baby isn't supposed to be happening now. Not with the way things were currently in the air.

I move around the bathroom, making myself a bath, heating the water until it's almost too hot to bear. I pour some soothing lavender body wash and oil into the bath water and then slip into the warm water, laying my head against the rim of the bath and wishing I'd thought to get some wine to drink.

Except I can't drink wine anymore, can I? Not for the next nine months, at least. I tip my head back, sliding back until I'm completely submerged in the warm water, praying the lavender manages to soothe me soon.

I close my eyes and hold my breath underwater. My lungs start burning pretty soon, and I sit up, coughing and choking as I drag air into my lungs. I realize I'm crying, fat tears cutting a line on my face like a train on a track.

I wipe the tears and sink back into the water, my skin burning from the heat. I place my hands over my stomach, but this time, the warmth from the water reminds me of the heat I'd felt when I'd first held Lucian in my arms.

This baby will not be any less loved. I smile as I remember the way he'd wound his fingers around my thumb, his eyes squeezed shut as cry after cry had broken from his small lips, the sound startlingly loud despite the tiny bundle of joy it had been coming from.

I must have fallen asleep in the water because when I wake, it is to the sound of footsteps in the bathroom. I throw my arms over my breasts and dart my eyes to the dark shadow staining the doorway.

Xander has his gaze on my body and looks down to find that all the bubbles in the bath are gone. The water is a clear stream, barely hiding anything from his wandering eyes.

The heat in them sear at me, and I allow my hand to fall away. His eyes caress my skin as they skim my body, my stomach, the curve of my hips, the junction of my thighs, and then back up past my navel, past my breasts, and then up to my eyes again finally.

I shudder. A quick quiver of my body as though someone has stepped over my grave. He walks into the bathroom, closing the door behind him. The click of the lock has me sitting up, the water swishing all over me.

"What are you doing?"

He settles beside me and rolls his hand through the water so it stains the cuff of his dark shirt. He cups my hips through the water and then just stares at his hand against my body. I can't breathe, I don't move. I want to but I can't seem to break the spell he's weaving.

He meets my questioning eyes. "I hurt you this morning, didn't I?"

My heart beat spikes as though I've taken a plunge from a hill. "Why would you think that?"

An emotion that I can't read swarms his gaze. "Your eyes. They looked bruised. As though I'd stomped on them."

He stands and removes his shoes then slips into the bath water, fully clothed and I feel how cold the water has become. As cold as he was this morning. "What do you want me to say to that Xander? I had no idea I was pregnant. I mean, we're still not certain I am."

He drags me against him, turning me around so my breasts push into his chest, the fabric of his shirt scratching against my nipples. "I'm sorry, il raggio di sole."

It's the first apology coming from him that I have no doubt he means. I bend my forehead and let it drop against his. He presses his into mine. "You hurt me a lot. A whole fucking lot than you should be able to Xander. I didn't get pregnant to make our fathers happy."

He nods and whispers against my lips, his breath intoxicating like aged whiskey. "I know. I was fearful. Worried I'll ruin it as always, and I went ahead to do it anyway."

I pull back an inch, and he lifts his head to meet mine again. I smile softly. "You love Lucian. How could you worry about that?"

He tips his head so his nose rubs up against mine, the action so sweet that my heart rolls in my chest. "You already brought him up to receive love, Sole. That had nothing to do with me. He's lovable just by existing. How could anyone not love him?"

I wring my arms around his neck and grind into him. He groans and locks his arms around my waist. I slip a hand between us and pull his belt off gently, the air between us tender with heat and energy.

His pulse racks harder, a vein throbbing in his throat that I bend my head to lick at, sliding my tongue all the way over the pulse. He inhales sharply, his eyes darkening and going flinty with lust.

He lets me go to curl his fingers over the edges of the tub as though giving me permission to do with him as I want. I go soft with need. "You look like a lord surveying his kingdom."

An indolent look crosses his face and he smirks. "Chicago belongs to me. And so do you. You're not much farther from the truth."

I laugh, the sound exploding from my chest and taking with it the tightness that had resided there all day. It's insane that he's able to heal the pain that he had caused himself.

Being vulnerable with me this way is all the antidote I needed for the hurt. I drag his pants down his legs, brushing my palms over his firmness through his shorts.

I stroke him, stoking a fire between us that flares in his gaze. "And you're mine, aren't you?"

His throat moves again, a promise in his eyes. "Anytime you want Sole. Any fucking time."

I fist him, stroking from the base of his cock to the tip, grateful for the clear water so I can watch the way he thickens and lengthens in my grasp, grateful for his open eyes so I see the way his feverish, hungry eyes feast on me, needy with the way he hisses and grunts when I tighten my hands around his balls.

"Think I can get you off this way?"

"Honey you just keep doing that and there won't be any question of the fact." He growls the words.

I sit back in the water and wish I could have him between my lips, suck his girth between my hungry lips. But I can't so I pump faster, drag my fingers up and down him, bending to him so he grazes his fingers up my sides, ghosting them over my nipples, while I jerk him off.

I pump faster and faster until soon, he's pushing himself into the cup of my palms as I massage his balls again, as I beg him to cum for me, as I suck at his lips, my hands between us pleasuring him.

He jerks once, his entire body going stiff under me, his eyes blinking close as he groans loudly, capturing my lips with his to stifle his groan. I swallow it, kissing him back as I stroke faster, sinking my teeth into his lower lip as I slide my fingers down over the tight bunch of muscles at his ass.

His eyes snap open fast, and the fire in them burns brighter as I press my fingers into the muscles and he comes, spilling his seeds over my fingers, the water washing them off before I can think of licking them off me.

His chest rises and falls, and watching this lumberjack of a man coming undone from my hands is enough. I stroke him once more and let him go. I lie back against him in the tub and let him stroke my sides with his gentle fingers.

It is almost twenty minutes later, when the water is so cold I almost shiver that he steps out of it, his clothes dripping. He watches me, a soft glow in his eyes as he undresses, dropping the clothes into the water in the tub.

I allow my eyes to trail over the hard ridge of his flat stomach, over the thickness of his thighs as he drags the pants down. When he's naked, he turns away and walks from the bathroom, dripping as he goes. I watch his tight ass, my core melting.

He's got to be the most desirable specimen I've seen. Actually to be honest, he's the only male specimen I've seen this way. I like it that way.

He returns to the bathroom with a towel which he hands to me. I lift my eyebrows at him and he bends to the floor, sweeps his arms into that water and lifts me up against him. Then when I think he'll towel me off, he nods at the towel again.

I giggle, and he laughs. And my heart feels like it just might explode in that moment. The laughter leeches from me when he holds out the pregnancy test I hadn't noticed he'd been carrying this whole time.

"You should try it."

I nod. I know I should but I hesitate a second before taking it from him.

The plastic wrapper crinkles as I open it, revealing the stick that holds the key to so many unanswered questions. I glance at Xander, who is watching, his expression almost hopeful.

The silence between us is palpable, so thick I could cut it like cake.

I follow the instructions, peeing on the stick and carefully placing the test on the counter. The minutes drag on, each tick of the clock I can't see almost echoing in the small room. The only other sound is the rhythmic beating of my heart, quickened by the unknown.

Xander takes my hand and drags me against his front and I snuggle into him, sinking my head into his shoulders and closing my eyes as we wait.

As the seconds pass, I can't help but steal glances at the test. The control line appears first, a reassuring sign that the test is working. But the second line, the one that will change everything, takes its time to materialize.

The quiet tension in the room amplifies the rustling of the shower curtain and the insistent hum of static. I keep my eyes fixed on the test, unable to tear them away now they're open. Xander's gaze never leaves my face, his presence a grounding force in the uncertain moment.

Finally, the moment of truth arrives. A faint, yet unmistakable, second line emerges on the test. A surge of emotions floods through me – disbelief, joy, fear, and excitement all at once. I look up at Xander, and our eyes lock in a shared realization.

I'm pregnant. I'm carrying his baby. There's a new child nestled in me in this moment. I run my fingers over my stomach and then bite my lip to hold back the surge of emotions.

Ecstasy engulfs me as I fling myself into his arms, the positive test forgotten on the counter. His strong embrace envelops me, locking me in a tight hug. I can feel the warmth of his chest against mine, the steady beat of his heart echoing the newfound rhythm of ours.

Xander sweeps his hand over my bare ass, then drags it up my sides and locks them around me again, pressing a kiss to my wet hair. His words are simple and soft. "Thank you Sole."

26

XANDER

I LIFT THE FLOWERS OFF THE BED WHERE I'D DROPPED them and hand the bouquet to Mel, who bends her head into the yellow petals and sniffs at them. She lifts her head to meet my gaze, sniffles gently, and then crushes herself to me.

The flowers get squashed between us and I don't fucking care. It's more than worth it to have her in my arms like this. "Do you like it?"

She nods against my chest. "I love it."

"You're my sunshine Melissa Sedric. You always remind me why you are every time I make a pretense of forgetting. Like what you have done for the charities."

She'd made time even with our busy schedules to visit the hospitals the charity was associated with, she'd even made me go with her once, dragging me half the way and sticking by my side the entire time.

She lifts her head off my chest and glares playfully up at me. "You bought that ticket didn't you?"

I plant a small kiss on her lips and she pulled back, laughing when I tuck my hand into her hair and hold her still. "I had to. No one was getting that lunch with you."

She'd suggested auctioning lunch with someone to make more money for the hospital. It had been a bad idea, first because it was unsafe for her to be out there where danger might get to her, second because I didn't want anyone getting lunch with my woman.

She is mine. If she is having lunch, it would be with me.

"It would've made me a lot more money." She quirks her eyes up at me.

I lift my own brows. "Do you need more money?"

She slaps her open palm against my chest. "It's not about the money Xander!" She laughed.

I tip her head up to mine and then press it into my beating chest. "The charities are supposed to be secret. I don't want the rest of the world finding out. I like you running it, I like seeing you with those children, I love how the adults adore you, that you treat it like your baby, that you shine so bright, my sunshine but I'd like to keep it under wraps. It'll help me feel better knowing you're safe."

She drags a deep breath into her lungs and looks away from me, when her eyes meet mine again, there's tears in them. "I understand. But you still overpaid for lunch."

I shrug carelessly. "Whatever's mine is ours. You overpaid."

"She pulls away, a soft smile lingering on her full lips. "Do we tell the family I'm pregnant?"

"Yes. I'll inform my family tonight. I'm guessing you'll want to talk to your family too."

"Do you think we should? It's early days yet." Melissa asks looking up at me, her forehead creased in question.

I plant a small kiss on her lips and pull her into my arms again. "Father's sick. I think we should. The news won't make it out of the family. We can depend on them for that."

She plants a kiss on my lips too. "Father will be so glad. We should tell Lucian, too."

I shake my head. "Give me a little more time with him first."

My phone rings on the bed and I go to take it. She starts dressing while I get on the phone with Ryder, who seems a little hurried as he informs me about the arrival of another shipment of our merchandise.

I nod and reply as I watch Mel sink her head into the flowers again, a tiny smile curling her lips. As we'd both been expecting, the pregnancy test had turned out positive. The relief I'd felt in the moment had been instant.

I end the call with Ryder and decide it'll be good to spend some time with the family. "We should head over to my father's. I'm sure he'll love hearing the news from us instead of over the phone."

It's been a while since the family has been together. We haven't had a family gathering since my father's illness had been outed by Gabriele. I'd been too busy keeping everything afloat with my brother's help.

She drops the flowers to the bed finally and nods. "I'll ask Father if he'd like to come over."

I walk over to her, tip her head up and plant a soft kiss on her lips. She kisses me back with no hesitation. It feels as though something is crushing my heart. It's tight as though filled to the brim. It's an odd feeling, but it's good.

I pull away and she moans, a gentle hum that ends with a mewl when I nip at her lips gently. "You've got to be the best thing that has ever happened to me Melissa."

She leans forward and spears me with a long look full of meaning. "Good. I better be."

MOTHER HEAPS some peas over Father's plate, and when he grimaces and shoots a look at the rest of the table with her head bent, we all laugh. Father looks as though he's aged ten more years since the last time I saw him.

He's weak, so much so Mother is feeding him a part of his meal. It wrenches my heart to see the once strong man so weak. It's also a reminder of the futility of it all. Some day, we all will slip from the earth like stardust disappearing in the sky.

Sedric shakes his head like he understands and scoops up his own peas, which he heaps on Lucian's plate. The laugh explodes again.

"I can see you all are having fun at my expense, but he's going to eat what the doctor says is good for him."

We all shut up. Knox is smirking at me. "Of course he will, Mother. We all know how much he needs it."

Mother finds a pea on the platter and in a move that surprises everyone at the table, throws it across at him. It hits right on his forehead and a laugh rings out along with a steady applause which mom accepts with a queenly wave.

Mel flicks her hair back and leans closer to me. "Do we tell them now?" She smiles. "I'm sure they're all thinking why we invited them to dinner at your parents."

I let my hand drop to her thigh under the table. "Let's let them stew in it a little while longer."

Knox's voice breaks into the conversation. "Are we too boring for you, brother?"

I lift my eyes to his to find the rest of the table already staring at us. Mel blushes a furious pink and returns her attention to the half eaten chicken on her plate.

I roll my eyes when Declan snickers. "Quite frankly? Maybe you are Knox."

Alec laughs. "Oh, I see how it is then."

I bare my teeth in a smile, my heart somehow even lighter. This feels familiar. "You do? Pray tell."

Mother taps at the table, and glares at the four of us. "You will desist from such behavior at the table, especially not when we have guests."

Sedric meets Mother's eyes and chuckles. "You don't count us among guests, do you? We already are family."

Daniel nods and gives his sister a playful glare. "Especially since those two were being very obnoxious with it too."

Mel winces. But before she can get a word in, Gianna jumps in. "And he looked a second away from kissing her right here." She giggles and slaps at the table. "The insolence!"

That's Gianna, alright.

Mel grimaces this time and glares at her sister. They stay locked in a stare down until Mel laughs and looks away. She rolls her eyes and mutters "asshole" into her food.

We finish the meal, Mother making sure Father gets as much fiber as he can, Father muttering all the while about controlling women. Daniel and Alec are discussing something I can't hear, while Knox has a smile on his face as he recounts some story to Mel.

She tips her head back and laughs. A shot of possessiveness attacks and I beat it down, instead, I call on Hailey and distract Lucian with ice cream. He follows her out of the room and I tap my fork against the crystal of my glass.

Everyone's attention comes to me, and I slip my hand into Mel's. I press a kiss to her knuckles, and Mother smiles softly. "I know dinner tonight was impromptu, but we've barely had time to spend with each other, so

I thought the news we have to share was a good enough excuse to gather here today."

"We don't need an excuse to gather Xander." Mother mumbles.

"No, we don't. But we're all here today." I nod at Mel. "You tell them."

She tilts her head to the right and then presses a kiss to the corner of my lips that I feel everywhere. She slides the smile to my father and then to her father. "I'm pregnant. We found out just this morning."

A shocked silence fills the gap her words leave. Mother's eyes widen even as she comes around the table to hug Mel. "Oh, my goodness. Are you certain?"

Mel hugs her back. "Yes, I am. The test was pretty positive."

Gianna comes around the table next, and she glares down at her sister first before squeezing her arms around her. "You lied to me."

Mel loops her arms tight around her. "No I didn't. I said there's nothing wrong. There isn't."

"Oh Sissy. This is such great news." She comes over to me and hugs me just as hard. She bends her head and whispers right into my ears. "For the first time, I don't think I want to be responsible for your murder anymore."

I chuckle. "You never would've been."

She pats at my shoulders. "Well, you had to go ruin it, huh?"

Father holds his hand out to me, the other to Mel, and I take her hand as we walk to him. She tips her head to his, and he presses a kiss to her face, his sunken cheeks twitching in a smile. "I'm so happy to see the day Mel. You will never know how truly glad this makes me. Maybe we cannot rewrite history, but the future is a blank slate."

Mel nods and shifts away so I can receive my own kiss. We go over to her father, who stands and hugs her hard, pressing a kiss on her forehead. She hugs her father, sagging into his arms. He pats her back and whispers something to her that makes her laugh.

My brothers are next, and soon, the table is rowdy again, Lucian the only one among us who is utterly focused on his ice cream. Mel watches him eat, and I watch her watch him.

This is a future I'd never once envisioned. Especially after she'd left me. It had been a question of surviving her, of waking up every morning with the singular focus of going an entire day without any thoughts of her. I'd put all of me into the business, into growing it, into making sure that the Amory name deserved the tremble that it evoked.

But to have her here beside me, holding my son, carrying my son or daughter inside her, it is a blessing. I take Lucian from her. He swings his arms around my neck. "Do you want some Ice cream, Papa?"

Papa? It's the same name I'd called my father growing up as a child, and to hear it from my own son, sitting at the same table where I'd grown as a child, it smothers the air from my lungs as though it has been sucked out. "No figlio, you enjoy."

He returns his attention to the ice cream and I huff out a hard breath. He's a lovely boy. Downright, the best thing to happen to me ever. He along with his mother provide the warmth I need to chase away the cold that clouds my days at work.

Mel shifts closer and swats at something off my shoulder. I hitch my brow at her and quirk my lips. Bending my head towards hers, I whispered right into her ears. "Did you just miss getting your hands on me?"

"Best bet I plan on doing a lot of that when we get home." She runs her tongue over her plump lips. "And yes. Yes, I just did."

I groan softly. "You'll be the end of me, Sole."

27

MEL

"Why are we going? I want to stay here with you. This isn't repeating itself!"

Xander's shirt is open at the throat, dark hair peeping at me through the gap, a packed box beside him that Rosa had filled with my clothes. I've just returned from Amory Corps to find him at the door, a car idling on the curb.

He's trying to convince me Cabo is a good idea. I don't believe it is. He jerks me into him. "I didn't say I'm staying here."

Oh. That's a different story then. I sidle up against him. "So we're taking a vacation?"

"Yes. To Cabo. You need the rest and I could use the breather. Things are rolling here too fast."

He hasn't spoken about work in a few days. Which is either an indication that things are so terrible he doesn't want to scare me or he's back to hiding the facts of the business from me.

"You should've started with that. I thought you'd be sending me away." I make air quotes. "For my protection."

"It's a vacation, and we're leaving right now. You've just about made me ruin the surprise, but you'll love the cabin."

Lucian comes down the stairs with Hailey behind him. Rosa brings up the rear, with Romero lugging a box with him. I smile up into Xander's eyes. "How long have you been planning this?"

"A few days." He walks away to swing Lucian into his arms. "Come on, or we'll miss our flight."

"Considering the fact that I'm certain it's a private flight, they really can't leave without us. Now can they? Don't you think I should change?"

He trails his eyes over my figure, his eyes chasing a shiver down my spine. "Like you said, it's a private flight. It doesn't matter if you're dressed in that or something else."

He holds his hand out to mine, and we walk out of the house together into the heat of the sun, which is smiting this afternoon. My heart feels light, my body almost weightless.

We're going on a vacation. As a family. Together. And it's been completely planned by Xander. Nothing else matters at this moment but that.

The drive to the airport is long and quiet. Ryder sits in front, silent, except for when he has a question for Xander. I sit with my head against Xander's broad shoulders, tickling at Lucian, who giggles.

By the time we arrive at the airport, Lucian has fallen asleep in my arms, and I hold his head against the curve of my shoulder as we walk towards the private plane, idling at the private hangar where we end up.

"You own this?"

His shrugs. "Amory Corps owns it. Anyone who is family is welcome to use it."

He leads the way into the large plane, and the entryway welcomes us with a sweeping staircase adorned with a plush, custom-designed carpet that extends an invitation to explore the luxurious interiors.

The Amorys never do anything by half measures, and that means that the plane is the very apex of luxury. The main seating area features oversized, sumptuous leather seats arranged to encourage relaxation as much as to add to the beauty of it all.

I take one of the leather seats by the window and Xander slides in beside me. He takes Lucian from me, cuddling the sleeping boy to himself without a word. Ryder hands him his phone and leaves the plane.

I watch him go, scrunching my face up in confusion. "Isn't he coming with us?"

Xander's hand slips into mine. He's been doing this a lot lately—taking my hand, curving his hand around me, slipping closer, or tugging me into him. So much so that he's grown comfortable doing it when it's safe, even if we're not alone, I can't deny that I like it. A lot.

"He's not coming with us. I told you this was a vacation."

"Oh."

"Yes, Melissa. Oh is right."

I turn to take in the plane in its full glory. The Amorys have opted for a neutral color palette with tasteful accents, creating an atmosphere of understated elegance. The plane lifts into the air, and soon, we're flying away from Chicago.

Large windows along the sides of the cabin provide breathtaking panoramic views of the sky, enhancing the overall sense of openness.

And I spend the flight looking out, at the soaring birds, the large clouds rolling lazily past.

Xander takes Lucian into one of the sleeping spaces and when he returns, he spends the flight working, typing away on his computer with the occasional look at me, sipping away on his glass of wine which the hostess had poured for the two of us.

It's enough to sit in the silence with him. To watch his long lashes feather the skin under his eyes. I could do this all day and not tire. He looks up to catch me staring. "Do you need something to eat?"

I give him a saucy little smile. "Are you on the menu?"

He smolders at me. "Unfortunately not. I do cost a little more than the rest of the meals."

I swallow to wet my dry throat, fanning a hand across my chest to the buttons on my dress. His eyes follow the motion. "I think you'll find I won't mind paying."

"I'm not tempted. Not at all."

I spread my legs, one dainty move at a time. "You're certain?"

I can feel warmth staining my lingerie, feel the way my body strains for his touch. He leans back in his chair and spreads his legs, too. "Come get it then."

The words are a challenge, and with his men here with us, maybe I really shouldn't have been tempting him to begin with. But he's made me happy, and I want to give him just a little of what he's given to me.

I leave my seat and settle on his lap. He drags me into him, but he doesn't touch me as I'd expected. Instead, he curls his arms around me and just holds me to him. As though to protect, to hold dear.

I spread my fingers over his chest and feel the steady throb of his heartbeat. He tightens his arms around me and leans back, almost as though it's just us in the entire world and we're cuddling together in bed back home. I press a kiss against that thatch of hair I can see through his open buttons and then relax into him and close my eyes.

Just being held by him drains the tension from my shoulders, and my thoughts rattle around, settling on everything that has happened the last few days. His angry words when he'd found out I'm pregnant, his soft hold and apology later that evening, the large bouquet of flowers I'd left in a vase in the kitchen so I could see every time I cooked.

I fall asleep to his musky scent floating around me, his body warming mine. I wake to the softness of sheets over me, Lucian tucked against my side. He's still sleeping and we're obviously still in the air because this doesn't feel or look like a house.

I get out of the bed and leave the room gently so Lucian doesn't wake. The sound of laughter reaches me, and I follow it to find Xander on a call, his grinning face tilted up.

The men are quiet, a few of them asleep, two of them playing cards since there's nothing to do with the plane in the air.

I take the seat beside Xander, who looks up at me and grins before saying his goodbyes to whoever was on the phone. I'd guess one of his brothers. Xander never laughs that openly with no one else. "How'd you sleep?"

I stretch, the cut of my blouse riding up over my stomach. My bones creak and when I look back at Xander, he's just lifting his gaze from my skin. "Very well. Thank you. How long was I out?"

He takes a look at his watch. "An hour at least. You didn't say you were tired."

"It's probably the baby." I wiggle until I'm comfortable in the seat. "I'm hungry too."

"We're a few minutes from landing. I've had a meal prepared at the cabin. We'll eat together."

Just as he'd said, the plane begins to land a few minutes later, and soon, we're driving towards the cabin, through a landscape where the arid desert meets the deep blue waters of the ocean.

I stare out that entire time with Lucian's face right next to mine. This is my first time here, but I have a feeling it won't be the last.

The beaches are postcard-perfect, with golden sands stretching along the coastline as far as my eyes can track them. I turn to Lucian. "Do you like it?"

He nods and presses his nose to the window. We pull away from the main road and pass through land beaded with large houses that stand right by the edge of the water. I slide my hands to Xander. "How far away from the cabin are we?"

"Not much farther." He murmurs, his eyes on his phone. He's right; a few minutes later, we pull up to a beachfront cabin that blends seamlessly into the warmth of natural elements. One of the men opens my door, and I lift Lucian into my arms as I step out of the car.

We're far enough from the water that the beating waves don't wash too close to us but close enough that the sound of the waves and the scent of the sea wash over me.

The entrance welcomes us with a solid wooden door, intricately carved with traditional patterns, offering a preview of the meticulous woodwork that awaits within.

Upon stepping inside, the open-concept living space unfolds, showcasing a symphony of rich, dark woods that create a cozy and inviting atmosphere.

The living area is dominated by bespoke wooden furniture, each piece a work of art in itself. Plush, handwoven textiles in earthy tones complement the wooden surroundings, creating a harmonious balance of comfort and elegance.

Large windows frame wide views of the turquoise waters, allowing natural light to flood the space. It's a beautiful space. Damned near perfect with that view of the water.

I let Lucian go and watch as he runs up the stairs, Xander nodding at Romero who goes after him. He slides up behind me and I turn to face him, his hooded eyes staring down at me. "Do you like it?"

I nod. "Yes. I love it. It's beautiful. How much did you pay for that view?"

"It came to me as part of a deal."

I look up at him, the air halting in my throat. He's a fine man. His deep voice is rough and gritty as he holds me. "Thank you for planning this."

"We both needed the time away. I've had a doctor's appointment booked for you here too."

I tip my head up. "Is that really why we're here? Because you're worried someone outside the family will find out about the baby?"

He runs his fingers at my sides, his thumb digging at me, so I giggle softly. "No. We're here because we deserve a break. I certainly need one."

Lucian comes running down the stairs and we pull apart. He hurtles to a stop beside us and jumps up and down and I wonder what's got him so excited. "I found my room." He spreads his hands out to the side. "It's this huge."

I'm sure it's a lot bigger than what he's pointed out, and I wink at Xander, who laughs as he follows Lucian back up the stairs to show him what he calls a box of toys.

The men are pulling our bags into the house behind me, and I walk over to the kitchen, where I find dinner has already been cooked and is idling in the microwave. Whoever had prepared it is gone, though, because I don't find anyone in the kitchen.

Apart from the men Xander had brought with us, it's just my family here with me. The air halts in my lungs as I think of that. Father and son upstairs, together, the laughter of their voices spilling to me down here.

There's nothing I could want more than this. I place my hand over my stomach and inhale the scent of sea and salt. It's a gently soothing feeling, and I revel in it.

28

XANDER

I RECEIVED THE CALL IN THE AFTERNOON. MOTHER'S voice had been thin and clogged with tears. She'd asked if I'd been alone, and then she'd whispered the words I'd half been expecting. "Your father's dead. He's finally gone."

I'd gone cold, tightening and redrawing into myself. I'd called the airport, had the plane prepared for a flight back, and grateful Mel had gone out on the town with Lucian, I'd driven to the airport alone.

It was evening now, the air still as my brothers and I huddled around the family house. Nobody was saying much, and the space seemed chillingly quiet for the number of people gathered in the living room.

Mother sniffles and wipes at her eyes. "Do any of you need anything? A meal? Some coffee?"

Her eyes are pleading, as though she's asking us to give her something to do with herself. Her green eyes are cloudy, filled to the brim with tears that she holds back. I shake my head no; my stomach is too knotted to let anything slip past my clenched lips.

"I'll have some coffee, mother. Actually I'll come with you." Knox says. He stands and follows Mother, hugging her gently to his side as though to offer her strength. I watch them go, then close my eyes and lean back into my chair.

"It's your turn now." It's Alec. His voice is quiet, a confirmation of something I already know. The weight of leadership, of responsibility, now rests squarely on my shoulders.

"Can we not talk about this today?" Declan rasps out.

I open my eyes and run a hand through my hair. "I'll inform the Famiglia by morning. Get ready for the meeting."

"We should bury him first." Declan's voice breaks the heavy silence. He stands and walks to the window.

For the first time in a long fucking while, Declan doesn't look put together. His hair isn't slicked back perfectly against his skull, and his agitated pacing shows not an iota of control.

He paces the room, a caged restlessness that mirrors the storm within. The loss of control, the unraveling of the carefully crafted facade, is a testament to the depth of his grief.

I turn to him, frustration lacing my words. "We will. But the meeting will be held tomorrow. We always knew this would happen. We've been preparing for it for years now. We will not hide our faces in the sand and pretend reality doesn't exist." I snap at Declan, who glares at me.

I fist my hands at my sides and stand. "Do you understand? You will be at the meeting bright and early."

He nods and I leave the room. The men of the Famiglia will be here soon. The most high ranking members at the table will want to know if he is dead. Truly and fully gone.

And they will want to sniff like sharks at the smell of blood, searching for a weakness they will never find in me.

I'm glad Melissa is gone. That she's away safe and tucked away in Cabo where none of this will get to her.

I'll call her later when I have a better grasp on my emotions. When I know how to tell her the man who trained and reared me is dead. When I don't feel this cold fist of air in my chest strangling my every breath.

I am relieved that she is spared from the intricacies of our dark world, shielded from the machinations that now require my undivided attention. Even more so, that Lucian doesn't have to see this.

Exiting the house, I feel the cool night air on my face, a stark contrast to the heated emotions within. The famiglia will demand answers, and I will provide them. My father's death marks a shift, a transition that we cannot afford to stumble through.

Alec follows beside me as I walk to the car. "He's right, you know."

I glare at him. "The responsibility doesn't fall to you. Do you know what happens to men who don't protect their ranks? They get trampled by rabid dogs who want their share of the meat."

"It doesn't mean you're not allowed to mourn Father."

"You're right it doesn't. But it does mean I have to protect his legacy. And that's what I'm doing. Protecting what he chose over us time and time again."

Alec doesn't argue with me. And I walk away from him to the car, where Ryder has the door already standing open. I slide inside. "Straight back home."

As I prepare to face the Famiglia, the weight of the legacy we carry bears down on me. My father may be gone, but his influence and his teachings live on within the Famiglia.

It is my duty to ensure that the foundation he built remains unshaken, even in the wake of his departure.

As the heavy wooden door creaks open, Alec, Declan, and Knox enter, their footsteps echoing in the solemn silence. I follow behind them as a hushed acknowledgment sweeps through the room as the brothers position themselves behind me.

Tradition demands their standing until I take my seat, a symbolic gesture of respect for the ascending Capo. There's no pretending we don't all know why we're here.

I approach the ornate chair at the head of the table, the weight of expectation settling on my shoulders. As I seat myself, the subtle rustle of fabric indicates the unanimous acknowledgment of the Famiglia.

The dimly lit room buzzes with tension as the men of the Famiglia occupy their positions, each one a cog in the intricate machinery of our world.

Five figures, distinguished by the weight of authority they carry, sit in a calculated arrangement, their faces etched with the stoic demeanor expected in these hallowed chambers.

These five men are the men who hold up the Amorys. The same way the pillars help the foundation hold a building aloft. We are the foundations, they are the pillars.

At the head of the table sits Lorenzo Moretti, the Consigliere, his sharp mind and shrewd calculations guiding the Famiglia through the labyrinth of alliances and power dynamics within the criminal underworld.

Beside him, Marco Rossi, a man known for his cunning strategies and ruthless execution of orders, observes the proceedings with an unreadable expression.

On Lorenzo's left, Giovanni Russo, the Caporegime responsible for orchestrating the Famiglia's lucrative racketeering ventures. His eyes, cold and calculating, survey the room, acknowledging the weight of the moment.

Opposite Giovanni, Carlo Vitale, the Enforcer, a man whose reputation for swift and merciless justice precedes him. His presence alone would normally send a subtle tremor through the room. But all the men here today are powerful, he's just another man.

Completing the assembly, Antonio Lombardi, the Accountant, maintains a meticulous record of the Famiglia's financial endeavors, his ledger a testament to the delicate dance between legality and criminality that sustains our existence.

The air thickens with the hold of unspoken words as Lorenzo begins the proceedings.

"Xander, we gather today to discuss the transition of power, a solemn moment in the history of our Famiglia. Your father's legacy demands a seamless continuation, and we look to you to find a guide through the challenges that lie ahead."

The dim light casts shadows on the faces of those assembled, the gravity of their responsibilities etched into every line and furrow.

I nod at him. There is no hesitation in me. Even a whiff is enough to bring any of these men to the conclusion they can overthrow me. "And I am ready to lead."

A dissenting murmur emerges from Marcello Russo, a brash and impulsive soldier known for his recklessness. His eyes bear a challenge, his posturing suggesting an unsettling desire for confrontation.

As the murmurs gain momentum, I lock eyes with Marcello, a silent warning passing between us. "Marcello," I address him with a steely resolve. "Is there anything you wish to say at the table?"

"Are we truly together in this? Your Father, bless his soul, had kept us tight. And he kept tight with us. Are you willing or ready?"

I do not give him my attention as I answer the question. "Questioning the unity of the Famiglia is a dangerous path. We are bound by loyalty and tradition. Disrupting that harmony jeopardizes not only your position but the stability of our organization. And every dissent will be squashed. There should be no question of that."

The room falls silent, the unspoken threat lingering in the air. The other men exchange glances, recognizing the gravity of the moment. Tradition dictates respect, and any deviation breeds consequences.

Lorenzo, sensing the need to redirect the focus, interjects, "Let us discuss the Famiglia's future under Xander's guidance. The challenges may be formidable, but so is our resolve. We have watched him lead. Nothing changes now."

The shadows dance on the walls as the discussion unfolds, the fate of our Famiglia hanging in the balance. The room holds a loud silence before Giovanni Russo breaks it with a gruff voice, "Xander, your father held this Famiglia together with an iron grip. Can you do the same?"

My response is measured, "Giovanni, I aim not only to maintain but to elevate our standing. My father's legacy demands nothing less."

Carlo Vitale leans forward, his cold eyes locked onto mine, "Legacy means nothing if you can't enforce it. We need strength, not aspirations."

I meet his gaze evenly, "Strength is earned through respect, Carlo. A united Famiglia is an unstoppable force. Division is our only weakness."

Antonio Lombardi's voice holds a hint of skepticism. "Earning respect takes time. Time we may not have. What's your immediate strategy, Xander?"

Alec speaks up, "Antonio, my brother knows the value of time. We're not starting from scratch; we're building on a foundation our father laid meticulously."

But Marcello Russo, brash and insubordinate, can't resist challenging, "Building on foundations is for architects, not Capos. What's your plan, Xander, besides pretty words?"

My patience wanes, "Marcello, loyalty is earned, not demanded. If you question your place, perhaps you need to reassess your loyalty."

Declan, always the voice of reason, attempts to diffuse, "Enough, Marcello. The Capo has spoken. We move forward as one."

Giovanni, not easily deterred, adds, "Actions speak louder than words, Xander. We need to see what you're made of."

With calculated calm, I lean back, "Then watch closely, Giovanni."

The meeting ends soon and as is tradition, I lead the men back to the house to give their final respects to Mother. The house is already crowded with the men who work for us. Sandro is by the door, a cigar stuck to the corner of his lips.

I ignore him, heading straight to Mother with my brothers. Sedric is off by the side, speaking to his son.

I head towards them, but movement by the stairs catches my attention, and I lift my head to look, the air freezing in my icy lungs. What the fuck is going on here?

29

MEL

IF LOOKS COULD KILL, I'D BE A MELTED PUDDLE DRIPPING down the stairs to the pool by his feet. Xander stills just for a second by the bottom of the stairs, and I keep my eyes on him, reading the look of anger just as he wishes me to.

There's a reason he'd left me in Cabo. There's a reason I'd heard about his Father's death from my own father. That reason is staring me in the face right now.

I curl my fingers around the rails as I slowly head down the stairs, the sudden quiet in the room very loud.

Xander heads towards Father as he's about to before clocking me on the stairs, a strained smile on his face that slams my heart into my chest.

I head towards him slowly, hoping for some sort of reaction from him, praying he doesn't snap at me for wanting to help. Hoping he isn't so hurt he's already shut down.

The room is filled with the men of the Famiglia, a few whom I've seen before, most whom I've never before seen, but all of them are staring at him, waiting for his reaction. He's, after all, the new Capo by virtue of his Father's death.

"My condolences, Xander. We came over here as soon as we could." Father pats Xander's shoulders awkwardly before smiling at me as I arrive at the circle. I stand beside Knox, who is dry-eyed, his lips twisted in a sour smile.

"I wasn't expecting you." He whispers, shifting closer. I turn towards him and loop my arms around his back, hugging him tight, my eyes on Xander, who twitches imperceptibly but doesn't give me his attention.

"Father called. I'm so sorry about this, Knox."

He hugs me back and nods against my cheeks. "Of course he did. I'm sorry, too. But we were expecting it."

I bite my lip, my eyes watering slightly. Expecting it or not, it didn't make it any easier to know I'd never see him again. He hadn't been a smiley man, but he'd been good to me. He's protected me when I needed protection, too.

Knox pulls away, and I give Declan a hug, too, who stands stiffly in my embrace before smiling just as stiffly. Alec hugs me tighter but pulls away just as fast. I wipe at my eyes as their Mother makes it to us, a single line of tears tracking its way down her cheeks.

Xander shifts to make space for her in the circle, but when I step towards him, he stiffens and steps back. I stop, undecided about what to say or do.

He's obviously avoiding me right now. I stop beside him anyway and go to hug him, but he gives me a sharp shake of his head.

Father notices the action and raises his eyebrows but doesn't say a word. He turns and whispers something to Daniel, who looks at Xander but doesn't say a word to either of us. Declan curves his arms around his mother, and she bends her head into the crook of his shoulder.

I take a step closer to Xander and settle beside him, throwing a look around the room. His men have created what constitutes a line, and I know, according to tradition, that soon those men will want to speak to him and will want to give their condolences to the family.

Very soon, he will have to go away. Without saying a word to me. I won't let him. I'm not a line on a contract; I'm his fiancée, soon to be his wife. The mother of his son. Of his children.

"How are you holding up?" I lean into him, slanting my head and lowering my voice so the words are only for him.

His face tightens, but he doesn't reply; instead, his fingers lock around my waist, and he tugs me closer. His fingers sink into the fabric of my dress and press into my flesh. I lift my face to his to catch him watching me, his eyes cool. "Where's Lucian?"

Of course, that's his first worry. I smile. "I sent him with Romero to Father's. He's safe."

"I had no doubt that he was. You wouldn't be so calm here if he wasn't." He bends his head so his lips graze my ears, his brand on me obvious to the rest of the room. "And while we're on the topic. Why the fuck are you here, Melissa?"

I jerk away slightly, his angry whisper raking over my skin like cat claws. Why the hell is he so angry?

I lick my lips and shift closer. "Can we talk? Alone?"

He pulls away and, turning, walks up the stairs without a word. I send a look to Father and excuse myself. I find him upstairs, in his Father's study, the door just pulling shut behind him.

He's sitting, a look on his face that I immediately recognize. It's anger mixed with worry and dread. And there's pain there, too, in the scrunch of his brows, in the slight hunch of his shoulders, in the way he holds out his arms and welcomes my embrace. Now, it's just the two of us in the room.

I fold my arms around him, pulling the skirt of my flared dress up so I can straddle him. He allows himself to relax into the chair so I can fix myself to him, my chest flat on his, his hair against my neck, my ass resting on his thighs. "I'm so sorry, Xander. I'm so very sorry this is happening."

He tightens his arms around me, his chest hitching on a deep inhale, and the tears finally drip out of my eyes. He's hurting. Which means I'm hurting. "Why are you here, Melissa?"

I go to lift my head, but he presses down on the nape of my neck, wounding his hand in my hair in a move that isn't altogether painless.

"You're supposed to be in Cabo. Where I know you and my son and my baby in you are safe, where none of this can get to you. How am I supposed to handle the Famiglia and worry about you, Melissa?"

It doesn't escape my notice that he keeps using Melissa instead of Mel. Or that his chest is rising and falling against mine with each worried exhale.

"I needed to see you, Xander. I needed to know you were fine."

He grunts, his eyes finally lifting to meet mine. They're hot with anger, traces of worry floating through the blue depths.

"I can't be perceived as weak. I can't let the Famiglia doubt me. Not right now. They're waiting for the slightest sign of weakness. Each of those men would kick me to the ground if they thought they could get away with it."

I bend my head so my nose rubs against his. "But they won't. They're not getting away with it, Xander. They're your men, and you will lead them. It's not them you should worry about. It's the Russians."

He bares his teeth in a sardonic grin. "What do you know about the Russians?"

"Only what Daniel told me on our drive over. They're trouble, it seems. But let's not talk about them. Not today."

"What would you rather talk about?"

I swat his hand trailing up my side away. "You."

He bends his head so his forehead laps against mine and then holds himself still, just watching.

"I'm fine, Mel. I've been expecting this. I've made my peace with him. I forgave him. He knew about his grandchild, the one growing in you. The family will go on."

A knock comes at the door, and Declan calls out. "Mother is ready, Xander. You need to come down."

He stills and sniffs before sitting up and slowly pulling me off his lap. I allow him, shifting away to settle on the table. He stands, straightening his clothes around him before bending his head to press a soft kiss to my lips. "You stay here."

I slant my head back and glare at him. "Is that a command?"

"Yes, Mel. I'm happy to see you, but I worry about your safety. I have to be strong now, and you are my weakness, Sole."

I give him a fierce scowl, leaning forward so he knows I'm serious. "I can be your strength, too. I'm not so weak that I can't take care of myself, Xander."

He grazes his thumb over my lips, a slight smile at the corner of his lips that sends relief rocking through me. It's the first smile he's worn since I'd seen him. "I know, but I want to take care of you. The same way you want to take care of me, Mel. Stay here."

He kisses me hard and fast, his hands locked around my body on the table before he pulls away and is gone, the door closing gently behind him.

It opens almost immediately and Daniel strides in, a grim look on his face. I walk over to him, and he opens his arms, allowing me to sink into him.

We stand quietly that way for a while, his fingers strolling up and down my back. "Did he send you up here to make sure I stayed put?"

Daniel pulls away and nods. "And I understand why. He's got to keep a tenacious grip on things."

I stop and look away. Why is everyone starting to sound like a broken record? I have no wish to keep Xander from his responsibilities to the Famiglia. "I would never stop him."

He pats my shoulder and nods. "You wouldn't. But sometimes, he needs to handle some things himself. You can't always solve his problems. As much as you want to."

I could try my damndest. Any pain he feels ricochets in me, too. "I'll be expected to stand beside him. Chicago already knows we're to be married. Why can't I be with him now?"

Daniel shakes his head back and forth. "You will be with him. But his priority is to keep you safe. He's surprised to see you. Give him time to deal with this. You'd need the same if you were in his shoes."

I sag into myself and dab at my eyes. He's right. Much as I hate to agree. Sometimes, having time alone is necessary to heal. "Will you stay here till they're done down there?"

"Do you need me to?"

"Not really. I think I'm fine. I'm just worried about him. He's not allowing himself to feel a thing. It's all bundled up somewhere inside, and soon, it's bound to erupt."

"He can't be any different, Mel. He's been trained and reared to be just that way. His Father didn't allow for an expression of emotion growing up, and now he's dead, the Famiglia will not allow it either. But I promise you he's happy to see you."

I know he is. That kiss just before he left had made that pretty clear. But coddling me here isn't any way to show it. "I know he's happy to see me."

We're quiet together for some time, Daniel browsing through the books on the shelves when the door opens again, and Xander steps in.

His eyes track the room, and when they land on me, my heart does a weird little flip, and I stand fast from the chair I'd taken.

I hurry towards him, worry clawing at the base of my spine. "What's wrong?"

He's not smiling, his eyes hard and flinty. "Me. I'm what's wrong."

I look up at him, already stepping into his arms. "How could you say that?"

He pulls away, takes my arm in his, throws Daniel a long, searching look, and then walks back to the door, his fingers twining through mine. "You're mine, Melissa. I think it's time the world knows it."

Like the world didn't already. But the possessiveness in his voice does something potent to me. I stop, tug at him gently until he stops, and when he turns to me, I bring my lips to his, nip gently at him, and then kiss him so softly I barely feel the imprint of his lips on mine. "I love you, Xander. I never stopped. I know I never will."

Then I stroll by him, my chest too tight to breathe, my heart hammering, my palms suddenly clammy, wondering where I'd gotten the boldness from.

But my boldness must have infused him with some because, for the rest of the day, he keeps his arms around me, glaring at anyone who gives me so much as more than a second look.

30

XANDER

Finally, we're alone. Mel has just taken a shower and is now lounging on the bed, her legs tucked under her as she watches me on the phone with Lucian, who is staying the night at his grandpa's with Gianna and Romero.

"I'll come get you tomorrow, figlio. You sleep well." I place the phone between my shoulder and neck and walk towards the bed, holding my hand out to Mel, who crawls towards me, her eyes wary, her wet hair sticking to her head in places.

"Good night, papa," Lucian says sleepily. My heart flips over. I'll never get used to him saying that to me.

"Good night, champ. Let me talk to Uncle Daniel." I press a kiss to Mel's hair, a soothing scent of lavender seeping into my nose from the wet strands. She looks up at me and presses a kiss to my bare chest.

I'm feeling too many things all at once. Hurry to take over from Father even as I mourn his death, fear for Mel and my son, and anger at the Russians, who it seems have not stopped digging at us. Not that I expected them to.

"How can I help Xander?" Daniel's voice is mellow and calm. The calmest I've heard from him so far. I guess he can be pretty calm when he's not threatening me over his sister.

"You can keep my son safe. I'll come get him in the morning, but I'd like to keep the news of his grandfather's death away from him as long as possible." I grunt into the phone. I have no idea how he'll feel. He's still a child, but it doesn't mean he won't notice his grandfather missing at the table. Especially because he had more of a relationship with the man than he did with me.

"I promise you, he'll be safe. Even if that means my own life is at risk."

I nod. I know he will be. Daniel is as good as dead if anything happens to my son. "Good. I'll see you in the morning."

I hang up the phone and drop it on the bed, running a hand through my hair. It's been a long fucking day.

The men had left the house sometime after seven; we'd gotten Mother to stop crying and go into bed by nine. Daniel and Sedric had returned to the house earlier for Lucian, and I'd had to fight the urge to go with them for my son.

I wanted him in my arms; even Mel had looked longingly at the door as though she was feeling the same way. But she stood by me. Hadn't moved from my side the entire day.

I don't know how to feel about her. But I do know how I feel about her words. Her declaration to me just before she'd stepped out of Father's study and spent the entire evening pretending she hadn't just made my knee buckle under me.

I sweep her into my arms and walk down the stairs, grateful it's just the two of us at home tonight, apart from the men standing guard outside. She smiles softly up at me, and I can almost guess the question on her parted lips.

I shake my head no. I'm fine. She's asked me a thousand times already. But I am as fine as a man can be when he's received news of his Father's death and also had the woman whom he loves tell him she loves him. I'm all over the place, but I'll be okay.

Especially because her words have put me on cloud nine.

I clatter down the steps, and when I reach the kitchen, I let her slide down my body. I tip her head up and blow a stream of air across her lips. She closes her eyes, and I watch her, my pulse spiking. If anything were to happen to this woman, I'd be a caricature of myself.

She opens her eyes. "What are you worried about?"

I quirk an eyebrow and kiss her lips gently. "Who says I'm worried?"

She lifts a hand and wiggles it between us, brushing at my forehead. I realize I've bunched my brows together. "This right here."

I could tell her about the threat by the Russians. Ryder seems to think they've got something planned. Alec doesn't know, and neither does Declan or Knox. Not while they're mourning Father.

But I've had the men prepare for an attack. If the Russians do decide to attack our shipment or our men, we'll need to immediately retaliate. They can't ever think our ranks are open to attack.

But I don't want to think about it tonight. Tonight, I want to sink into Mel's warmth and let her remind me that there's life for a living. Death will always hang over every human, but it doesn't mean we have to live as though we'd die tomorrow.

I shake the somber thought from my head and tune in to find Mel still watching, her fingers gently stroking my forehead. "Nothing's wrong, Mel. Nothing could be wrong with you here."

She laughs gently, and I allow myself to seep in her warmth. I allow myself to be here in this moment with a woman I love. I twine my arms around her back and tug her closer. "Tell me again."

Her brows tip questioningly, and those inviting lips clasped between her teeth. "Tell you what?"

"That you love me. Always will."

She pulls out of my arms and turns towards the stove. "Are you hungry?" She says, refusing to answer the question.

I walk over to her. "Yes. But not for food."

She leans against the counter, smiling, her face tipped up. There's a hungry look in her eyes that I know for a fact is reflected in mine. "What are you hungry for?"

I press my front into her, my erection grazing the junction of her thighs, already dragging the robe she'd thrown on away. "Do you need to ask?"

She puts her arms around my neck and laves at my neck, her wet tongue licking at the pulse at the base of my throat. She sucks at it and then bites down, drawing a hiss from my guts. The air sticks in my chest, refusing to allow me another breath without her lips on mine.

I drag her head up and slam my lips down on hers, slipping my tongue between her lips, tucking her tight into my arms, lifting her hair off her neck, and hitching my hands around her waist to lift her onto the counter. "Have we christened this room yet?"

She wiggles and giggles in the back of my throat, the sound flowing over me like a cold waterfall. Washing away things I don't want to think of. "I don't know. Why?"

"I think we're about to."

She bites down my lips, sucking at my bottom lip and hissing as I cup her breasts in my hand, hefting it through the robe. She mewls and goes to tilt her head back, but I don't let her lips go.

I slip my arms around her back and tug her so her ass is on the edge of the counter, pull away and bend my head towards her thighs, pulling the robe off as I go.

I press a kiss to her thighs, spreading them wide so I can step fully between the sleekness of her smooth legs. "Tell me you love me."

She leans back on her elbows, but her eyes are hot on mine. "I'd much rather you just took me."

I skim my finger over her clit, bending my head to tug gently at the nub until she cries out. I tease my fingers over her wet folds, stroking and skimming and caressing until her legs are spasming.

I roll my tongue over her core, licking at her like she's the tastiest, most moist dessert in the world, and I'll never tire of it.

She's moaning, her legs tightening around my head, her hands in my hair, tugging at me. I lift my head and kiss my way back up her stomach, kissing a trail to her breasts where I bite down hard, her groan of pleasure causing my cock to jump in my shorts.

When I reach her lips and kiss her hard, she bites down just as hard on my lips. "I want you to fuck me, Xander. I know you want to just as much."

I want her; it's driving me to the brink of distraction, not sinking into her warmth, into the blistering heat of her body, but I've been thinking about this all day, craving it all day, needing it all day. "I think I want to hear you say you love me much more."

She pulls away from my lips, and her hands stroll down my body, slow and telling until she runs them over my chest, and I stand still until finally they rub at me through my shorts. "I think you're lying, Xander."

Her eyes are questioning, her voice tuned low. I watch her eyes, but she doesn't look up at me. Instead, she keeps her eyes down on me, rubbing and stroking until I have to swat her hand away for fear I'll come before I'm seated as deep inside her as I can go.

"Why the hell would I lie about this? That was the one thing I had to look forward to today; kept thinking about your eyes as you'd said them, the certainty in their depths. I want to hear it again."

She bites her lips and lifts her head finally, hurt and something akin to temper swimming in them. What have I done now? "You didn't say anything."

I chuckle, incline my head, and suck at her neck, right at the pulse she so enjoys sucking on my own skin. "Did that piss you off, baby?"

"You're a jerk, Xander Amory!" She snaps, leaning back to give me more access to her.

"And you're mine." I push my shorts off my hips, my heart pumping blood too fast, my cock thick and ready on my fists.

I bring myself to her folds, slap my cock against her clit, and watch as she fights the pleasure rolling through her. She doesn't want to give in first. I chuckle again.

I line myself up at her entrance, slamming into her just as I whisper a truth she never should've doubted. "I love you, Melissa Sedric. I think sometimes I can't breathe because of how much I worry about you. The way I want to keep you with me is crazy. The way your smile heals my world, the way I love our son is indescribable, the way you care about me, the way you crave me, it's just the same way I want you."

I punctuate each of the words with deep, settling, speaking thrusts into her, slamming into her tight, sleek warmth, pulling out despite the way she clenches around me with each stroke, with each pull back, she pushes against me, pulsing around me, needy in much that same way I was.

Her eyes are watery. "You didn't say a word."

"Because we were in a hurry. I needed you this way, totally with me, to let you know that I love you. That you're mine. That I'm yours. That I'm not going anywhere you aren't."

Her chest rises and falls rapidly, her nipples tightening right before my eyes. "Oh, Lord. Fuck me, Xander. I think I'll go crazy if you don't. I need to come. Right now!"

That was a wish I could fulfill. I jerk my hips into her, our bodies slapping together, her fluids making it so easy to fill her. Her face flushes, and her breathing becomes harder, more erratic, more in touch with my ragged one. The pleasure torching my body, dragging me closer and closer to my orgasm, must be in hers too.

"Cum for me baby, I need you to come now." I grunt, snapping faster and faster into her, stroking at her nipples and bending my head to bite at her nipples and bring her closer to the brink.

She nods, becoming wetter and clenching more. Her body almost makes me come; it's taking all of my control not to blow inside her.

She parts her lips and shakes her head, lifting her head to scream her orgasm against my lips. She sinks her tongue in but doesn't move.

Feeling her fluttering and pulsing against me, I slam into her once more, my body tingling from my fingers down, spreading white-hot pleasure like heaven over my skin.

I slide into her and spew my seed into her, bending my head into her neck and falling over her heaving chest. I allow my head to rest on her, breathing in time with her loud gasps. She kisses my ears softly. "I LOVE YOU." She whispers.

I know she does. She's home. And finally, the pain spills over my skin, rash and hot; they sting at my eyes. I pull away, my body inside hers, and finally agree that I'll miss my Father. "I wish he didn't have to die now." Not now, when I am just getting closer to him. When I am old enough to understand why he'd been the way he'd been. When I might just have to be the way he'd been.

She tightens her arms around me, and tears spring into her eyes. "Oh, Xander."

That night, we fall asleep together, her arms flung over mine, my hands over her stomach, her breathing singing in my ears.

31

MEL

Xander's mother, a figure draped in black, moves with a grace that belies the pain etched across her features. She acknowledges condolences with a nod, her eyes betraying the depths of her grief yet remaining steadfast in the face of the funeral traditions that envelop us.

The burial ceremony unfolds with a solemnity that echoes through the space. A priest in rich vestments intones prayers in Latin, the ancient language weaving an aura of reverence for the departed soul.

Incense wafts through the air, carrying with it the aroma of centuries-old traditions that bind us to our heritage.

Xander stands beside me, his eyes straight ahead while the priest blesses his father's soul.

The cemetery is a sea of dark attire and muted whispers, each mourner bearing the weight of grief as they gather to pay their respects.

The air is thick with the heavy scent of lilies and the sorrow that clings to the atmosphere as if the very heavens weep for the loss of a man whose presence commands respect in both life and death.

My hair ruffles gently in the breeze blowing through the trees as I stand, my arms around my body, my heart breaking for the man beside me.

He's wearing a stoic mask on his face, his body so still I would believe he's hewn from marble if his chest wasn't rising and falling every few seconds.

He closes his eyes as the priest says the last stream of prayers, and soon, it is time to let his Father into the dark earth. Tears stream down my face, and he gives me a long, soft look. "Hey, it's fine."

I nod. I know it's fine. But he's hurt. He's in pain as much as he won't agree he'll ever miss the man. "I know. It's just so sad he's gone now when things are looking up for us."

"He fought long and hard. He deserves a rest." He looks at the dark casket placed in the center of the gathering, and his lips curl in a soft smile. "I like to think he's at peace now."

But is it possible? Amory had spent his entire life with violence just around the corner from him. He was responsible for more than a few deaths, for drugs on the streets and guns in homes. Is there rest for him, or is it judgment?

The funeral mass is taking place just a few steps from the family mausoleum, where his father will finally be laid to rest. There are a few snuffles and sniffles from the females, but most of the men keep their faces blank. Death is an accepted end to the journey of life.

The priest ends the prayer, and six men heft the casket, and we trail behind them to the mausoleum, the guests behind us. Not all of them will make it inside; the burial itself is reserved for family only.

I tug gently at Xander as we step through the large wooden door at the entrance of the mausoleum. He gives me his attention, and I ask softly. "Are you okay?"

"As okay as I can be. Don't you worry." He smiles softly, but his eyes are bright, and they bring an ache to my chest.

We stop before the large crypt where his father's casket will be laid, and the six men step in, slowly, slowly, letting the casket drop until it lands with a thump on the granite surface of the elevated platform.

A loud wail cuts the solemn silence, and I turn to find his mother sagging into Alec's arms, her face hidden away. Alec's jaw ticks hard, and Xander's nail bites into the skin of my hand, but I don't pull away.

Knox is looking up with an effort to hold his own emotions at bay. Only Declan is sobbing quietly, a line of tears running down both his cheeks.

He leans against one of the statues scattered around the room. It's a gloomy day outside, but inside, it's almost warm, with bright lights spilling from the chandeliers above.

Amory Vittoria has been laid to rest. Finally, I turn away and sink my face into Xander's shoulders, and he holds me tight, but his body is restless and shifty under me. He sinks his hand into his pocket and comes up with his phone, checks it for a second, and returns it to the pocket.

By the time I lift my head, he's already directing the men out of the crypt with instructions, the keening cry when the men step out loud enough to meet my ears inside the mausoleum. Knox leads his mother outside.

I feel queasy immediately as I step outside, already wondering if there will be a repeat of my time in the bathroom from this morning.

I turn my head to find a man staring. He's almost...normal, apart from the flask, which he lifts in a salute and drinks from. He looks harmless enough, but for the rest of the time, he just stares at me.

"I'll be driving over to the house to receive the guests for the feast. I want you with me. I don't want you out of my sight." Xander takes my hand, and together with his brothers, we walk over to the car, where I slide into the back beside him. Ryder is absent, and I realize I haven't seen him all day.

I don't ask Xander because he places his hand on my thighs and leans back into the cool leather. I relax into him and allow him some time for himself. We sit in a comfortable silence till we arrive at his parent's.

We arrive at the house to find guests milling around. There are about two hundred people who have come to feast for the last time at Amory's table.

His mother is already at the door, thanking the people for coming, and Xander joins her. I try to walk away, but his hand tightens around mine. "I'll be inside with your brothers. You don't have to worry."

"Make sure they don't lose sight of you." He grits out. He lets me go, and I walk away, thinking he's being more protective than usual. I find Knox sitting on the sofa alone, his eyes closed. Beside him is Declan, who is dry-eyed and scowling.

"What's wrong?" I ask, settling between the two of them.

"There's too many fucking people. Where the fuck did they come from?" He growls, his eyes darting around

317

the room, which is buzzing with the loud silence of people eating and talking quietly. "It's not safe."

Weren't they expecting this many people? "It's your father's funeral. Of course, there's going to be a lot of people, Declan. They're here to pay their respects."

"They're here to sniff out the competition. I'm certain a few of them are fucking spies too." He sounds disgruntled, and I don't argue with him. He's most probably right.

Rosa arrives from nowhere, a plate of fruit in her hand, which she hands to me. She has a frown on her face, and a hurried look lingers in her eyes. "I know you haven't had a meal all day. That can't be healthy for you. And stop worrying; he's going to be fine."

I bite my lip and nod. Of course, he's going to be fine. It doesn't mean that I worry any less. "I didn't know you were here. I haven't seen Ryder all day."

Her reply is very cryptic. "He's keeping an eye on things."

I want to ask what he's keeping an eye on, but Alec interrupts us. Most of the guests are settled, a few eating, most standing around discussing with familiar faces. Father is somewhere around, but I can't see him now. As is Daniel.

Alec has Lucian in his arms. He hands me the boy, and I clasp my arms around his struggling body and press a kiss to his hair. He wants to be let down, but there are too many people around for that.

Xander and I had made time to sit with him and tell him his Grandpa was dead. He didn't understand everything but at least it would explain why the man wouldn't be seated at the head of the table anymore. Why wouldn't he be able to see him when he wanted to? My heart squeezes and wrenches and I'm the one holding back tears.

I've just dabbed at my eyes and swung my head to try to find Gianna in the throng of humans when my eyes clashes with the man from the funeral. He still has the flask in his hands, and he doesn't look away now. Same as earlier. This time, there's a sly smile on his face that sends a slimy shiver of discomfort skittering through me.

He presses a finger to his lips and then turns and limps away. I watch him until he steps out of the door. I look away, somewhat chilled, and hug Lucian harder against my frame, relieved when he pushes his head into the crook of my shoulder and settles somewhat. Xander walks inside, people parting without question to let him pass.

He walks towards us, his eyes trained on Lucian, who's suddenly restless again, sticking out his hand for his father. He wiggles in my arms to be let down, and I let him, watching as he runs to his father. "Papa."

Xander sweeps him into his arms and hugs him tight, closing his eyes for a second and inhaling his hair deeply. That and the fast blink of his eyes for a short second is the only streak of emotion across his blank face.

I see him relaxing into the comfort that our son brings, and it makes my heart swell with joy.

His phone must ring in his pocket because he finds it, lifts it to his eyes, and stiffens. His entire body goes rigid, his arm around Lucian going so tight that the boy wiggles.

I stand, noticing the flurry of movement everywhere in the room. All his men are alert, as is Rosa, who has her eyes on her phone.

He stomps towards me, hands me Lucian without a word, and bends towards my ears. His words are a panicked whisper, barely loud enough for me to hear. "You head back home with Romero right now! You do not leave the house without hearing directly from me. Do you understand?"

I gulp and bite down on my lip, my eyes tracking the room. Most of the men are already heading toward the door, and the few left are taking up strategic positions around the room. It's easy to see that something's wrong. "Are you going to be safe? Xander, please, I need to know."

He takes my fingers in his, and his eyes clash with mine. "I'll come back to you. I can't promise in what state, but I'll be back."

XANDER

BETWEEN THE CHURCH AND THE WAREHOUSE, I DON'T have time to worry about whether or not Mel made it home safe.

I have to trust that she did.

The phone call at my father's funeral was Ryder, letting me know that the Russians were finally making their move. As we roll up, there's a spray of bullets. Ryder quickly takes the gunman out, but it feels like an ominous welcome.

I have a feeling that this is not going to go well.

"Damn them," I hiss as Ryder and I get out of the car. "Of course they'd do this today."

"It's a smart move, I have to say," he whispers back.

"Not smart. Stupid and brash," I rage.

We creep into the warehouse, and unsurprisingly, there's yet another gunman around each corner. Ryder and I manage to subdue them, but once we get toward the cargo that we're trying to protect, something becomes painfully apparent to me.

It's going to get a lot worse before it gets better.

Briefly, my thoughts turn to Mel and Lucian.

I promised her that I would come back.

I have no idea if I'm going to be able to keep that promise.

The melee of bullets ricocheting off the walls is almost deafening. The sound of boots stomping back and forth fills my ears, and I pull another gun from my hostler, so now there's one in each hand.

Ryder has his back almost against mine, keeping his eyes on my back while I make sure nobody gets us from the front. I can't see most of the people shooting, but I can hear them. They're whispering, some screaming as they nurse injuries.

The Russians are dumb. It's a pretty obvious move to try to use my Father's funeral as a distraction while they overtake my men and steal from us. We've got a lot of them shot and on the floor, but the occasional bullets still come from some of them too stupid to give up.

"I want as many of them alive as possible." I snarl at Ryder, angry beyond measure. My forehead aches from scrunching it so much, and my fingers are curled around my gun's trigger.

Anyone who's stupid enough to step into the line of fire and dumb enough not to be one of my men is going to get a nice little gift on the legs.

"Yes, capo."

"And not one of them escapes the warehouse, dead or alive," I grunt at him. I don't watch, but I know he'll relay the information through hand gestures to our men behind him.

I can feel a stinging pain in my legs, which either means I've been wounded or a piece of shrapnel got me. I can't tell. I don't have the time to check either. The warehouse is dark, with large container boxes creating safe hiding places for men with guns.

I sink my elbow into Ryder's side, and pointing, whisper to him. "I'm going to shoot somewhere off to the right of the red one. You take off anyone who sticks their face out."

My heart is in my throat, sweat dripping off my forehead. If the Russians make it out of this fight with even a hint of a win, there will be nothing to stop the Cambodians from trying and possibly every other fucking gang in Chicago.

They were going to be a lesson to anyone stupid enough to think the Amorys have lost their prestige just because my Father is dead.

I had known that there was some risk of something like this. After all, when powerful people die in this world, others are always willing to take their place.

I wasn't sure, however, that it would be this soon.

I wait to receive Ryder's nod against my back, and then I point my gun at the red container and release too-fast shots. I roll away, and Ryder shoots almost immediately after. The silence is punctuated by a sharp scream, and the sound of a thousand bullets spills into my ears in the silence.

I jerk away and run a few steps, my eyes tracking the men's positions even as I roll and find cover, taking out a man who isn't dressed in the standard Amory color of red and black stripes.

All our men are dressed the same way. It makes it easy to avoid taking out your own man in the heat of battle.

I find a corner, and a shot rings out just a few inches above my head. I grimace and turn to the left where the bullet had come from. The man has his hand in the air, and a look of realization flits across his face just seconds before he falls to the floor, a dead man.

He doesn't get to threaten me and live. I have a wife and kids at home waiting. And that's the only reason that I've come here, away from them. Only because I know they're safe. My home is like a vault, there's no way to get in unless you're let in.

We'd found about twenty of the Russians here; there shouldn't be that much left to take out. I can't wait to get back to them. But I also have a responsibility to the famiglia, and this is that responsibility.

This reminds me of Father. He never would've stayed with the family, either. He would've been in the thick of the battle. Same as I am now. Maybe I am a lot more like him than I've always believed.

You promised her you'd come back.

Father always promised too.

I hope that I get to make it back to her.

I wipe a line of sweat creeping toward my eyes away with my sleeves and listen for footsteps around me. There's nothing, but it doesn't mean someone isn't creeping towards me.

I spread my feet and slink forward, darting my head quickly back in when I find a man looking in my direction. He lifts his gun, but I'm already gone. I cock my gun again, stick my head out and take him out with one shot. He drops his gun and buckles, sinking almost comically slowly to the floor, his scream piercing the air as he folds his hands over the wound on his leg, spurting blood.

I'm still watching when Ryder appears, his forehead sweaty, white debris all over his dark grey suit. He hands me my phone, his eyes bloodshot. "You need to leave right now. I've had the back entrance cleared."

I glare at him, wondering if a bullet to his own legs will teach him a thing or two about subordination. "I don't take orders from you."

He shakes his head, frowning himself. He looks around and steps closer. "No, but you said to let you know if anything goes wrong at home. Everything just went wrong at home."

My heart drops right to the bottom of my feet, my stomach roiling and twisting around itself. I blanch when I take a look at the picture on the phone screen. I feel hazy for a moment, as though all the blood has left my head and gone south, as though there's no substance holding me up.

On the screen is a picture of Mel, her arms tightly wound around her back and tied to a pillar in the living room. I don't see Lucian anywhere, and my heart skips as I think the worst.

Where the hell is my son?

I look back at the phone, my eyes drifting to my wife.

If looks could kill, Mel would already have flayed him. But since it can't, when I get home, I'm going to cut his arm off; then I'm going to feed it to him. I allow the rage to clear from my eyes, and then I turn and walk away, Ryder behind me.

"What happened to the fucking men at the house? Where's Romero?" It didn't matter much where he was; he'd better be dead when I found him.

No one came near my wife.

No one came near my son.

And I was going to teach them exactly why.

———

33

MEL

TWO HOURS EARLIER

I have my arms around Lucian, who has finally fallen asleep, his body lax against mine. Rosa is in the car riding shotgun beside Romero, who has his fingers clenched around the wheel.

"Can you go faster?" Rosa snaps at him, her body bent forward, her phone pressed to her ears.

"I'm going as fast as I can. Unless you want to explain to the Capo why his wife and kids were found in a ditch somewhere." Romero snaps back, throwing her a sharp glare. She grimaces and looks away, frowning.

Whoever she's trying to reach on the phone must not be getting through because she takes the phone from her ears, her hands wrapped tight around it like it's a neck she wants to squeeze. "Good gracious. Why the hell do they never take up the fucking phone."

"Language Rosa!" I lean forward to glare at her, too, my nerves stretched taut. She lifts her hands in the air, throws me a look of apology, and taps at the phone again, placing it right back against her ears.

She growls and jerks the phone from her ears, throwing it into the console. "Something's very wrong. I can feel it in my guts. We need to get these two to safety right now."

Romero presses down on the gas, and I run my fingers through Lucian's hair, praying in my heart that he stays asleep through all this. "Where's Xander?"

Rosa doesn't mince words. "Killing the Russians. I should be there too, but as per the boss' instructions, you're more of a priority."

She says the words begrudgingly with no rancor in her tone. Her eyes are on the road as we hurry home, and I add another line to my mantra of prayers. I pray he comes home safe to me.

We arrive home, and the gate opens automatically, as always. We go up the driveway, Romero's eyes darting right and left. We're almost at the door when I notice the cars. The only problem is none of the three look familiar, and none of our men are standing guard.

Rosa must notice the same thing because she stills and winds her glass down. "Where are the men? There should be at least three in sight."

She's barely spoken the words before the sound of footsteps hits my ears. I gasp and hug Lucian tighter against me. He heaves out a long breath and shifts restlessly in my arms, and I pray he really doesn't wake up now.

Romero finally turns to me. His eyes are hard. "Get off the seat. Get on the floor. Don't move. Not a sound."

He opens the door and steps out just as I push off the chair carefully with Lucian in my arms. I'm sweating, the air sticking in my throat, my blood pumping a million times a minute.

The sound of voices and footsteps comes closer. In a minute, the passenger car door snaps closed and I know Rosa has left the car too.

I shudder as I stay hidden in the car but soon, the footsteps head towards the car. Towards me.

The tears pool in my ears and I bite my lip to hold back the cry in my throat. I'm mewling softly when the door opens, and someone barks an order I can't hear. Hot air sweeps into the car interior, and I stifle the sob building in my chest.

I quiver, suddenly cold, folding my body around my son, who snuggles into me for safety I can't offer. The man grunts and growls at me. "Get out or I'll take you out myself."

I lift my head slowly and look up into laughing eyes. It's the man with the flask, which he still has in his left hand. He curls his lips and indicates that I step out.

I beg with my eyes and my words. "Please, not my son. Whatever you want with me is fine, but not my son."

He chuckles, but his eyes flash wickedly. "Anything I want with you, huh?"

My heart seizes at his tone.

I lift my chin. "Just leave my son alone."

"We'll see about that," he says with a dark chuckle.

I step out of the car, holding Lucian. I can feel him stirring and I hope he's not waking up. I look down to find Rosa flat on the floor.

There's blood dripping from her shoulder, and she's groaning and grunting, but I know she's not going anywhere without help. Her gun is gone... and I don't see Romero anywhere.

The man fists his hand in my hair and tries to take Lucian from me but I tighten my arms and he lets go, instead jerking his head to indicate that I move. My heart sinks, and I want to scream at him to leave us alone.

Lucian is wiggling in my arms, and definitely awake. "Mommy, what's going on?"

"Daddy has some friends over," I say, hoping that he won't notice the fact that they're distinctly not friendly.

The man's lips curl into a smile. "Yes, we're all just friends."

The color leaks from my face, and I want to strike him, want to sink my hands into his shirt, and claw that look of superiority off his fucking face.

He walks into the house, leading three other men who all have weapons in their hands. I almost shout when we make it inside.

Only the thought of my son in my arms keeps the scream from exploding out of my lips. Romero is hog-tied, blood dripping from his forehead. He's not moving, and I think he's dead. Because of me.

I hold Lucian close so he can't see.

The man holds out his hands, and smirks. "Hand him over."

"Lucian…"

"Hi," Lucian says. "Who are you?"

"A friend," the man says.

The glint in his eyes tells me I need to let go, so I do.

He takes my son from me finally and I cry softly, the tears dripping down my face. If I survive this moment, I know this man is surely going to be hurt badly. By me. But if he hits or hurts my son, I'm going to kill him.

"Not my son," I whisper again.

"I heard you. I'll take that deal. How about you go upstairs with one of daddy's friends, and you can watch a movie? How does that sound?" he asks Lucian.

"Okay," Lucian blinks.

My son is too trusting.

The man looks at me. "See? Not your son. But you…"

My heart crumples.

It gets even worse when he swings his head to a woman who steps out of the hallway and nods to him. He growls at her, his brow hitched in question. "Is the room ready?"

She sends me a long look and then holds her hands out for my son. "Yes."

34

XANDER

WHEN I FIND ROSA OUTSIDE, HER GUN MISSING, HER shoulder still seeping blood, I experience a level of rage that I've never felt before.

The car door is open, and Mel is missing. As expected. There are about three cars scattered around the driveway, and none of those cars are mine. What did they do with the cars?

What the fuck do I care about the damned cars anywhere? I know I'm trying to distract myself from what could be happening to Mel right now.

It's a rookie mistake to leave the house unguarded, and they have to know I'll be coming, which leads me to believe they have something planned.

They planned this. They knew where I'd be. They knew Mel would be here, and they knew who would be with her.

This is all too well planned to just be a random attack. This is something that took time. Money.

Information.

"It's not a good idea to step in there unprepared, Xander." Ryder has his gun in his hand, already lifting his hand to halt the men we have arrived with.

"Do I look like I give a fuck, Ryder? They've got my wife! They've got Lucian." I growl at him. We're finally by the front door. I move, pressing it open. The expensive hinges don't make a sound, something that I'm grateful for now.

I move my head, glancing around the corner, trying to get a peep down the hallway. There's no one. I step forward.

I can't believe this is happening.

Mel.

Lucian.

Where are they?

My heart is beating too fast, and I can't drag air into my lungs. If they harm her, I'll make sure not one Russian survives in my territory.

I'll burn down the fucking world if need be to make sure not one of them survives. I've only just found her again, only just fallen for her again, only convinced her she could trust me again.

I'm not losing her for anything. Not even to save myself. Ryder jerks his arms around mine to hold me back. I glower down at the fingers curved around me.

"Let one of the men go first. You are capo. You cannot take a bullet today. Or ever."

I want to spit at him. "Are you stupid, Ryder? You've two seconds to get your hands off me."

He hesitates and throws a look at the hallway ahead of us. "I'm your right-hand man. Let me do it."

I pull away and hurtle forward. From the picture, they're in the living room, and that's exactly where I head for. The heavy wooden door is locked when I go to open it, and I knock the butt of my gun against it.

The sound thuds and echoes, and in reply, the report of a gun hits the door. I pull back, but the bullet doesn't pierce through the door.

I hit the door again and growl, hoping Sandro can hear me through the door. "You've got something of mine, Sandro. Actually, you've got two things. I need them back."

I hear footsteps heading towards the door and then the sound of a click as the door is unlocked. I don't let the door open completely before pushing it; I'm already shooting.

There's no one behind the door, but the sight I find is enough to freeze the blood in my veins.

My men are bunched together in the middle of the room, their arms splayed out. Romero looks dead, unmoving and stiff beside them.

Even worse, she's gone. As is Lucian. Both of them are missing from the room.

Sandro is smiling. He tips his head back. "Whom are you more worried about?" He grazes the gun at his jaw thoughtfully. "The son? Or the wife? Who do I do away with first?"

My heart stops beating for a sharp second, and I can't move, can't breathe, can't speak. If he hurts my family, he's as good as dead. As is the rest of his lineage.

"You don't want to do that, Sandro. It won't be safe for your family. Where are they?"

He sucks his teeth loudly, and an angry flush turns his face red.

"You mean the same way it wasn't safe when you sold me to the fucking Russians? The same way you left me out to dry?"

"Is that why you turned and betrayed me? Because you weren't strong enough to stand the brunt of war?" I twist my fingers more securely around my gun, shifting my attention slightly to Ryder behind me. "Where's my family, Sandro?"

They have to be somewhere in the house. I hope that the men we brought with us have the good sense to spread out.

Sandro's jaw tightens, his face twisting into a snarl. "I turned nothing. You, Xander Amory, did me dirty first."

"Let my family go, and I just might consider letting you leave here alive." I let the words seep from my tightly clenched lips. He won't listen to them. But it's a choice.

He laughs hard, his body rocking back and forth on his heels. "You're stupid, Xander. Stupid and conceited. But surely you don't think I'm just as worthlessly stupid. That would hurt...a lot." He waves the gun in the air.

"This took a lot of planning, you know. Getting the Russians to trust me, to see we had a common enemy in you. And your Father, he died almost as though he was offering to help."

Ryder shifts behind me and hurls his words angrily at Sandro. "You're a sick man, Sandro. And I'll enjoy feeding you your own intestines."

Sandro rolls his eyes. "Shut the fuck up, Ryder. You're only as good as Xander says you are; you lickspittle."

I'm tired of listening to his voice, tired of watching him swing a gun around. I want my family and I want them now. "Go ahead. Kill them then."

The air seeps from the room, a creeping silence blanketing the room. Sandro stops. "What did you say?"

I shrug carelessly, my eyes sharp on his. I give him a dark, hard long look. "Kill them. You've had a lot to say. I find I'm tired of the words. Show me some action." I point down the hallway with my own gun. "Go in there, find them and put them out of their misery."

I force the words from my lips, hoping and praying Sandro doesn't call me out on my bluff. If he's truly working with the Russians, and I have no doubt that he is, then they won't want to get my family killed. They would want them in their control. So they can control me.

Sandro can't kill them. And he's about to box himself into a corner trying to prove it.

"You don't mean that. And that reverse psychology bullshit won't work on me. I'm not that fucking dumb."

I step forward, strolling towards him, my eyes on his as the space between us shrinks. "I think you are, Sandro. As a matter of fact, I think you're the dumbest person in this room. I'd also prefer that you don't cuss in my house."

I see the moment the fear spikes in his eyes, and that's the moment I give Ryder the signal to shoot. The sound of the gunshot unleashes sudden chaos; one of Sandro's men yells, falling down. I look over at Sandro, who is glaring at me.

"Prepare to fucking die, asshole," I snarl at him.

I move forward, my gun pointed at his heart. He backs up. "Listen to me, Xander…."

I don't listen.

I shoot him in the hand.

Sandro yells, the gun falling out of his hand. He curls over his wounded fingers, gasping for air.

"Where is my family, Sandro?" I snarl.

He glares at me, his body bristling. He growls at me. "Russians or not. I'm gonna fucking kill them if you make me. There's a man with a gun to their head if you don't listen to me right now. The Russians want control of Amory's territory."

I'd known it as surely as I know the back of my hand. As I'd recognize Mel in the dark. They wanted what the Amory's had and they were willing to play dirty to get it.

Holding my family to force my hand. I release a shuddering breath and allow my shoulder to relax slowly.

I smile at him. I've cornered a desperate man. I have no doubt he'll harm Lucian if pushed too far. I can't even think of him killing my son. "Where is my family, Sandro."

Sandro stands.

He walks away backward, sticking his head down the hallway to wave his remaining fingers at someone I can't see. I take a step closer, willing to jump him if I have to.

Sandro gasps. "If you just sign the fucking papers, I'll tell you where your family is."

I know what it is. But I ask anyways, a sarcastic lilt to my voice. I pray it masks the panic that's lodged in my throat. "What papers?"

He looks at me as though I'm dumb. "What do you think, Xander Amory? It's an agreement. And you'll damned well sign it."

"Why would I do that?"

He waves his wounded hand at me, blood spattering from it, and I wonder how one man can be so carelessly stupid. "Because you might as well count your family dead if you don't."

I don't believe him.

I lunge forward, ready to end this. "Tell me where my fucking family is."

Sandro looks at me.

And he runs.

I follow after him, shooting out at his legs so he drops slowly to the ground, screaming and groaning. His loud "fuck!" Is very satisfying.

I stand over him for a second, snapping a finger to Ryder who comes running up to me. I only then realize most of Sandro's men are either dead or about to very much be dead.

"Take care of him. Call the doctor for Romero, then come with me."

I don't wait to see my instructions carried out. I run up the stairs, checking all the doors in the hallway till I stop before the master suite, and the adjoining room beside it.

All the other rooms were empty. All of them are not holding the treasure of my family.

Ryder is breathing hard beside me. I raise my brow in question. He nods sharply. Sandro is dead. It doesn't give me any relief. Not until I find my family.

I push the extra door open to Lucian watching a movie.

He blinks at me. "Hi daddy," he waves.

"Hi. Have you seen your mommy?"

He shrugs. "No, but I watched a movie!"

"That's great, buddy. Give me a minute, okay?"

He nods, his gaze going back to the television.

I've never been happier for an addictive screen.

Finally, I come to our bedroom. For a second I'm terrified of what I might find inside, and my hand hesitates on the door handle.

Then, I open it. Mel is tied up to our bed post, just as much panic in her eyes.

I sprint over to her. "You're okay, you're okay baby," I murmur at her.

Ryder is already beside Mel, pulling ties off her arms. As soon as he does, she's off the bed rushing towards me, tears in her eyes, tears on her cheeks, tears dripping off her face. She hurls herself at me, her arms locking around me.

"Lucian?" she breathes.

"He's fine. Looks like he was watching a movie the whole time," I whisper.

She sags in relief.

"Mommy?"

Lucian walks in, and we gather him into our arms.

The door crashes against the wall, and my brothers spill into the room, but the fighting is already over. Mel pulls her face from Lucian's hair and gives me a trembling smile. "I love you. Thank you for keeping our son safe."

I watch her, a stunned look on my face. "You don't hate me?"

"I hate this. I hate myself for letting them take advantage of us. But never you."

I step closer to her and jerk her into my arms. "Don't you dare say that. You're my weakness, and I don't care. I want you to be. I like how I feel about you. I like how much it is that the thought of you and me heals something within me. I would never change that!"

She swallows and says with relief. "I know. I love you too, Xander."

I hold her tightly. I almost lost her. I almost lost both of them. Everything that I've done... it would be for nothing if not for them.

They are my everything.

"It's okay," I whisper in her hair. "It's okay. We're safe. Everything is okay. We're here together and we're safe, and it's all going to be okay."

I'm not sure how long I hold the two of them. It's clear that for all three of us, we just need to hold on. We just need to be together.

We just need to remember that we're okay.

In that moment, with my wife in my arms, holding onto my son, I make a decision.

I'm never going to let anything happen to either of them again. We have one life, and we have each other.

Damn it, I'm going to make the most of every second with these two.

I only hope Mel will still let me.

THE NEXT MORNING, I wait for her to come down to the breakfast table. I've been up all night, and I have come up with a plan. I want Mel to know that I don't just care about her.

I love her.

And I'm never ever letting her go.

I touch the box in my pocket, hoping this all goes the way that I want.

"Morning," she says sleepily.

"Good morning, amore mio," I reply. She settles in, and my hand goes to the velvet box that I brought down stairs with me this morning.

"You okay?" she asks, looking at me.

I look her square in the eyes. "I will be."

Mel stills.

I take a breath. "Yesterday was terrifying."

"I know," she whispers.

"If anything had happened to either of you…"

"Xander," she cuts me off. "We don't have to talk about it."

I shake my head. "We do, Mel. We do because it's important to me that you know, I would never put you and Lucian in harm's way. I will never do it again."

"I know."

I shut my eyes and heave a huge breath. "All I could think of was our promise. The one I made you, to come back."

Mel looks like she's hardly breathing.

I look at her. "I may not always come back."

"Xander…"

"I may not always come back," I continue. "But I can promise you that when we're together, we will have the best life we can possibly imagine. I will make all of your dreams come true. I love you, and I need you to know that I love you, every second of every day."

"Xander," her voice breaks.

I take another deep breath.

And this is not the perfect moment, but it's the one I've chosen. I grab the ring box that's in my pocket. I push my chair back and turn Mel's so it's facing the room.

I lock eyes with her, grateful that we're the only two people in the room. I want to do this right, so I get on my knees before her. I grab the ring box from my pocket and open it.

Her eyes widen and the tears that had seemingly dried up come hurtling back. Her eyes shine as she glances back and forth between me and the ring. "What are you doing, Xander?"

"Asking you to marry me," I whisper.

My heart is in my throat.

I'm not sure what she's going to say. I know that technically, we're already engaged.

But we didn't make that decision. Someone made it for us. Life pushed Mel and I back together. This time, however, it's different.

This time, I'm asking her to choose me.

And I'm terrified to hear what she'll say.

She looks down at me incredulously as though I've gone off my rocker. "We're already getting married. You can't ask me now," she whispers.

I shake my head. She needs to know that this is important. That I need her like I need oxygen, and I want to know that she's just as passionate about me as I am about her.

"I can. I will. I am." I open the ring box and the lights glint off the canary yellow diamonds nestled in the black velvet of the box. She bites her lips and lifts her eyes to mine. I know she's thinking of the red rubies. The one she's still wearing, though she hates it.

I'll never make her do anything that she hates ever again.

I look up at her, and my throat feels tight. "I need to ask you, Mel," I whisper. "I need to ask you because so much has changed from the first time we did this."

"Which time?" she laughs.

I smile. "When you agreed to be my wife. When I gave you that dress and that ring. When I put that together, I honestly thought this would be something political only. Something to keep our businesses and families intertwined. I didn't think it was possible for me to fall for you again. I thought there was no way I still felt a thing for this woman. At most, maybe I'll hate her. But when you stepped through the door, wearing that red dress and that damned ring that I hated giving to you, I'd should have recognized that even then, hating you just wouldn't be possible."

She sniffles and glares down at me suddenly. "Why'd you send me the ring then? I thought you'd forgotten I hated rubies. Still hate them," she says with a meaningful glance at the yellow diamonds nestled in the box.

I wince and wish I didn't have to answer that question. But we're starting out on a clean slate, and everything needs to be out there.

"I know, baby. I'm sorry. But I wanted to prove to myself I was over you. Wanted to hurt you as much as you hurt me by leaving."

She rolls her eyes and throws her hair back. "That's a dumb idea, Xander."

"I know. I was dumb. I was the biggest idiot on the planet, and if I have to spend the rest of my life making it up to you, I will. I gave you the rubies. I did all of those things. And my only hope right now is that you'll give me the opportunity to do just that."

She sniffles. "To do what?"

"To start over. I know I gave you rubies in the beginning, but things changed. You changed me, Mel," I whisper. "I started this marriage in bad faith. But I had this ring, one that I knew you would love, made. I was going to ask you in Cabo." I lift my shoulder and drop it back. "Things got out of hand, and I didn't have the time."

She snorts. "You can say that again."

"I'm so damn sorry, Mel. So sorry that we didn't have this sooner. That I didn't ask you then."

She watches me for a moment as if she's making up her mind about something. "So ask me now"

I put my heart out there. "Will you marry me, Melissa Sedric?"

"You know what?" She asks, tilting her head back and sending dread and love keening through me. How is it possible that she is able to elicit a thousand different emotions, all counter to each other at the same time within me? "I think I will."

She holds out her hand and I slip the large ruby off, throwing it behind me so it pings off a surface and rolls away. I slip the ring out of the box and slide it on her finger, loving the way she bends her hand immediately to watch the light glint off it. "I like it. It's lovely."

I blow out a relieved breath and hug her tight, almost squishing her. "I love you Melissa. I hope I'm able to protect you as much."

She presses a kiss to my cheeks. "I hope you don't have to."

EPILOGUE

MELISSA AMORY

"I pronounce you husband and wife!"

As soon as the preacher says them, I kiss Xander with everything I've got.

He kisses me back, and the church erupts into hoots around us.

The moment is a blur. The ring on my finger feels solid, a diamond band that has absolutely no hint of a ruby in it.

We're on the way from the church to our reception before I know it, and I change into a smaller, less cumbersome dress. When I open the door to the hallway that will lead to the reception hall, Xander is there.

I smile at him. I was hoping that Xander and I steal a quick moment together, since we waited so long for this.

I want to really savor the moment.

I've waited five months now to hear those words. Five months of long days and nights planning our wedding, five months of hiding the wedding dress from Xander's eyes; I'm wearing my mother's dress, which I thought that would be a perfect way to have her here with me.

Xander smiles down at me, a wide open smile with nothing to hide and I know I've seen him smile before, but this feels different.

"You're my wife now." He whispers into my ears, his fingers rubbing at my waist.

Finally.

The words have been something we've thrown around a lot. But finally, now, we have them. We mean them.

It's true, it's real.

Forever.

I place my hand against his chest and nod. "And you're my husband, to have and to hold as long as we both breathe."

He returns my smile. "Which I plan on making a very, very long time."

"No more Russians in random warehouses?"

He shrugs. "Well, it is my business, my dear."

I laugh.

He places his hand on my chin and tips my head up before kissing me soundly, his kiss possessive and soft all at once, his tongue brushing against my lips but not penetrating, his hands moving towards my stomach where our twins are nestled inside me, growing.

I've saved a little announcement about that for this moment too.

I pull back and smile at him. "Hey."

"Hey yourself," he whispers.

"How's it going?"

Xander throws his head back and laughs. "Pretty good, how about yourself?"

I bite my lip. I've been saving the big news about the pregnancy to tell him about until after the wedding, not because I have any kind of thing about telling him.

Honestly, we just haven't had a chance.

However, telling him…

It's all so different than with Lucian. With him, I didn't get to have this fun moment of a gender reveal, or knowing more about the baby. I have the sort of irrational fear that when I tell Xander there's more going on with this pregnancy, he'll freak out.

But I know that's not true.

I know that Xander and I are meant to be together, and that nothing could ruin this moment.

Still…

I take a deep breath.

There's nowhere to go but up.

"Hey, can you do something for me?"

He smiles. "Anything, amore mio."

"I think we're going to need to invest in some different cribs."

"Why?" he frowns. "What is wrong with the crib we got?"

"We're going to need double of everything," I say, hoping he'll catch on.

Xander's eyebrows pinch together in confusion. "Double of everything? It's one baby, my love. Why does one baby need two of everything?"

He still doesn't get it.

He's a badass mafia boss. The leader of a whole crime organization.

And he can't figure this out.

I sigh. He's cute when he's like this. "Xander, we aren't just having one baby."

I can tell the moment when the words start to make sense to him. He squints, then his eyes go wide. His pupils blow out and he looks down at my stomach. "Not just one?"

"Yes," I laugh.

He kneels before me, framing my belly with this hands. "How… How long…"

"I just found out. A boy and a girl, the nurse told me at my fourteen week appointment."

"Fourteen…" he pauses.

Xander looks up at me, his eyes like saucers.

"A boy… and a girl?"

I nod, my joy impossible to contain.

"We're having twins."

"Twins!" Xander shoots up and picks me up in his arms. I laugh as he twirls me around, kissing me and murmuring words of affirmation in my ear. He tells me I'm beautiful, he calls me his wife, and eventually, he figures out that spinning a pregnant woman isn't a great idea.

He puts me down. "Mel," he breathes. "Why didn't you tell me?"

"And miss this reaction? Absolutely not," I laugh. His eyes are a little hurt, so I stop. "We haven't had time, Xander. Between the wedding and everything else…"

He nods. "I see. I know, amore mio. I am so happy right now, I don't even know what to do or say."

"You don't have to say anything, love. Let's just enjoy the moment."

Xander laughs and kisses me again. "I enjoy all of our moments, and this one? This one is the best of all."

He pulls me into his arms in a hug, and I sigh and lean into his arms.

What could make this moment more perfect? I don't believe I'll ever find out.

I pull away, breathless and smiling. Xander takes one of my hands, kissing my fingertips before putting my palm flat against his heart.

I can feel the beating underneath my fingers. Strong, steady.

Xander.

"I love you Melissa Sedric Amory," he whispers.

"I love you Xander Amory Vittorio. With all my heart and soul and body."

He leans in, pressing a kiss against my forehead. I tilt my face up, waiting for him to kiss me. He does, and then whispers into my ears. "Can't wait to have you fulfil that promise to me later tonight."

I shake my head and slide my arms into his as we begin the walk to the reception hall together. "What promise?"

He shoots me a wicked grin. "Your body."

I snort. "That's not new, Xan."

"It's great every time."

I laugh. "You're such a guy."

He pauses and takes my hand. His eyes look deeply into mine. "No, Mel. I'm not. I'm going to think you're sexy every day. I'm going to want to fuck you every day for the rest of our lives. I need you to know that you're the most beautiful woman that I've ever seen, and I will never get tired of seeing you naked."

I lean in, a silly smile pasted across my lips. "Babe, that's so sweet."

"See how sweet it is when I'm…"

A throat clears in the hallway behind us.

I look up and see Ryder, waving us forward into the reception hall. "Where have you guys been?" he hisses as we get closer.

Xander shoots me a look. "We had some things to catch up on."

I grin back.

Ryder shrugs. "Whatever. Get ready for the gauntlet though."

I roll my eyes at him.

Nothing could ruin this moment for me. Ryder's sarcasm, an earthquake...

Right now, everything is perfect.

We enter the reception hall to the applause of our friends and family, and for a minute I just bask in the love that's surrounding us.

Gianna waves at me from the front row where she and Daniel are seated together. On the opposite row is Xander's family, Knox smiling just as widely as I am certain I am.

Their mother has a soft look on her face as she watches us. The rest of the crowd are the members of the famiglia who were important enough to be invited to our wedding.

Xander squeezes my arm. "You still want to enjoy the day with all of these people?"

I roll my eyes at him, straight up at the high ceiling. "I think this is just kind of part of the deal."

"You know, since we're the ones getting married, we could decide to just leave."

I laugh at him. "Xander. We can't leave our own wedding party."

"I know," he wrinkles his nose at the crowd of people milling about, ready to congratulate us. "But we also definitely could."

Without warning, Lucian comes running towards us, a flower in his hand which I'm almost certain Gianna had given to him as a sort of distraction. "Mama!"

His voice is loud and happy but the smile on his face as I bend to sweep him into my arms answers my question.

This moment is perfect just as it is. With my husband beside me and my son in my arms, and our babies kicking in my belly. Nothing else could beat this.

It's the wedding I've always wanted.

With the man I've always loved.

We haven't had an easy road, Xander and I. But, as I let my husband hold me, I bask in the moment.

I don't care how the road brought us to where we are.

All that matters is that we're here.

THANK you for reading my book, please leave me a review, they help me out a lot as an independent author.

Dive into my recent release The Arranged VOWS and meet Leland and Catriona as they take you on a rollercoaster ride to a heart warming happily ever after. Their story is an Age Gap, virgin, arranged marriage romance full of drama, angst, danger and instant chemistry as these two meet as strangers on their wedding day...yes prepare to swoon and fan away.

Click Here to Read now

HERE IS AN A LITTLE TASTE...

THE ARRANGED VOWS

CATRIONA

. . .

THE APPLAUSE after our first kiss was nearly deafening. I felt . . .I don't know what I felt. Wild, excited, a little scared.

It was one hell of a kiss.

He tasted a bit like coffee, and faintly of something else. Mostly, he felt huge, like his tongue was filling my mouth. It was exhilarating, and a little frightening. Kisses, in my experience, had been a peck on the cheek, a touch of the lips.

Obviously I knew that they could be more, since I had seen many people kiss who cared deeply for each other, but I hadn't ever put much thought to what it would feel like myself. This was in an entirely different class!

During the kiss, my body responded as well. Something else was happening. My leather vest felt too tight, as if my breasts were swelling. It almost hurt as the fabric of my chemise rubbed against my nipples.

My underwear feels damp, and I have the strongest desire to stretch against Leland, as if I am a cat trying to mark a favorite human.

I do know what is expected of me, in terms of procreation. I know what goes where and how it all works.

What I did not expect is how it would make me feel. Hot and heavy and uncomfortable but exhilarated and light at the same time.

It's overwhelming. It's consuming.

And I want to do it again.

The bearers carry the sleigh bed out the door and into the bridal yurt, then the brazier is brought in, followed by a small table, then a basket that smells of fresh bread and smoked meat follows and is placed on the table.

My mother and father come in, and kiss each of us on the forehead — their blessing. They are followed by the twelve village elders, who (thankfully) do not kiss us. Instead, each leaves a small packet on the table beside the basket. The last leaves a bottle of wine, chilling in a bucket of ice.

Then everyone goes out, closing the door of the yurt behind them. Outside, there was a great yell. Then bells jingle, a bagpipe starts squalling, followed up by chorus of fiddles, and a drum that throbs with a highly suggestive beat.

"Are we married now?" Leland asks, looking a little alarmed at the din. "I hope they don't disturb the elephant. If he gets started moving. . ."

"Hand fasted," I correct. "Good for a year and a day. If we like it, we can renew next year." Part of my frenzied feeling abates with the quiet conversation. It is both a relief, and kind of a disappointment. "The animal pens are soundproofed. We get sonic booms here, when the big jets go over. It makes the bulls crazy, so we started doing that a few years ago. Your Lord Whatyoucallhim won't hear a thing."

"Ah, good," he says. "One less worry. Next question. Do we go on?"

"Go on?" I ask blankly.

His cheeks darken, and he seems embarrassed. "With our, uh, wedding. Consummation, I mean."

"More kissing?" I ask. I'm nervous to ask about anything else.

"Yes," he says, flashing a bright smile. "We can certainly start with kissing."

I blink.

Oh, wow. That smile! It lit up his face, and those strong mobile lips were certainly made for kissing.

He leans forward and presses his lips against mine. I'm aware of everything... his lips on mine, his hand where it pulls me tight against him. Even the fur on the bed beneath my fingers feels softer, like I'm more aware of it.

Leland's kiss is tender, and when he pulls back, it seems, more tentative, as if he is asking a question. He smiles at me before asking a soft question. "Have you ever done this before?"

I am surprised by the question. "You mean kissing?"

"No, Catriona," he says with a little laugh. "The part that comes after kissing."

I blink. Was he expecting to marry a more experienced princess? "You'll be my first, of course," I reply. I tilt my head, curiosity burning through me. "Have you ever done it?"

"Once," he says. "I can't say that I was impressed. My step-father brought in a woman to instruct me and my half-brothers. She was a priestess from the temple of Ultimate Desire, and she was supposed to be an expert in instructing young men. She set up a lot of instruments, then went through a ritual that was supposed to be enticing before lying across a bed and presenting herself. At the time, I thought my hand gave better value. In retrospect, it is possible she was simply tired. It was the year of the G8 summit that addressed AIDS/HIV and Tuberculosis relief assistance."

I nod my understanding. I have read the history of the Global AIDS and Tuberculosis Relief Act of 2000. However, it seemed odd to me that this handsome of a man, who was a few years older than me, had never had another sexual experience. A thought struck me. "Do you like men?" I ask.

He stops, thinks, then says, "Not like that. But the woman didn't seem happy about what she was doing. It wasn't . . . encouraging. In all fairness to her, she might have been enormously skilled, but the priestesses in the Temple were hit hard by disease that year. Only those certified free of any kind of contagion were allowed to visit the royal youth. There were rather a lot of us," I add wryly.

"That seems strange," I say. "Did your father pay her for her work?"

He laughs. "I doubt it. Servicing the nobility was her sacred duty. I made such service voluntary my first year as reigning prince regent. And when there was an Ebola outbreak, I issued a decree to close the temple. I think it probably cut our casualties by at least two-thirds."

"What happened to your father?" I ask, now a little worried by all this talk of illness.

Leland's smile turns brittle. "He was dying of cancer, not any kind of sexually transmitted disease," he replied.

"Even so, I saw plenty of illness caused by close personal contact, so that temple priestess twelve years ago was my one and only sexual encounter. Andrew and the naval doctors have tested, poked, and prodded me until I am a mere shadow of myself. I promise, Princess Catriona, that I bring only my untalented, inexperienced, and possibly uninspiring self, minus any sort of contagion."

I take my unbound hand out of the furs and touch his face. "I'm sorry," I say. "I will try to make this time more memorable. But I'm afraid that all I know comes from reading romance books."

"I'm not far ahead of you," he says. "How about if we try kissing again?"

That seems like a good idea. So, we try that.

It feels good. The sensations of my body are back, the heat and the way my skin seemed to come alive under my touch. When Leland's mouth broke off to kiss my neck, it felt better.

Then the warm, happy feeling I'd had in the hall was back again, and my body was doing the talking, just as my mother had told me it would.

Panting, I pull back to look at Leland. "I have too many clothes on,", I murmur with what I hope is a seductive look.

"Shall I help you with that?" he purrs in that deep, velvety voice.

It melts me, and I say, "Yes, please."

368

He tries to undo the laces to my leather vest. I have to show him that the knots are really tiny buttons. Once we get past that, he undoes them slowly, one by one.

He then peels back the vest, exposing my lace trimmed chemise. It was made special for this night. The fabric is thin, not quite see through. It brushes my nipples, and they stand up, crinkly and hard.

He brushes his unbound hand across them, and cups one breast in his palm. I get a strong, warm flowing feeling that rushes into my armpit and down my side, straight to the area between my legs. I give a soft little moan, and he flashes that amazing smile. "Feels good?" he asks, shyly.

"Yes," I say. Then, thinking that I should be polite, "What can I do for you?"

"Another kiss?" he asks.

The smoke from the brazier swirls around us, filling the night with mystery, honing our desire.

I tip my face up to him, and he settles his mouth over mine. He runs his free hand down my back until he meets the resistance of my leather pants. He makes a soft sound of frustration.

I run my free hand down his bare back. He is a thin layer of skin over whipcord muscle and bone, with scarcely any flesh over it. His cargo shorts seem to be worn perilously thin. He shivers under my touch, like a nervous horse.

Instinctively, we arch our pelvises toward each other, leather meeting fabric, both unyielding to our mutual desire. I wrap one leg around his, pulling us closer together. I ache for him, for the bulge I can feel straining against the thin cotton of his pants.

"This would be easier if we weren't tied together," he says. "Is there any way to get this cord off?"

"Only one good way," I reply. "We trade our bloody wedding linen for having the knots undone."

"Our what?" he gasps.

"Bloody wedding linen," I repeat, my heart warming at his reaction. "I'm a virgin. There is a special cloth on the bed to protect the sheets. I should bleed a little. If I don't, Mother put a little bladder of chicken blood in our basket, for just in case."

"Oh," he says. Then, "Oh!" as comprehension hits. "What's to keep us from just using the chicken blood?" he asks.

"Nothing," I say. "But do you really want to?" The smoke swirls thicker around us, the spices in it stirring my blood. I'm vaguely aware that what I am feeling might not be quite natural, but it speaks to desires long repressed.

Something fierce lights up in his face.

"I want to. I think that you are a remarkable woman, Catriona. You're gorgeous and I definitely want to pursue this further. But maybe today... today we can put some of this on hold. We have tomorrow, and the next day, and all of our lives for more. But today I want to hold you in my arms, and we keep getting in each other's way. And there are trousers — on both of us."

He looks so irritated, fierce, and childish all at the same time, I bury my face in his shoulder and giggle. He smells warm, masculine and enticing.

"What?" he says. "I'm funny?"

"In the sweetest sort of way," I assure him. "One thing the binding does is force us to work together."

"I see," he says. "If we can get rid of the pants, we can accomplish what we need to do. I think I can get mine off one-handed. What about you?"

"I'll need your help," I say. "These are special wedding pantaloons. They are laced in the back. Just, be careful. The strings are tied in a bow, but if you pull the wrong one, they will end up in a knot."

"Your people have some strange customs," he grumbles, as he undoes his fly one-handed.

I help him wiggle out of his trousers, and he slips his feet out of his sandals. I discover his skin is darker above his belt and below his cargo shorts, as if the areas in between have been shielded and saved for me. As his trousers slide down, his equipment pops free, almost right against my nose.

He smells of strong soap, and something else — something distinctly masculine. The aroma that goes straight to my desires. *Pheromones* I think to myself. *Just pheromones and the incense*. But the science of it does nothing to lessen the impact on my emotional self.

I reach up and touch him gently, running one finger up the skin of his most private area. He seems... large. I haven't looked at too many naked men in my life, but the ones that I've seen from a distance are not quite so big. For a moment, panic overwhelms me. How would I fit all of this inside my body?

"Catriona," he whispers. "The look on your face doesn't give a man much confidence."

I glance up. "How so?"

"You're looking at something quite personal to me with quite a bit of confusion."

I laugh. "Sorry. I was just wondering how... it's going to work."

"Oh darling," he says in a throaty voice that sends heat shooting through me. "We will work. I promise you."

I purse my lips and consider him again. Beneath my gaze, his length twitches, like he can feel my eyes on him.

"Perhaps I need to explore a little more," I say as I grin up at him.

"Darling, you're going to kill me if you do," he says in a hoarse grunt. I pause, but he nods. "Please. Do whatever you want. It's a hell of a way to die."

"Dramatic," I laugh. But I continue. My hands run over his thighs and the flat plane of his stomach. He groans in a way that makes me want to touch him more. I slide my fingers into his pubic hair. It is wiry, yet soft, like a nest of young reindeer moss, or beautifully combed lambswool.

"Easy there," he says, catching my fingers.

"Did I hurt you?" I ask, surprised.

"No, just making sure you don't," he says. "Vulnerable area. Let's see what we can do about that backside lacing, eh?"

"All right," I say, standing up. I'm not ready to cease my pursuit of him, not yet. Despite my apprehension, I'm excited to see how it will work.

And mostly, what it will feel like when we do find each other.

I start to turn so he can see, then realize I can't go that direction because of our joined hands.

Leland guides me the other direction, then carefully undoes the bow. He then unlaces the closing to my leather pants and helps me slide them off. Or at least he tries to do so.

When we get to my feet, we have a fresh problem. I am wearing leather leggings, and they will not pull off over my shoes.

I begin to laugh, feeling both ridiculous and frustrated, standing there with my pants around my ankles. I overbalance and fall forward onto the bed, pulling him down onto my back.

He catches himself on his free arm, just managing not to wrench the shoulder of my bound arm. He says a string of several words. I don't understand them, but the sense of them is plain. "Are you all right?" he asks.

"I'm not hurt," I say. "But can you untie my shoes so I can get them off?"

"I think so," he says. "You'd think they would have taken these off before tucking us in. Talk about . . ."

"Planning guaranteed to make us both super frustrated," I say.

"Yes," he agrees. He carefully positions my bound arm so he won't pull on it, then gently unties my shoes and helps me off with them.

"If I'd thought about it, I would have worn slippers," I mumble into the furs.

I hear first one shoe drop, then the other. Leland leans over me, his penis brushing my behind. I feel helpless, face down on the bed, with one hand tied to his.

He slides his free hand around to my front, fumbling and exploring. "This isn't too bad," he says. "I think I can get to everything from here."

I spit fur, feeling as if the situation has slipped out of my control. "The cloth," I protest. "We need to do it on the cloth."

"Sorry," he says. "I forgot. His weight lifts off my back.

Using his free arm, he helps me stand up so I can kick off my leather pants. While I am standing, with him behind me, I flip back the furs so that the sheet with its special pad is exposed.

"Shall we dance?" he asks playfully, lifting our bound hands, turning me to face him. Then he must have seen the fear on my face. He helps me sit down on the pad and kneels before me at the edge of the bed.

This puts me above him, and him between my knees. He looks up at me, his expression concerned and gentle. "We don't have to do this," he says.

I swallow hard. "I think I want to," I say, "I just don't do well with feeling trapped." Having our hands bound is making the whole thing more difficult than I feel necessary.

And, I don't like to be reliant on others. Having my hands bound to Leland means that I have to ask him to do anything, and that feels... challenging.

He looks ruefully at our hands. "I can understand that," he says. "Why don't we lie down on that pad thing, with our free hands on top, and just talk a while."

"That sounds like a good idea," I say, scooting backward onto the bed, then turning so my bound hand was under me.

He followed, easing over to me so we lay face to face. "What shall we talk about?" he asks.

Suddenly, my mouth is dry, and I can't find a single word to say. Then I pull myself together. "Us," I say. "Let's talk about us."

I want to know everything there is to know about this man.

And I want to tell him everything about me.

. . .

LELAND

She is scared.

I can tell she is scared, and I have no idea how to make her feel better.

I have no experience calming frightened women, especially if they're partially naked in front of me. I feel like I could easily rush Catriona off of a battlefield, but here, with our hands bound together in our bedroom, I'm at a loss for how to support her.

However, if working with elephants and other animals has taught me anything, it is when they are frightened, it is time to slow down.

If I understand her correctly, we have a year and a day to get this accomplished thanks to her mother's thoughtful gift of a bladder of chicken blood.

If I'm being honest, I'm a little scared too. The rush of emotion that I have here is what I had always envisioned for myself, if I were to marry someone I loved.

I didn't choose Catriona. I don't really even know her.

I am duty bound to bed her, but beyond that…

I too am confused.

"All right," I say. "We can talk about us. Let's trade questions and answers. What would you like to know?"

I notice some of the lusty haze disappear from her gaze, but at least the fear diminishes as well. "When you have time to yourself, would you rather read, watch a movie, or play a game?" she asks.

It wasn't the kind of question I expected. "That's almost three questions," I tease, trying to cover up my own fears. *This was so strange. But then, my life had been strange ever since I woke up in a hospital tent and a blond stranger said, "Hello, Leland. I am your younger brother."*

"Can you answer the question?" she teased back. "Or are you afraid to?"

I deepen my voice to imitate an old television character from one of the few programs I ever watched, "I fear nothing!" I intone. Then I drop back into my normal register and smile at her.

"It kind of depends. If I'm on safari, I like to read at the end of the day. Or I make notes in my journal, make rubbings of plants I've not seen before, or just watch the campfire if I'm in a group, or the stars from my hammock tent if I'm alone. I like movies, but our television reception was spotty, and the cinema in town was only open one day a week. Games...well, I guess solitaire doesn't count?"

She laughs at that. "It is a game," she says, wrinkling up her nose. She has a cute nose, and the freckles across it are like a tiny constellation of stars.

Her eyes are an odd sort of hot brown that seems to match her fiery hair. Altogether, her features are becoming more familiar to me. And, I find that I'm seeing them as much more dear.

"Which one do you like best?" she winks.

I click my tongue at her. "No fair," I say, "That's a new question. It's my turn. What do you like to do in your spare time?"

She sighs, and shifts her shoulder, trying to find a comfortable position. "I don't have much spare time these days. But when I have a minute, I like to take a book and climb the reception tower. It is quiet there on the maintenance platform, and I can see the whole island if the day is clear."

"The reception tower?" I ask, picturing some sort of place where people and things go in and out.

"We get satellite reception," she says, "But we have to get the dish up above the mountains and the glaciers. So on top of the tallest tower of the castle is a reception tower."

"Oh. That kind of reception," I say, realizing that she is talking about a wireless tower. "Do you get good reception?"

"My question," she says. "What kind of journal do you keep?"

I think about how to answer that. I am frequently writing and reading, and I have some that are personal to me in ways I can't quite describe to her. "It's a combination personal journal and botany observation journal. I have a degree in ecological systems, and was doing an ongoing study, before . . ." I stop and swallow hard.

She touches my face gently. "Maybe this isn't such a fun game," she says. "I don't want to remind you of things that hurt."

I sigh and run a finger along her lips. "It's kind of why I'm here. I don't need this for myself. I need it for my people, the animals we were able to rescue, and I'm told you need my skills here."

"Maybe," she says. "But I don't want to talk about that now. This is our wedding night. If we do this right, it will be our only one, so I don't want to waste it."

"All right," I say, and kiss her gently on the forehead.

She pulls me to her and kisses me on the mouth. She is so sweet, I want to give her more. I'm not sure what she will be ready for, but slowing down and talking appears to help her with her doubts.

I gently explore her mouth with my tongue. The peppermint flavor has worn off a little, but she still tastes sweet.

She kisses back, and my cock, which had gotten a little limp while we were talking, rises once more to the occasion.

She strokes me gently, exploring, and being careful. Encouraged by this, I touch her. I use my fingers to map this unknown territory and find that her opening is moist and relaxed. I try inserting a finger, and muscles clamp around it, pulsing.

I shiver, thinking of how she will feel when we do... more. She scoots toward me, then rolls on her back, opening her legs, inviting me in.

I am not sure if I should wait longer, or if I should try to enter her. After all, I have only done this once... Father kept all his sons close, almost as if we were daughters in a seraglio.

Perhaps I should thank him, since it means that most of us made it through our teens without contracting a disease or accidentally getting a girl pregnant.

Then there was the business of my mother having been married before, and to a man with a pale skin. I look different from my brothers and cousins.

I had a harder time getting girls to dance with me at the few parties we attended. Add that the girls were as closely guarded as a king's ransom, and I'd had little opportunity to improve on that first time.

When Father became too ill to set close watch on us, I was the oldest and responsible for the rest, which meant whatever example I set my brothers and cousins would follow. I was nearly as inexperienced as my bride, even though I was at least ten years older.

Catriona is not just lying there, nor is she limp. She tilts her pelvis to me, trails her fingers across her opening, and uses two of them to open wide for me. It excites me so much; I nearly disgrace myself by exploding right then.

"Please," she says. "I think I'm ready. Do it quick, before I get too scared to let you try."

The comment isn't exactly a turn-on, and yet it is. She is a virgin, exploring unknown territory. And this is only my second time.

Neither one of us knows what the fuck we are doing, yet that's exactly what we need to do. I take comfort in the fact that, if nothing else, we are here.

Together.

And together is how we will figure this out.

I ease myself in her entrance, fighting every urge not to explode immediately. She is warm, wet, and tight. She whimpers a little, and I pause. "Are you all right?" I ask.

"Yes," she says, "Don't stop. Keep going. I'm ready." She tilts, and wiggles, and I nearly lose the connection, so I plunge in all at once until I reach a sort of barrier.

She gasps and gives a little cry. But she clings to me, and says, "More. Please, more, and deeper." The fear has left her eyes, and she gazes at me in a way no other has ever done. It melts me in a way I cannot describe. Pleasing her has become the most important thing in the world.

I will not fail to make her feel as incredible as I do.

I pull back just a little, and plunge in again. The barrier gives way, and she wraps her legs around mine, locking her feet behind my knees so I cannot escape if I want to.

I don't want to. Suddenly, the entirety of the world has focused on our joining. Outside, the bagpipes are keeping up a wild screeching and the drums are beating an insistent rhythm.

They've been doing it all this while, I realize. I let them guide me, I match them. I slide in, retreat, slide in again, over and over, my excitement building.

Catriona lifts her pelvis to meet me, welcoming me, pulling me down with her legs,… continue reading The Arranged Vows available on Kindle Unlimited, Audible and Paperback Click Here to Read now

ABOUT THE AUTHOR

VIVY SKYS the author of Steamy Contemporary Romance novels, featuring smart, strong, sassy and witty female characters that command the attention of strong protective alpha males, from Off limits, Age Gap, Bossy Billionaires, Single dads next door, Royalty, Dark Mafia and beyond Vivy's pen will deliver.

<u>Follow Vivy Skys on Amazon</u> to be the first to know when her next book becomes available.

Made in United States
North Haven, CT
10 April 2024

51144060R10233